DUPLICITY

DUPLICITY: A SMOKE & MIRRORS BOOK - 2

Copyright © 2012, 2016 by H. D. Thomson

Previously published as Shrouded in Mytery in 2012 by Bella Media Management

This is a work of fiction. Names, characters, places, and incidents are products of the author's imagination or are used fictitiously. Any resemblance to actual events, locales, or persons living or dead is entirely coincidental.

Published by Bella Media Management.

DUPLICITY

A SMOKE & MIRRORS BOOK

2

A Tale of Murder, Mystery and Romance

H. D. THOMSON

True heroism is remarkably sober, very undramatic. It is not the urge to surpass all others at whatever cost, but the urge to serve others at whatever cost.
—Arthur Ashe

CHAPTER ONE

HE CAME TO with a jolt. Wind rushed through the broken windshield and slashed vicious tentacles against his face, while shattered glass and snow lay scattered across the dashboard and his lap. Pain cut into his skull and the back of his neck. With a tentative hand, he touched his brow and came away with damp fingers.

Blood.

He blinked several times, unable to understand why he sat behind the wheel of a car.

Some type of car accident? He couldn't remember.

The vehicle rested at an odd angle, its nose dipped downward, and the driver's side tilted toward the pine tops. Waning light turned a cloudless sky to a dirty gray. Dawn or dusk? He didn't know. He couldn't think. How had he gotten here?

Lifting his hands, he peered at them. They were large, long-fingered, and free of calluses. Fine brown hairs dusted their backs. Stranger's hands. His hands.

He wrestled for answers—a memory, an image, a clue to his identity—anything.

Nothing but a black, empty slate.

Panic welled in his throat and cut off the air to his lungs. He couldn't remember anything about himself. He didn't have a name, a past, a family. He didn't exist.

Finally, he managed to drag in a lungful of air, but its frigid sting rushed past his throat and into his lungs too fast. Oxygen flooded his head, and white sparks danced across his peripheral vision.

No. He needed to stop. Now. And focus. Think.

He forced himself to relax, to calm the wild thump of his heart. After a moment, he managed to breathe in a slow, steady rhythm, and the panic eased. He turned and noticed the passenger to his right. A man sat slumped, silent, his body thrown forward and held in place by his seatbelt.

"Hey, are you okay?"

No answer.

He nudged the man's shoulder with a hand. "Can you hear me?"

No response.

Something wasn't right.

He unbuckled his seatbelt and slapped a palm against the dashboard to stop from pitching forward. Awkwardly, he twisted in his seat, eased forward and ducked to get a better look at the person's face. That's when he noticed the hole above the passenger's open and unblinking eye. For several long, heartrending seconds, he stared at how the blood pooled from the wound, and then dripped, again and again, slowly but steadily onto the person's jean-clad leg.

A gunshot wound. Had to be. "Jesus!"

Until now, he hadn't noticed the pungent odor of death and how it clung to the interior of the car. At the stench, his stomach lurched but kept from heaving its contents.

The passenger wasn't even a man but a kid in his late teens. A dead one at that. And the boy sure as hell didn't die from a car accident with a bullet hole in his head.

Repulsed by the idea, but determined to find something of importance, he dug inside both outer pockets of the teenager's jacket. He needed something to tell him what the hell was going on or at least who sat dead in the car with him. Next, he unzipped the kid's jacket and felt around. His fingers caught on something jutting from a shirt pocket. He pulled it out and lifted it up to get a better view.

A picture. He managed to make out that it was a photo of the passenger and a woman with her arm draped over his shoulders. They stood in front of a building of some type. He turned the photo over and read:

Me and Katherine at the Morning Dove.

At least it was something. But not nearly enough to tell him who either one of them was.

Had he been the one to kill the kid?

There'd have to be a gun.

Quickly, he stuffed the picture inside the pocket of his down jacket and started searching. The fading light forced him to grope around the seat and floor by his feet and that of the dead teenager. He reached for the glove box, the most logical place for a weapon, and kept his gaze away from the body.

He didn't find a weapon inside, but he did find a flashlight, which he flipped on and aimed at the car's floor. Still no gun. The relief was almost immobilizing. Because if he'd found a gun, he'd have proof that he'd murdered the boy. The idea of sticking the barrel of a gun into that kid's face—

No. He didn't want to go there.

He aimed the light in the back of the car where the beam caught on a navy blue duffle bag. Finally something. Not liking the idea of reaching over the back and brushing up against the dead teen, he decided to go outside and around. He opened the door, jumped out, and landed in a foot of snow, which seeped under his pants and bit into his skin.

Suddenly lightheaded, he bent over and rested his hands across his knees. Eyeglasses, he hadn't noticed until now, slipped from his nose and fell to the ground. He plucked them from a snow as gray and lifeless as the sky and put them back on. When he rose, a wave of dizziness seized him. He swayed and latched onto the car's roof with one hand. God, he was weaker than he'd thought.

After he regained his equilibrium, he opened the back door, unzipped the duffle bag and aimed the light inside. And froze. He'd hoped for some clue to his past—anything—but what he discovered was far from what he'd imagined.

Cold, hard cash. The bag was stuffed with bundles of it, all tied by bank straps. With the flashlight trained on the bag's interior, he lifted one bundle out and fanned the top edges and did it again to ensure he wasn't hallucinating. Hundreds. Every single one of them. The bills trembled against his fingers, while his heart rate kicked into a rapid rhythm. At the very least, there had to be more than a hundred thousand in front of him.

How? Why? What type of person carried this amount of money around with them?

He dropped the bundle back into the bag, opened the sides wider and realized he wasn't done. Far from it. Something large rested inside. He wrapped his fingers around the handle and pulled the item from the bag. Beneath, the flashlight's beam, the dark silver gleamed as if recently polished.

A gun.

"Holy Shit."

Something big had gone down, and he'd been involved. But what?

He hated the feel of the gun beneath his fingers as he shoved it back in the bag. But even though he disliked touching the weapon, he'd obviously found it important enough keep one around.

What the hell type of person was he?

Then he heard something other than the wind through the pines. A cry. It had a distinct rhythm, growing low, then high, increasing in intensity as it approached.

He stilled.

The murdered teen, the cash, the gun. All incriminating, all unexplainable. The police or paramedics would never believe him. He didn't even believe himself.

Fear shot him into action. He grabbed the bag—he might have lost his mind, but he wasn't stupid enough to leave something like that behind—pivoted and stumbled away from the car and the dead boy.

He left a visible trail in his wake, but he didn't see any other option with a deep carpet of snow covering every dip and mound of dirt. Even though it should have impeded his movements and momentum, he dodged trees, jumped over snow-crested logs and jogged his way through the thick, white powder with astonishing speed and agility.

After a good half-hour, he slowed to a walk, surprised at how his lungs and limbs quickly recovered from the demanding pace he'd forced on both.

The siren had long since died, while darkness had descended in its entirety. Surely if he'd been followed, they'd have found him by now. Even though somewhat reassured by the thought, he continued through the forest.

A noise crashed from behind. He jerked around and searched the darkness, moving backward with cautious steps. Another sound. He stopped and listened. He heard the flap of wings and a rustle of leaves.

A bird.

He laughed and turned back around. His feet hit black, wet tarmac. Headlights flashed and blinded him. He stumbled back. A horn blasted. Wind hit him in the face.

A car sped past, feet from where he stood. His heart hammered against his ribs. Two more steps and he'd have been coating the car.

The moon broke through the clouds, illuminating pines and snow on either side of a two-lane highway. He kept to the edge of the road, his rubber-soled boots scraping against small rocks and broken asphalt. Maybe being visible to anyone who drove by wasn't the smartest move but getting lost in the forest wasn't any better. If he didn't find some form of shelter soon, frostbite would be the least of his worries.

The duffle bag against his side felt reassuring yet unsettling, while the gun inside felt a whole hell of a lot more than unsettling. Shivering, he stuffed his hands into his coat pockets and flexed his fingers to try to work the stiffness from their joints. When he brushed something from inside one of them, he pulled out a plastic rectangle, possibly a card of some type.

Even with the moon as a source of light, he couldn't make it out. He grabbed the flashlight from his back pocket and pointed its beam on the card. After a moment, he realized it was a driver's license. He didn't know why the I.D. was in his coat pocket instead of a wallet. He was too damn thankful to have some type of identification.

He glanced at the picture. The person in the photo had gray eyes, short, brown hair, thick-framed glasses and a wide jaw—none of it familiar—which didn't mean anything. He didn't think he'd recognize his own reflection if he looked in the mirror. Aloud, he read the first name on the license.

"Clark."

He repeated it along with the last name, rolled the syllables between his tongue and lips and tried to get a feel for it. There was no dawning realization or understanding, no sudden burst of recognition. The name didn't mean anything. But there was an address.

"Boston. Finally, I've got something!"

Getting there didn't bother him. He had enough cash to hire a pilot if he needed to. And once in Boston, he should be able to get some answers.

With a sense of purpose now, Clark stuffed the license back in his pocket and searched his other ones for a wallet or any other form of identification. All he found was a package of spearmint gum in his pants' pocket, and he could barely make that out because his glasses had filmed with moisture. No wonder he'd had such a hard time reading his driver's license.

With the flashlight cradled beneath an armpit, he used the collar of his flannel shirt to wipe the lenses and the same frames like the ones in the photo. When he put them back on, Clark noticed his vision, even with the aid of the flashlight, hadn't improved. Puzzled, he took his glasses off again and aimed the flashlight's beam at the lenses. He scowled. They were nothing but plain glass.

Why was he walking around with non-prescription glasses? Were they a disguise? Even though none of it made sense, there had to be some rational explanation. Well, until he learned the reason, he'd keep wearing them.

A faint rumble disturbed the evening air. The sound grew louder as Clark moved along the road. A car's engine. He thought of diving back in the woods, but if he didn't get out of these harsh elements, he was liable to die from exposure. Tense, expecting the worse, he turned and relaxed somewhat. A pickup, not a patrol car, appeared around the bend in the road.

Maybe his luck was turning around. Hell, it couldn't get much worse.

Hitching up a thumb, he waited and hoped for two things: one, the driver hadn't witnessed any police or paramedics with sirens, and two, they were kind or naive enough to pick up a hitchhiker.

The pickup rushed past, and then slowed and rolled to a stop a couple hundred feet away. Without giving the driver a chance to change his mind, Clark ran down the road, opened the passenger door and peered inside.

A heavy-set man with a baseball cap, in a desperate need of a shave and shower, sat behind the wheel. He took one look at Clark and whistled. "You okay buddy? Your face looks like it met up with a two-by-four."

Clark heard the suspicion in the driver's voice and explained, "More like a steering wheel. I had a tire blow out a couple miles back and hit a ditch."

The man snapped a piece of gum between his teeth and seemed to hesitate as if weighing his options. "Hop in. I'm going as far as Pinetop."

Thank God. Clark slipped inside the interior's warmth and slammed the door behind him.

"Not the best place to break down." The driver shifted his rear against the vinyl seat and steered the truck back onto the road. "Since we're going to be up close and personal for a while—the name's Stu. And you're?"

"Clark. Clark Kent."

CHAPTER 2

W HAT'S WRONG?"

Katherine Spalding placed the receiver back in its cradle. She looked up to where George, her assistant, stood by the doorway to her office of Morning Dove's Youth Shelter for the Homeless.

"Kincaid's donation hasn't come in this month, and I'm getting the runaround from his office. He's dodging me as if I were the Black Plague."

George leaned a jean-clad hip against the door frame and rubbed at his gray beard. "It could be bad timing or a busy schedule."

"I don't think so. Until now, he's always returned my calls."

"Maybe it's time we started looking around for another company with some spare change. But right now, it's late. Worry about it tomorrow. You've been here since six this morning, and it's almost six now."

She looked at the clock on the wall. "Oh, shoot. I'm going to be late if I don't get moving. I promised to have dinner with my parents. They've invited some of the family over tonight."

"There you go. Get out of here and have some fun."

"You don't know my parents."

George raised a thick, gray eyebrow. "Then, all I can say is 'best of luck'."

Her lips twitched. "Thanks, I might need it."

After she shrugged into her jacket and grabbed her purse from under her desk, Katherine followed George down the hall and into the lobby. At the front door, she paused and glanced back at George. She'd almost forgotten. "You haven't seen Brian today, have you?"

"Nope. Sorry. He'll show up."

"Hmm. I hope so."

But she wasn't so sure. She hadn't seen him for weeks, and even if he'd ended back on the street, word would have gotten back to her. There was a close-knit network out there. She'd checked with the police, and they'd put out a missing person's bulletin, but it hadn't helped. In their eyes, hunting down a homeless teenager was the least of their worries.

The sad part was Brian had shown so much promise. He'd been off crack for a month and searching for a job. Now it looked like he'd either gone underground or moved out of the city.

George's weathered face turned somber. "Get that look off your face. You should know more than anyone that you can't save the world. So don't start getting yourself trapped in that mindset. Otherwise, you won't be much help to anyone. Some of these kids are beyond hope by the time they find this place, and no matter how much support we give them, it doesn't mean they'll make the right choices. They all have free will."

"I know. But it doesn't make it any easier—"

"Will you stop—"

"Okay. Okay. I'll stop worrying. I'll see you tomorrow." She waved a farewell.

After stepping outside, she pulled her collar up against her neck, stuffed her bare hands into her pockets, and huddled deeper into her coat. Mid-January in Boston and she was already tired of the winter and all it entailed. Other than Thanksgiving and Christmas, this was the busiest and saddest time of the year for her.

Shivering, she pushed her thoughts to the evening ahead. Her mood didn't lift. Dinner with her parents was always an ordeal. She didn't know why. All her life, they'd supported her.

Maybe she was just discontent, a selfish emotion, to say the least, considering what life had given her.

She glanced down at her jeans and realized faded denim was out for tonight. Before she went home to change, she'd have to stop by the drug store down the street for some shampoo. She'd completely run out.

Head bent, still focused on her legs, she slammed into something hard. The air left her lungs in one loud whoosh. She stumbled. Tilting precariously on the heels of her feet, she grabbed for something solid and found a jacket. She dug her fingers around hard-muscled biceps and held on. An arm swept around her back and pulled her up against an unyielding chest, while her legs tangled with strong, solid legs.

Oh, my.

Katherine caught a glimpse of a strong throat and a wide, clean-shaven jaw. The light from a store window illuminated the most incredible gray eyes she'd ever seen. They were rimmed silver and flecked with charcoal closer to the pupil. His breath, scented with peppermint, brushed against her cheek.

Then he stepped backward, and she stood alone, shaken, unharmed, but unable to look away.

The same light touched his skin to smooth honey and glittered off his brown hair, highlighting their strands to warm mahogany. He had a strong, angular, almost austere face with a hard, inflexible jaw. He looked exactly the way Katherine had always envisioned a man should look like.

He brushed away a thatch of hair, but it fell back against his brow. "I'm sorry. I wasn't watching where I was going. Are you okay?"

His crooked smile did strange things to her pulse. Absently, she rubbed a hand along the strap of her purse draped over her shoulder. "I'm fine."

He nodded, then bent down and picked up a pair of thick-framed glasses that must have fallen to the ground from their collision. Slipping them on, he paused with his hands by his ears and peered down at her.

There was something about his expression Katherine couldn't quite make out—almost a mixture of curiosity and caution.

"Have we... Do I..."

"Do you what?" she prompted.

"It's just that—" A muscle pulsed along the ridge of his jaw. "It doesn't matter."

"Okaaay." She nodded. "Sorry about your glasses."

He smiled sheepishly. "I really should get them tightened. They have this terrible habit of falling off my nose."

"Yes, well—"

"Oh...of course. Excuse me."

He stepped aside and nodded as she walked past. She felt his gaze along the length of her—how else could she explain the prickle of awareness across the base of her neck? But she stopped herself from looking over her shoulder and double-checking.

Incredibly handsome, but very strange. He'd acted like he knew her. She slowed on the sidewalk and almost knocked into another pedestrian when she tried to remember what she was supposed to be doing.

Oh, yes. Shampoo. She needed to get some. Her stride determined, she walked the rest of the block to the drug store.

After completing her purchase, Katherine rushed home, showered, applied a thin layer of makeup and changed into a black, Ann Demeulemeester, stretch rayon dress. Then she swept her hair into a loose bun, grabbed a suede jacket and left the house. Key in hand, she hurried to her car and saw Ethan, her neighbor, getting out of his own vehicle two parking spaces away from her Mazda.

"Hey, gorgeous. Where are you off to?"

"Dinner with my parents."

"And here I thought you had a hot date."

"No such luck." She smiled. "Want to join me?"

Ethan laughed and shook his head as he walked over to her. "Oh, no you don't, Katherine. The last time you dragged me there, they found out what type of marriage material I was. I could have sworn I saw your mother's face lose a couple of shades of color."

"Sorry. My mother's in a phase where she thinks I should be married with children, or at the very least have a couple of prospects lined up."

"Ah, mothers. Don't we just love 'em?" With an index finger, he flicked a loose strand of hair that had slipped from her bun. "How about skipping the parents and instead the two of us go wild tonight? Dancing, dinner, and later we can steam up my car windows with some heavy necking."

"And what about Ken? I don't think he'd like me moving in on his territory."

Ethan appeared to think about it. "Maybe another time. He can get a bit jealous."

She chuckled. "That's what happens when you date a younger man. It's called high maintenance." She turned serious. "Well, I've got to rush. Otherwise, I'll be later than I already am."

Something Katherine didn't want to be—not when it came to her mother.

~~*~~

Clark stood beneath the shadows of an old elm tree and watched the couple from a distance.

After crossing the country from Arizona—Clark still didn't have a clue why he'd ended up in the mountains there—he'd checked into a hotel in Boston and searched for the address on his driver's license. He didn't find a house but a three-story building, which housed the local newspaper. Frustrated, he'd gone inside *The Boston Globe* and almost got kicked out by the security guard when he insisted on talking to someone.

He'd next looked up the Morning Dove in the phone book and came up with another address. This one held a hell of a lot more promise. He'd immediately recognized the building as the one in the teenager's photograph. He didn't know if he'd once walked through the doors—it didn't feel like it—but a strange sense of foreboding had grabbed at his insides when he'd first spied the building.

Then he'd stumbled into the blonde, and when he'd seen her face, he realized she was the woman in the photo. And the oddest part, he'd felt a connection, as if he'd known her. But if so, then why hadn't she acknowledged him? It didn't make sense.

Not about to let the woman get away without uncovering something about her, he'd follow her here to skulk behind a tree and watch for...he didn't know what.

"Katherine," he whispered, repeating the name the man had called her.

Suddenly, Clark stiffened and flattened a palm against the rough bark of the elm. A vision of the past flashed across his mind's eye. He saw Katherine grin up at the sky and toss her thick, blonde hair over her shoulder as she rocked back on her heels. She stood talking to a tall, heavy-set man in front of a gray brick building. The man rubbed an affectionate hand against her shoulder and said something undecipherable. Clark tried to grasp more from the memory, but the image vanished as quickly as it had appeared. But he recognized the place as the shelter.

Why? Why did he remember that and nothing else? What was it about her and the Morning Dove's Youth Shelter for the Homeless? Or was this sudden memory a false image fabricated because of the photograph? All three questions kicked at his gut and elevated his blood pressure.

Patience. Clark needed to remember that. In time, he'd find out, but right now he'd watch and wait, and weigh every situation that crossed his path. But then, Clark thought of the wrecked car, the dead teen with a bullet hole, how close he'd eluded death. He couldn't afford to be patient. Not when he needed to find out if a murderer was running loose.

Hell. He might be a walking target. Tomorrow, he could find himself facing the person who killed the teenager and not know it. Or—worse yet—he might be the murderer.

A cold breeze kicked up snow and whirled it around his ankles. Shivering, Clark stuffed his hands into his coat pockets and watched Katherine wave goodbye before she unlocked and opened her car door.

Clark couldn't get over the change in her. Less than a couple of hours ago, she'd looked like a college student with her braid and glowing complexion. Now her appearance and whole demeanor screamed elegance, confidence, allure.

Katherine was a paradox.

She also might be connected to the murder in Arizona, which didn't make sense. Not when she'd behaved as if she'd never seen him before. Unless...acting came as naturally as breathing to her. Clark frowned. The idea of her angelic face hiding something immoral and ugly didn't seem fitting.

Finally, after Katherine guided her car onto the street and disappeared from sight and her friend slipped inside one of several two-story townhomes, Clark stepped from the shadows. Overgrown elms and the soft glow of lantern-type streetlights hinted at red-bricked walls and gave the complex an old-world charm. A thick layer of snow tinted yellow-gold covered the sloped roofs and blanketed the common area. The place was new and upscale, and nothing about it looked familiar.

Damn. What did he do now? Introduce himself and start asking Katherine questions? Yeah, right. If she didn't run the minute he opened his mouth and confirmed his lunacy, she might pull a gun and splatter his brains everywhere.

Clark crossed the snow-covered lawn to the shoveled walkway and noticed the for rent sign on the lawn of one of the townhouses. The lights were off, and when he didn't see any signs of occupancy, he walked over and peered into a side window. The glow of one of the street lamps illuminated what appeared to be an empty bedroom. He hoped the owner hadn't found a renter yet. The townhouse would be perfect.

What better way to keep an eye on Katherine and not look like he stalked her every move? Plus, he needed a place to stay. He didn't want to live in a hotel indefinitely. And as to credit references, he could bypass that. Cash was a seductive incentive.

He'd look into it tomorrow.

CHAPTER 3

Double-checking her hair and anchoring her bun more securely with a bobby pin, Katherine paused at the front door of her parents' home. Then she stepped inside, draped her jacket and purse across the antique coat rack in the corner of the foyer, and followed the sound of voices coming from the dining room. They'd started without her.

When she walked into the dining room, five people turned to stare at her. Her father, Alex, sat at the head of the table, while her mother, Sharon, and her Uncle Paul bracketed his sides. Paul's son, David, and David's wife, Rachel, sat along the same side of the table as her mother. The only place setting available rested to her uncle's right. What luck.

The thick brocade drapes had been closed for the evening, while the muted light from the chandelier encompassed the room in an intimate glow and accentuated the smooth walnut table and gold leaf china.

Sharon raised a disapproving eyebrow. "You're late."

Her mother didn't add 'as usual', but Katherine heard the unspoken censure nonetheless as she sank down into the chair beside Paul. She wasn't going to feel guilty. Not tonight, at least.

"Sorry," she found herself still apologizing.

"You haven't missed anything," her father claimed. "Unless

you find a detailed discussion on several blue-chip stocks fascinating?" At her look, he smiled. "I didn't think so."

Her father and uncle were similarly dressed in dove white shirts, dark suits and power ties. Their clothing might be similar, but their looks were anything but. Her father, Alex, was blond-haired, blue-eyed and tanned, while his brother, Paul, was dark eyed, pale and had inherited the dreaded male patterned baldness from his mother's side of the family.

Her father hadn't changed much over the years. Because of a rigorous workout regimen each day and a capable plastic surgeon, the only signs of aging were a thickened waist and faint crow's feet. Time hadn't been so forgiving to his brother—or maybe Paul had never been concerned with appearances like his brother. As far back as she could remember, Paul had always seemed to have a harried look about him, more so since his wife's death five years ago. A sagging jaw, fleshy arms and legs attested to too many hours behind a desk and little else.

Minutes later, Diana, the Spalding's housekeeper and cook, wheeled in a cloth-draped trolley. She set a traditional Caesar salad before Katherine and replaced the empty salad plates with steaming caramelized mashed potatoes, grilled filet of beef and parslied carrots. The aroma twisted Katherine's stomach into a knot of hunger. She'd almost forgotten Diana's extraordinary culinary talents.

"How was your week, dear?"

As Diana poured a glass of wine for her, Katherine glanced across the table to her mother. At fifty-five, Sharon looked as good or better than a decade ago. Her updated hairstyle, short, wispy and feminine, complimented her large brown eyes and the smooth sweep of her nose and jaw. The dark gray suit and white, linen blouse were a typical example of her wardrobe— understated, conservative yet stylish. In all honesty, Katherine couldn't remember a time when her mother wasn't impeccably groomed. But then looks were paramount in her line of work. Image meant everything to her mother, from her leather pumps to her frosted hair.

"Frustrating."

"Oh, why's that?" Alex asked.

Katherine unfolded her napkin and placed it across her lap. "We have another missing teenager on our hands. That's three in the last year. Three I thought were going to be success stories. Then it looks like one of our financial backers is withdrawing his support. It wouldn't bother me so much, but this is the second company in a month that has decided to cut their ties with Morning Dove. I need funding from the private sector. The shelter can't survive on government subsidies alone." She smiled to lighten the mood. "It's all so strange that it's happening at once. If I didn't know better, I'd think someone had it in for the shelter."

"That's a shame," her father murmured. "But I'm sure you'll find another company willing to support the home."

"I'm sure I can—given time." Katherine sighed. "I don't like asking, Mother, but would you be willing to talk to Kincaid?"

"I'll see what I can do, dear, but I can't make any promises."

"Really, Katherine." Her father wiped a corner of his mouth with a cloth napkin. "You shouldn't ask that of your mother. You're putting her in an awkward position."

Knowing he had a point, Katherine nodded and glanced over to her uncle. He wasn't an option. Several times over the course of two years she'd hinted for help from his company, Miltronics, but nothing had come of it. Asking now would be like beating a dead horse, so she didn't even try. Sighing, she stabbed a Romaine leaf with her fork.

"Didn't you have financial problems when you first opened? And everything worked out fine then." Alex smiled with encouragement. "You'll come up on top this time, too."

"I know she will," Sharon said. "I think it's admirable how she spends her time." She met Katherine's gaze across the table. "Think what you could do if you had a wider vision. With your energy and enthusiasm, you'd be such a success in politics. You're young, your education's impeccable. You'd just have to focus in a different direction. Of course, there's the one drawback of being single ..."

Katherine shifted in her chair and set her fork down. The salad had lost its appeal.

Alex placed a hand across her mother's wrist. "We've been over this before."

"There's always hope."

Katherine lifted her chin. "I've never been interested in politics, and there's nothing wrong with being single. But then again, now that you've mentioned it, several bachelors have caught my eye. There's Ethan, of course. You've already met him. He's suave, attractive—"

Sharon's eyes turned cold. "That's enough. I find that far from funny."

Katherine flushed.

"I love your dress, Katherine," Rachel broke into the awkward silence.

Katherine plucked at the cuff of her sleeve. "Thank you."

"We have to go shopping together soon. I'm sure it's been ages since the last time. God knows, David hates it when I drag him along."

"That's not true," David protested with a half-smile.

"Always the diplomat," Rachel teased. "That's why you're so good at what you do, and why I married you."

Rachel patted her husband's forearm. The bulky diamond ring on her left hand sparkled against the chandelier's light and reminded Katherine how fate and fortune had touched a benevolent hand on all their lives. For three generations, the Spalding wealth had cushioned their failings, indulged their whims, and offered them opportunities given to very few, and she knew every person at this table had taken it for granted—including herself.

But tonight she felt like an outsider, an imposter. While she had the best food, the best clothing, the best home, the temperature outside was falling below freezing. No doubt, a woman, vulnerable, in need of medical attention, slept somewhere in a cardboard box. A teenage boy wandered the streets, prostituting himself to get his next fix of heroin so he could hide from the pain of his past.

Jason McFadden walked into the room.

"Senator. There's a call from Representative Harlow. He's

apologized for the intrusion, but he's concerned about the Carmel bill and needs to discuss a few issues with you before tomorrow morning."

Sharon's lips tightened with displeasure as she rose gracefully from her chair. "Excuse me."

Katherine watched her mother follow her personal assistant from the room, then turned back to her meal.

"You shouldn't bait your mother like that."

The distinct sound of a cell phone saved her from a reply.

Paul reached for his waist and unsnapped his phone from its leather case. "Hello. What? Are you sure?"

Paul rose abruptly. His napkin fluttered to his feet, while his chair crashed to the floor.

Katherine jumped, spilling several drops of Beaujolais on her hand.

"Are you at the scene? How bad is it?"

She raised a brow and met her father's gaze across the table. He shook his head and shrugged.

Paul disconnected the call, and, with a fumbling hand, pushed his phone back inside its case.

"Is there a problem?" her father asked.

"It's Miltronics. I have to go. There's a fire. Several employees are missing—possibly dead."

~~*~~

Early Friday morning, Clark, thinking a cup of black coffee and a newspaper might kill some time while he formulated a plan, crossed the street to The Coffee Company. The place was within sight of the townhouses where Katherine lived. Hopefully, he'd be able to get hold of someone regarding the rental there and move in within the week...unless the place had been taken already.

He paused by a newspaper vending machine and dug in his pants' pocket for some change. The machine took his quarters but didn't unlatch and open. He jiggled the change button. Nothing happened. In frustration, he yanked at the door handle. Metal groaned, and the door snapped from its moorings. Stunned, Clark stood with the door dangling from his fingers.

Well, hell. He hadn't pulled at the handle that hard. At least not hard enough to do that sort of damage. It must have already been broken.

He glanced around, but no one appeared to have noticed his little foray with someone else's private property. This time, he pulled a twenty from his pocket and rolled the bill until it was small enough to slip into the coin slot. Then after grabbing a paper, he placed the panel back on. Even though broken and misshapen, it somehow stayed.

Clark folded the newspaper in half, shoved it under his arm and tried to look casual as he walked the rest of the way to The Coffee Company. The aroma of freshly brewed coffee teased his senses when he stepped inside. While he waited in line, he unfolded the paper and glanced down at the newsprint.

The front-page photo consisted of a fire from the previous night. Suspected arson read the caption. Then in the headline, he saw the name in bold letters. Miltronics. Sights and sounds faded; his peripheral vision darkened and narrowed and colors drained to gray except for the lone article in front of him. His stomach rolled with nausea. Rage, inexplicable, and powerful, surged through him.

"Sir."

The filthy bastards! They'd done it.

"Sir!"

Clark looked up and snarled. "What!"

The teenager blinked at him. "I was asking what you wanted."

Heat crept into his cheeks. "Sorry. I'll have a coffee. Black."

He tossed a five on the counter, grabbed his coffee and lurched around the person behind him. After scanning the crowded place for a seat, he found an empty table by the aisle near the front door and dropped down in a chair. He set his cup down and flattened out the crumpled newspaper. The headline glared at him.

Miltronics.

Nothing else had gotten a reaction from him like that. Why

the rage? And against who? What had they done? Burned the place down? Is that why he'd been so angry? He closed his eyes and searched for a reason, a face, an image. He came up blank.

"A non-fat, café latte for Katherine!" a Barista called out.

Clark opened his eyes, snapped his head up and looked toward the counter. Katherine was retrieving a cup of coffee. Even though she lived across the street and probably frequented this place, he couldn't stop the way his heart did a free-fall to his stomach. For a panicky moment, he didn't know whether to run or duck behind a display case.

He did neither. Instead, he remained seated and watched her walk down the aisle toward him. She glanced his way, then again as recognition flared in her eyes.

He lifted his coffee and smiled. "Don't worry. It's safe. I promise I won't run over you."

"Hi." She returned his smile with one of her own, then searched the room.

He followed her gaze. It looked like he'd taken the last empty table.

"You're welcome to join me."

She hesitated in the middle of the aisle, while he moved the newspaper to make room. Just when Clark thought she'd decline, she glanced down at the paper on the table.

She dropped down in the opposite chair. "May I?"

When he nodded, she took the paper and flipped it around. Her hand had a distinct tremor to it as she took a sip of her coffee.

"Are you all right?"

"Umm. Yeah." She tapped a finger to the article and looked up. It took a moment for her gaze to clear. "It's only that—"

"What?"

"My uncle's the CEO of this company."

He couldn't have heard right. "You're talking about Miltronics?"

"Yes." She nodded at the paper. "It's a pharmaceutical company on the outskirts of Boston. He's worked there since he graduated from M.I.T."

He sat in his chair, afraid to move, afraid to react as shock and excitement assaulted him. Beneath the table, his fingers dug into the flesh of his thighs, and he forced himself to breathe in and out, slowly, calmly, while his heart crashed against his ribs with alarming speed. If he started acting odd, he'd lose whatever connection, however tentative, he'd established with her.

"I'm sorry," he said, his words husky with emotion. She couldn't guess that it wasn't sympathy that thickened his voice but hope at finding a possible link to uncovering his past. He glanced down at the newspaper and frowned. He hadn't had a chance to read the complete article. "There's a number of people mentioned here." He scanned the names and froze. "He wouldn't be Paul—"

"Yes. That's him. Paul Spalding."

Dread, fear and hatred rolled and twisted in the pit of his stomach. That name. It sounded simple and innocent, but not to Clark. Paul Spalding. Miltronics. They were bound together and linked to his past.

Clark now had a goal—to uncover why he hated them both.

"Are you all right?"

"Oh, yes." Clark grappled for self-control. "And your uncle? He wasn't in the building when it—"

"Oh, no! He was at dinner with us when it happened. When he left my parents' house, he was in a state of shock. I called a while ago to get an update from my mother, but she didn't have anything different to say than what's reported here."

Katherine frowned. "Excuse my rambling—seeing the front page caught me off guard."

He shrugged a shoulder and smiled with difficulty. "No need to apologize. It must have come as a surprise to see something so personal on the front page of the paper."

"I guess I should have expected it. What with twelve dead and three more missing."

He blinked several times to clear his vision. Damn. It was almost as if he'd known them.

Her large, brown eyes softened. "I didn't mean to bring down your morning." Straightening, she pulled the strap of her purse tighter around her shoulder.

Katherine planned on leaving. He couldn't have that. Not this soon. Think.

"Do you come here often?" At the inane question, his face burned. Talk about stupid. Couldn't he have thought of something more original than that? Obviously not. He might have been better off sticking the proverbial foot in his mouth. At least that way he wouldn't have sounded like a complete ass. "What I mean is—"

She laughed, a warm, throaty sound, which washed over him. "Yes, actually, I do. I'm a coffee addict. It's quite embarrassing how all the employees here know my name."

"Then I might see you around."

Nodding, she rose to her feet. "Thanks for sharing your paper and table. I've got to get to work."

Clark felt his smile congeal. "It was a pleasure."

He couldn't do a damn thing to stop her from leaving without causing a scene and alienating her. So he sat there and watched her go, a pleasant mask glued to his face, while frustration and helplessness gnawed at his insides.

CHAPTER 4

KATHERINE HURRIED FROM The Coffee Company and smothered the urge to look back over her shoulder. She hadn't known there were men out there who still blushed—until today. And he'd blushed because of her. For someone so darn attractive, he was refreshingly awkward and unsure of himself— even sweet.

By the time she'd reached work, she'd pushed him from her mind, but by Monday morning thoughts of a gray-eyed man with thick mahogany hair edged back into her thoughts as she stopped off for coffee. Katherine tried to tell herself she wasn't disappointed when she didn't find him inside.

Was she that desperate for male companionship? Honestly? Yes. It was quite embarrassing how little time she'd spent with the opposite sex when it came to dating. She'd only had one serious relationship, and that had been way back in college. If it came down to it, and if she needed a date in a hurry, she would come up empty-handed. There was Ethan, of course, but he didn't count.

After she bought a coffee and morning paper, she looked around. This time she didn't have any problem finding an empty table. She shrugged out of her jacket and slipped it over a chair, then sat down by the window and looked out at another overcast day where thick-bellied clouds, heavy with the threat of snow, shuffled across the sky.

She saw a man walk along the sidewalk across the street and straightened. He crossed the road and walked toward the coffee house. She mangled the corner of her newspaper with a fist and felt her heart do a crazy little flip. It was *him*. When he reached the sidewalk parallel to the wall of windows where she sat, Katherine glanced quickly down at the coffee cup in her hand, but she still managed to get a glimpse of him through the corner of her eye.

The door opened, and even when a cold breeze brushed across her skin, she continued to stare at her cup. But the battle didn't last long. Curiosity won, and she peeked beneath her lashes. He stood with his back to her while talking to a cashier. She'd forgotten how tall he was. A good couple of inches over six feet. He was big and broad-shouldered, too. The bulky navy jacket he wore emphasized his size even more. Its hem reached his waist, and the stonewashed jeans he wore hugged his long legs and small, tight buttocks. He sure had a nice—

He turned unexpectedly. Glancing up, she met his gaze across the room and felt her face burn with mortification. She'd been caught right in the act of staring at his butt.

He smiled, which revealed a dimple in his right cheek she hadn't noticed until now. All her embarrassment melted away with the pleasure in his face. He looked as happy as she felt when it came to seeing each other again.

He weaved through the tables until he stopped at hers. "Do you mind if I join you?"

"Not at all. I'm just trying to wake up before I drag myself to work."

He sank down in the opposite chair. "And where do you have to drag yourself to?"

As his knee brushed up against her own, she shifted in her seat. Approximately four feet separated them, but his proximity seemed even closer, the way his large frame dwarfed his chair and their table. She glanced down at the coffee he held. His left hand, capable looking, long-fingered and ringless, was in proportion to the rest of him. Large. He easily wrapped his fingers around his cup. What was that saying? "Men who had large hands had large—"

Okay. She needed to stop that. Just because her personal life rated a zero, it didn't mean she needed to act like a sex-starved idiot. Or was it this particular man that turned her brain into a narcotic induced stupor?

Then she realized he was looking at her with a question in his eyes. Oh, yes. Work. "The Morning Dove. I work at a shelter for runaway teens."

"That's admirable. I don't know of anyone else with such a selfless job." His voice was husky and deep, his gaze earnest. He acted enthralled, which she found both disconcerting and flattering.

Katherine shrugged and twirled the tip of her braid between her thumb and forefinger. "I wouldn't say that. It's very rewarding."

"What made you decide to get into something like that?"

"Oh, I guess I fell into it." Of course, not exactly the truth, but Katherine didn't want to go there. Even after all these years, she was liable to get too emotional over why she worked at the shelter.

"And you?" she asked.

"Me?"

"Yes. What type of work do you do?"

"What type of work do *I* do?"

He frowned and looked around the room. Then he glanced at the table where her newspaper sat unopened. For a moment, she wondered if he planned on answering.

"I'm...a reporter."

"Are you sure?"

His frown turned to confusion. "Why?"

"You don't sound too sure."

"I guess it's because I'm between jobs."

She grimaced. "That's never fun. I'm sorry—"

"Oh, I'll find something." His dimple reappeared with his smile. "This way I have a chance to see some of Boston since I just moved here. Actually, you can see my place. It's the end townhouse across the street."

Already guessing what place he meant, she still glanced over to where he nodded. She vaguely remembered a sign on one of the neighboring lawns but didn't know the details since the previous owner had kept to himself.

"If you don't find a job soon, I can ask around. I know a lot of people who—"

"No."

"Okay." It looked like she'd upset him. No doubt he had too much pride to ask or want help.

"My problems are insignificant compared to what your uncle must be going through. How is he coping with the aftereffects of the fire?"

She watched him rub a thumb along the edge of the table. "Fine, I guess, under the circumstances."

"From what I read in the follow-up, they never did find any survivors."

"I'm afraid not. At least the police caught the man."

His expression thoughtful, he continued to stroke the table's edge with a thumb. "Yes, they did. A janitor at Miltronics with a prior record for arson and, may I add, a man not too swift to leave all that evidence in his apartment. I'm surprised he slipped past with the company's strict screening policy. Even more surprised at how quickly the police were able to find and convict a suspect."

"What are you implying?"

Sighing, he met her gaze with sober, gray eyes. "I actually don't know." He smiled, but his face remained serious. "Well, anyway, I'm glad they found the person, but I'd be even happier if I knew the name of the beautiful woman seated across from me."

She was not going to blush at the compliment or the interest in his eyes. "It's Katherine Spalding. No nicknames, but plain Katherine. And you're?"

"Clark. Clark Kent."

She laughed. She couldn't help it. He couldn't be serious. "And you say you're a reporter? That's rich."

"I don't understand."

"You know, the superhero? The man in tights who leaps over buildings and sees through buildings?"

"I still don't understand."

This conversation was not going at all how she'd hoped. "You're making it sound like you've jumped out from some comic strip. That or some Saturday morning cartoon or kids show. How can anyone take you seriously?"

"You're talking about a cartoon character?" He looked offended.

"Yes."

"I didn't know."

"You're serious." Katherine knew she sounded incredulous, but this topped all the stories she'd heard over the years at the shelter. She'd caught herself a live one this time.

"If you don't believe me. I have my driver's license." He reached for his wallet.

"No. That's fine. I'll take your word for it." She looked at her wrist and realized she didn't have her watch. "I have to go. It was nice talking to you," she stumbled over the name "— Clark."

He was an absolutely gorgeous, take your breath away... nut. No doubt harmless, but still a nut. From appearances, her mother would keel over in ecstasy if Katherine brought him home. He was articulate, clean, well dressed. Then again, appearances could be deceptive. For a while there, she'd thought something could come of it. The chemistry had been there simmering beneath the surface between them, but if she stuck around, she was liable to get burned. Bad.

Standing up, she ignored the disappointment in his eyes, grabbed her purse and jacket and hurried from the coffee shop, leaving her coffee on the table.

~~*~~

Once again, Clark watched her walk away. Damn it. He scraped his fingers through his hair. Clark wanted to hit something, anything to expel his irritation at himself and the situation.

When Clark mentioned his name, the security guard at the newspaper had acted hostile. And now Katherine's response. Both thought he'd lost a few screws becomes of his name.

There might have been others with similar reactions Clark had missed; he'd been so self-absorbed with his own problems.

What was with this superhero? Clark didn't remember anything about a cartoon character. And why had the thought of being a reporter felt familiar? Was it a false memory he'd conjured up from his forgotten childhood? He closed his eyes against the insanity and slipped his fingers beneath his glasses to rub the bridge of his nose. A headache drilled into his temples and the base of his skull.

That same day Clark hunted down a comic and collectible store and found a book with a superhero in a cape and tights on the front cover. Once out of the store and on the sidewalk, he flipped through the magazine, and with each page, his embarrassment deepened. It was all there. His name in print. Reporter. Superhero extraordinaire. Able to twist metal with his bare hands. He even looked like the cartoon character right up to his fake glasses.

So Katherine thought him a lunatic, and could he blame her? When it came down to it, could anyone? In disgust, he tossed the magazine in the nearest trash bin.

What did he do now? Tell Katherine the truth? That he'd lost his memory, had over one hundred thousand dollars and a gun stashed away, but above all, he'd recovered a photo of her from a murdered teenage boy? Yeah, right. The truth sounded crazier than the character he'd impersonated. She'd run that much faster.

~~*~~

Paul Spalding walked into his office and flipped on the switch by the entrance, flooding the room with light. Although the house was empty, he shut the door and locked it, then walked over to the window and closed the shutters against the evening. One could never be too careful. He picked up the telephone receiver on his desk, punched in a number and waited.

"Hello," the person answered on the other end.

"I want the place closed down."

"I'm working on it."

"Not hard enough." Paul glared at the wall where an ornately framed seascape hung. "I want the screws tightened. Too much is at stake."

"You don't have to tell me that."

"She's starting to get suspicious. You know if she starts asking too many questions—"

"Calm down. There's no way she'll uncover the truth."

"You don't give her enough credit. She's smart."

"Not that smart. Plus, you can't off a senator's daughter without someone asking questions. It's not that simple."

Paul frowned. "I hope you're not getting soft on me."

A long pause followed, then, "Of course not. You know, if it comes down to killing her, then so be it. But it's not going to get that far."

"Let's hope not. I'm not the only one with their ass on the line."

"Don't panic. I'll take care of the shelter."

"You do that."

The phone went dead.

CHAPTER 5

THE SCRAPE OF a match cut into the night. The flame's light illuminated the haggard, sullen face of a man, who stood with a shoulder against a signpost by the entrance to the parking lot. After he lifted the match to his cigarette, he inhaled, and the glowing ember of the cigarette flared and retracted. Then he extinguished the match, thrusting his face back into shadow.

The sun had fallen over the horizon hours ago, and with its disappearance, night had formed, thick and filled with the scent of oil and fuel exhaust. Snow, wispy and steady, fluttered from the black sky and caressed her lashes, hair and cheeks as Katherine, having finished work for the day, walked toward the parking lot. She needed to pass the man to get to her car. Unless, that is, she wanted to look paranoid and leap over the metal chain that circled the lot and give the man a good laugh. She wasn't going to feel threatened. She'd crossed some pretty rough characters over the years and come out swinging. She also had the added comfort of her pepper spray hidden away in her purse.

But even after all her reassurances, Katherine still tensed when she walked past. Moments later, the scrape of shoes against cement echoed behind her. He was following her, she realized in alarm. From the very beginning, she'd known the shelter wasn't in the best neighborhood, but she'd foolishly thought nothing would happen to her. After all, she'd always led a charmed life.

Katherine sensed the predatory interest of the man behind as she crossed the lot to her car. It was too late to go back to the shelter; he blocked her way, and the stores and businesses within hearing distance had long since closed.

Don't hurry. Don't look like a victim. Above all, appear confident.

Slowly, and oh so very casually, she opened the zipper of her purse and slipped her hand inside to find her pepper spray in the side pocket. When she reached her car, Katherine clutched the small canister and glanced over her shoulder.

She jerked back. Only feet separated them. She didn't have time to react. He lunged and grabbed her wrist, pulling it up and around her back. The pepper spray dropped to the ground. Her purse fell and banged against her thigh; its strap caught against her inner elbow.

From behind Katherine, he rammed her elbow higher against her back. Pain blazed through her arm and ripped a cry from her throat. She shoved him with a shoulder, but he twisted her wrist harder and drove her against the side of her car. Katherine tried to protect her face with her free hand but wasn't fast enough. The metal border around the window smashed against her cheek. Then he wrenched her up from behind with such force her neck snapped back.

Something cold touched her throat. *Oh, please, no.* The flat of a blade.

"Move and you're dead."

Katherine froze, stifling the swallow lodged in her throat. One wrong step on her part and he could slice her neck. She didn't dare talk, didn't dare move.

He panted heavily behind her. His breath washed past her ear. He smelled of stale alcohol and evil. Katherine closed her eyes, wanting to vanish from the nightmare that evolved around her. She didn't want to die. Not yet. Not when she still needed to atone for Miranda's death.

His hand groped at her jacket and yanked the zipper open.

Buttons popped and scattered to the pavement as he tore open her blouse and bit his fingers into her breast. Her purse swung drunkenly against her leg.

"Hey, bitch. Feel like a big, hard dick between your legs?"

Rape. That's what he wanted. Maybe murder when he finished with her. She didn't dare lose control. Not with a knife at her throat.

Suddenly the blade vanished from her neck. From behind, the man grunted. Katherine, shoved to one side, caught a flash of movement, a whisper of sound. She stumbled and dropped her purse, spraying its contents across the ground.

Pivoting, she backed up against the side of her car and watched another man, larger and taller than the other, grab and lift her assailant. Fabric tore. Someone cried out. The knife, flashing silver from a nearby light post, arched through the air, tumbled to the pavement and skidded to a stop.

The smaller of the two dove across the air and crashed into the ground, where he remained. For a moment, her rescuer stood, head bowed, motionless. The faint rasp of his breath traveled the distance between them. Then he turned and walked toward her. Katherine tensed, not knowing if this new man was any better than the last. With each step he took toward her, his features grew more distinct. Dark hair, large jaw, and thick-framed glasses.

"Clark?"

"Yeah. Are you all right?"

Katherine sighed, feeling her body grow heavy with relief. "I think so. Maybe a little weak in the knees is all."

"Your cheek looks swollen and bruised. What about your throat?"

When he moved closer and grazed a knuckle against the side of her neck to nudge her braid aside, she stilled, fearful of what he'd find.

"You've got a shallow scratch, but it's hard to see in this light. We need to get you out of here. Do you know where your car keys are?"

When he continued to act concerned, Katherine relaxed a

little further. "They're on the ground somewhere. I dropped my purse. I don't know how we're going to find—"

"Here they are."

He bent down and dangled them from his index finger. How he managed to find them so quickly, Katherine didn't know— and didn't care. She just wanted to get out of here. After he retrieved her purse and the items that had spilled from inside, she followed him around her car on unsteady legs.

Clark opened the passenger door. The interior light broke through the shadows, illuminating the condition of her clothing. Her jacket hung off one shoulder, while her blouse gaped wide, exposing her torn bra. Four long, red gashes marked the top of her right breast. With shaking hands, she clutched her shirt closed.

The reality of the situation hit her. She'd been lucky. If Clark hadn't been around... Her legs buckled. Clark caught her by the elbow and urged her down in the passenger seat.

"I don't understand how you got here. Just what were you doing—"

A shuffling sound carried over the night air. Katherine glanced through the driver's side window and saw her attacker scramble to his feet. As he half ran, half limped across the parking lot and away from her car, his figure melded deeper into the shadows. Clark turned as if to go after him.

"No! It's not safe." Katherine lunged from the passenger seat and grasped his wrist, slick and warm against her fingers. "What in the—"

She snatched her hand away and looked down. Blood. Then she looked at Clark's hand and the thick, dark liquid dripping from his fingers.

"Clark, you're bleeding all over the place! We need to get you to the hospital."

~~*~~

Clark shifted away from Katherine's gaze, lifted his arm and pulled back his sleeve. The creep had slashed him across the wrist.

35

"It's nothing."

But it was. Blood flowed from the cut and had smeared across his arm and into the white shirt beneath his jacket. Even with the bad lighting, he could tell the cut was deep and close to the artery. Too close. Dizziness floated against the back of his eyes. Not a good sign. If he continued losing blood, he wouldn't be much help to anyone, but he'd worry about it later. Right now, he needed to concentrate on Katherine's safety.

"We need to call the police," Clark said.

"No."

"What do you mean, 'No'?"

"Later. I can't think. All those questions. I just—I can't deal with it all."

"Fine," he conceded, not wanting to upset her further. And in all honesty, talking to the police didn't appeal to him either. "Then let's get you out of here. Hop in."

When she sat back down in the car, Clark closed the passenger door and got behind the wheel.

"Hey, wait a minute. What about your car?" Katherine asked.

"I don't have a car, and anyway, even if I did, it wouldn't matter. I'm not about to let you drive. So how about you sit back and relax until I get you to a hospital?"

"I don't need to see a doctor. And anyway, if anyone needs help, it's you and your arm."

"My arm can wait. It's you I'm concerned about."

"But the blood—"

"It looks a lot worse than it is." Clark started to believe his wrist wasn't half as bad as he'd first thought. Strangely enough, the dizziness had disappeared.

"Then can you just take me home? I'm not up to waiting around for hours only to be given a prescription for painkillers. My stomach's already upset as it is. I just want to get home where I feel safe."

"I still think a hospital would be the best—"

"Please."

"Fine," he agreed reluctantly, going against his better judgment.

When she'd snapped on her seat belt, Clark started the motor and ran his good hand over the steering wheel to get the feel of it. Until now, he'd relied on taxis and the public transit system, but he knew at some point he'd driven because of the crash. He did fine, though, as he guided the car out of the parking lot and headed toward Katherine's house. During the drive, he eased his left hand down by his side to shield the wound from Katherine. With her already battered emotions, he didn't want her worried even more.

Clark pulled up in front of her townhouse and hurried around to help her from the car, but she'd already slipped out by the time he reached her side. Granted, she didn't look too stable the way she grabbed the side of the car for support.

"I don't think I'm feeling very good. I think—"

He swept her up in his arms, ignored her mumbled protest and carried her to the front door. Considering his wrist, he was surprised at how light she felt in his arms. The weakness he'd felt earlier had eased significantly, which reconfirmed his wound wasn't half as bad as he'd first thought. But he'd still get it dressed, and if bad enough, get himself to a doctor.

After Katherine showed him the correct keys to the house, he managed to balance her weight in his arms, open and unlock both the storm and front door without much struggle. He carried her into the house and kicked the door shut with heel of his shoe while Katherine snapped on the foyer light to his left. As he lifted her more securely in his arms, her blonde hair, thick and partially unbound from her braid, brushed against his cheek, and its fragrance, a hint of lemon and something elusive teased his senses. He'd never been this close to her. He'd thought about it, wondered about it, but not under these circumstances.

A wave of protectiveness surged through him. She didn't deserve what had happened tonight. No one did. He glanced down and saw the marks above her right breast. Several dark contusions fanned out from four, shallow gashes to her skin. Jaw taut, he glanced quickly away.

What type of man would do this to a woman? No. Man wasn't the correct word. Katherine's attacker was a sick creep, worse than any animal. At least with animals, they had their own code they followed. He should have gone after the bastard while he'd had a chance.

Thank God he'd been following her over the course of the last couple of days. To think what would have happened to her— No. What mattered was that she'd be okay after a good night's sleep.

The living room lay to the right. A loveseat and sofa circled a ceramic fireplace. Magazines were splayed out across a thick legged coffee table in some type of dark wood, while large potted plants were strategically placed to add a touch of the outdoors. The room was a mosaic of earth tones, warm and inviting. No doubt an extension of her personality.

When he moved to set her down on the sofa, Katherine placed a hand on his arm.

"No. Let me down here. I really need to—"

The minute her feet touched the floor, Katherine rushed to the bathroom, clutching her stomach.

Clark stood uncertainly by the closed door but decided she wouldn't much appreciate having him listen in, so he backed away, walked into the kitchen and flipped on the light switch. After he shrugged out of his jacket and placed it on the counter, he snapped on another light above the kitchen sink and pulled back the sleeve of his shirt. Frowning, he rubbed a thumb along his wrist. Dried blood flaked away from his arm, but the skin appeared fine. Odd. He moved his wrist beneath the faucet, he turned on the water and washed the blood from his inner arm.

When the water flowing over his arm turned from pink to translucent, he shut off the faucet and stared at his arm beneath the harsh glare of the overhead light. No scar, no wound. Nothing. The gash had completely disappeared. But his blood-stained sleeve still remained. Quickly, he rolled his sleeve to his elbow to hide the stain from Katherine, but Clark couldn't hide it from himself.

Too long Clark had ignored his situation, but after tonight, he couldn't. Something was wrong with him. And he wasn't talking about a cold or infection. This went way beyond normal.

Clark thought back to the car accident and how he'd run from the scene with such incredible agility, and this evening he'd been able to lift Katherine's attacker as if the man had been filled with air, not bone and muscle. Then there'd been the door to the newspaper stand he'd broken and now his arm. The gash on his wrist hadn't been a surface wound. So how could something of that magnitude disappear? It didn't make sense. Nothing about him made sense.

Who in the hell was he?

CHAPTER 6

CLARK HAD NO idea who or even what he was. Man or animal? Or something worse? The answers were locked somewhere in his brain. If he looked hard enough, there were clues all around him. He only needed to decipher them.

There was his name. Clark Kent. It was odd and easily recognizable. Was there any truth behind it? Was he named Clark Kent for a reason? Could he be some type of superhero after all? No. Impossible. He was talking about a damn cartoon character.

He looked around Katherine's kitchen. Several copper bottom pots hung suspended above the kitchen island. He took one from its hook and palmed the handle. He hesitated. Did he really want to know? No. Not really. But he *needed* to know.

With a thumb and index finger, he pinched the rim and pulled it toward the pot's center. The metal crumbled into itself. He jerked his hand back.

Holy, shit. It had felt like he'd been moving warm wax beneath his fingers. It had been that flexible.

He snapped his index finger against the pot's side and watched in horror as a dent appeared in the metal. And he hadn't even been trying. What could he do if he really put his strength into it? Would he be able to tear the metal beneath his two hands?

"How's your arm?"

The pot slipped from Clark's grasp and tumbled toward

the floor. With the flick of his wrist, he caught it in midair and turned to where Katherine stood by the doorway. She still wore a pair of faded jeans, but she'd changed her shirt. The black sweater accented the pallor of her face and the dark crescents below her eyes. She'd pulled her hair from her braid, and their waves flowed gold against the black material. The trauma of the night gleamed in her pain-filled, brown eyes.

"It's fine." He lifted his arm to show her, which was a mistake.

Her eyes widened with shock. "What happened to my pot?"

He glanced at the misshapen metal in his hand. How was he going to get out of this one without sounding nuts? *Oh, by the way, I thought I'd try my hand at modern art?* Or he could try the truth with *I only wanted to test out my special powers.* Yeah, right. She'd have his butt out the door before he had a chance to blink.

"I dropped it," he said finally.

Eying him and the pot with skepticism, she walked over and took it gingerly from his hand. "Really? It looks like you took a sledgehammer to it." She glanced around as if to find the alleged hammer, then frowned at the floor. "The tiles fine. I would think it would have done some damage to the floor."

"I guess they really don't make things like they used to." What type of lame comment was that one? He needed to change the subject and quick. "How's your stomach?"

Katherine made a face. "It's still there, but I took some Pepto Bismo, which helped a little."

Clark didn't like how she kept on staring at the pot. And he particularly didn't like the look of her neck or the bruise to her cheek. "Where's your first-aid kit?"

"It's in the master bathroom—under the sink."

After retrieving the pot from her, he placed it on the counter behind him and hurried from the room.

"Why?" she called after him. "I thought you said your arm was okay."

"Oh, it is." He walked down the hall, realized the floor plan was the reverse of his own rental and stepped into the larger of two bedrooms. In the bathroom, he pulled the kit from the cabinet beneath the sink and placed it on top of the counter. As he slipped an antiseptic pad from a package, he glanced over a shoulder and found Katherine by the doorway.

She arched a brow. "Do you always barge into a woman's bedroom without asking?"

Straightening, he caught her half smile and flushed. "No. Not unless I'm invited." He cleared his throat, amazed at how easily a pair of teasing brown eyes made him feel mentally challenged. "But we need to take care of your neck. There's also your cheek."

She laughed. "I'll take care of it later. All I need is a good night's rest, and I'll be good to go to work in the morning."

"You shouldn't be working. Your body needs to recuperate."

"Well, the way things are going, I may not have a job for very much longer."

"Why?"

"I don't want to bore you with the details."

"Tell me. I want to know."

She shrugged a shoulder. "Fine. It's called a problem with cash flow. The shelter's running out of funds, and I'm running out of options." Sighing, she shook her head and grinned. "Forget I said that. I'm sure everything will work out."

Katherine's smile and the buoyant tone to her voice didn't fool him. She was worried. It was there in her eyes.

"You never know," he mused aloud. "You might get that funding from the least likely source. Stranger things have happened. But right now, can you humor me and let me take a look at your face and neck? I'd feel better."

"I guess I can do that."

When she dragged back her hair and inched closer, he realized this wasn't going to work. The crown of her head barely reached his chin.

"If you sit on the counter, I can see better."

She raised a finely drawn brow but complied. "Anything else, while I'm at it?"

"How's your cooking?" Seeing how he managed to wipe the worry from her eyes, Clark smiled. "Don't worry. I'll ask for a home cooked meal another day."

"Oh, no. You're asking the wrong person here. Unless you like peanut butter and jelly sandwiches."

Clark laughed. She had a sense of humor. He liked that. "I'm sure you can make anything taste like *haute cuisine*."

He glanced at her cheek and sobered. "There's not much that can be done for the contusion to your cheek other than an ice pack to bring down the swelling. As for your neck ..." He wiped the antiseptic over her throat, gently edging closer to the cut, which was a horizontal line by the lower edge of her larynx. Thank God, it wasn't serious. "You were lucky. You only have a surface scratch with minor clotting. If he'd had a mind, he could have easily sliced through to your trachea ..."

When he caught her shiver, he straightened and realized that she was looking at him oddly. "Are you all right?"

"Fantastic, considering that I could have been sliced and diced by some sick pervert. You know, it's starting to hit me how lucky I was." She wrapped a strand of blonde hair behind an ear. "It's also reassuring to have someone so capable. I swear you sound like a doctor."

He dropped the pad into the wastebasket, and as reached for the Neosporin, he paused, his hand in mid-air. "Really?"

Leaning back with her palms against the counter, she closed her eyes and smiled softly. "Hmmm. Hmmm. A regular Marcus Welby."

"Marcus Welby?"

"You know? The doctor on television? I used to watch all the reruns when I was a kid." She opened one eye and then the other. A second later, both of them widened in wonder. "Oh, no. Don't tell me you've never heard of him either? You haven't, have you? That just tells me how much I need to get a life. Obviously, I watch way too much T.V."

"A doctor," he murmured.

Could he be? It was possible. He glanced down at his hands as he opened the Neosporin. What did doctor's hands look like? Like his? Hell. There he went again. He had to stop asking himself questions he didn't have answers to.

Determined to let it go for now, he concentrated on the task at hand, glancing down at the tube. The ointment had expired last year. "Do you have any other antibiotic cream?"

"It's in the medicine cabinet. No wait—"

But Clark had already opened the door. He immediately saw the box of condoms. Not just one. Four packages stared back at him. A party pack, no less—lubricated, flavored, colored, and yes, king-size. Trying to appear unfazed, Clark reached passed and retrieved the cream on the top shelf. So she had some condoms in her bathroom. So what if she had enough in there to throw a neighborhood orgy for a good week. Katherine's sex life wasn't his business. His glance skirted past her face and down to the tube as he unscrewed the top.

Okay, so it bothered him—a lot.

"They're not mine."

His hand tightened on the tube, squirting cream from the opening and onto the counter between her legs. Of all places. He grabbed a Kleenex from the box above the toilet and was about to wipe the cream off but stopped. There was no way of cleaning it off without touching her.

"Here." He offered Katherine the tissue and noticed her face had turned pink. "And about your cabinet—that's your business."

"I know, but it's just that I don't want you having this idea that I go around having sex with every guy I meet." Shifting, Katherine wiped the cream from the counter. "It was a stupid joke from a friend. His way of telling me I needed a sex life."

"And do you—?" Clark caught himself from mutilating the tube again.

"Have a sex life?"

"Yes. I mean, no. What I mean is do you have someone you're seeing?"

"No."

Clark relaxed. Until now, he hadn't noticed how tense he'd been. The idea of Katherine in a serious relationship with someone else had bothered him. If he didn't watch out, he'd get tangled deeper in her life, which wouldn't be the smartest move. She might be involved in the murder of the teenage boy in

Arizona. Then he realized how crazy that sounded. She worked at a shelter helping others. Someone like that didn't go around killing people.

But there was still the unexplained cash and gun. Both indicated a mysterious and possibly dangerous past—a past he had no right to involve her in, Clark realized, as he refocused on Katherine's injuries and applied a bead of medicine over the wound across her neck.

In time, the abrasion would fade and completely disappear. It would have been a shame to have a scar against such flawless skin. The sweater's low neckline exposed more silken skin and hinted at the shadowy valley between her breasts. He tried not to think how the material hugged her firm, full breasts or how close they were to his hand.

It wasn't working. Not when he was conscious of the heat of her body, the rise and fall of her breasts and how her splayed legs bracketed his hips. His groin tightened and the air around him thickened to where he couldn't catch his breath. Then he made the mistake of glancing at her parted lips. They reminded him of pink, crushed velvet.

Sex. He was tied up in knots, and he didn't know how to get himself untangled. He wanted to sink himself in her, drown in the sensation of having her legs wrapped around his hips and her mouth on his skin. This need was inexplicable, overpowering.

Why now? Why Katherine? Was he that inexperienced that merely touching a woman sent him into a tailspin? Did he even know what to do with a woman if he had one in his arms? And most importantly, did he even have the right to think of Katherine in any sexual light if he was involved with someone from his past?

No. He couldn't be married. It wasn't the lack of a ring or indentation on his wedding finger, but the feeling deep in his gut that he would remember someone of that importance in his life.

It took him a while to realize he'd finished applying the antibiotic ointment and had moved his palm to the hollow between her neck and shoulder and was rubbing his thumb absently along the line of her collarbone. As she shifted, her neckline inched lower, which exposed the beginning of a bruise.

How much of an ass could he be? He'd let his hormones overtake what little sense he had, while Katherine was probably feeling sore and battered.

"How's your..." He glanced up and met her gaze and was further caught off guard by the awareness in her large, brown eyes.

He dove right back into thinking of sex, tangled sheets, and long legs. Knowing a box of condoms was within arm's reach only aggravated the images.

She flushed. "They're fine. And no. I can take care of them."

"Yes, well...that's good." He was probably blushing as badly as Katherine.

Abruptly, he turned back to the kit, shut it with hands that had a distinct tremor, and cleared his throat. "You do know we need to call the police. We can't delay it any longer."

~~*~~

Katherine, so focused on his every touch and movement, didn't understand his comment immediately. When it finally sank in, she felt as if she'd plunged into a frigid bath on a January morning.

"I don't want to talk to the police," she managed to get out.

"You can't let something like tonight slide."

The room was too small, too stifling, too intimate while Clark was too big, too male, too obstinate. Sliding off the counter, she brushed up against his hard body, inhaled sharply at the contact, and backed away from him and the room. "I don't think it would be a good idea."

"Why?" He followed her out of the bathroom.

"I have my reasons, so can you drop it?"

If she wanted, she could be as obstinate as Clark. He, himself, had told her that he was a reporter. If she let him know that she was Senator Spalding's daughter, he'd have a field day—him and any number of other reporters if tonight leaked out. Her mother was having enough problems. Because of her mother's views on fetal cell research, her popularity as senator was on the decline. The last thing she needed was to have her daughter splashed over the newspaper.

"As long as you know that by not reporting this you're letting this creep go—"

"You don't have to tell me something I already know. And anyway, even if I did go to the police, do you actually think they'd be able to get the guy? He's long gone." She bit her lip, realizing she sounded antagonistic and ungrateful. "I want to thank you for everything. I can't imagine what would have happened if you hadn't stepped in. It was a miracle you were there in the first place, which all makes me wonder why you were."

She watched his expression change, almost as if the animation in his face had shut down. "I wanted to check up on you."

"Why?"

"Because you interest me."

"I interest you?" she echoed like an idiot. She didn't know whether to be charmed or alarmed.

"Yes. Everything about you and your life." Shoving his fingers through his hair, he didn't look thrilled with the idea. "If you only knew the half of it."

She hugged her middle. Something didn't add up. Then it dawned on her that all this time, their meetings had been planned. She'd met Clark too many times in too many places and all within a week. He even lived in the same complex. A coincidence? Fate? She didn't believe in either. Maybe if they'd only crossed paths once or twice... But he'd shown up at the coffee house, by the shelter twice, and lived on the same street.

"All this time you've been following me. I want to know why. Are you some sick stalker who—"

"I knew you'd react like that." A bleak look crossed his features.

"Why wouldn't I be upset? How else am I supposed to react?" she asked in disbelief. "And you didn't answer me. Why?"

"You wouldn't understand."

"Try me."

Clark rubbed the back of his neck and opened his mouth as

if to answer, but then he shook his head. "No. Not now. Maybe later. I don't know," he said the last in frustration. "I better go. You're exhausted. I just need to get my jacket, and I'll be out of here."

"I think that's a good idea." She didn't want him in her house. Katherine didn't trust him.

When Clark came back with his jacket, she'd moved into the hall by the front door. She tried not to flinch as he walked past and grabbed the doorknob.

Then Katherine stumbled on the only logical reason he'd been following her. "Are you doing a story on my mother?"

"Your mother?" He looked back at her in confusion. "What are you talking about?"

"Nothing." Katherine backpedaled. He didn't know. Even if he was a born actor, he couldn't fake that much surprise.

Clark opened the door and paused. "Are you going to be all right tonight? Is there someone you can call if you need to?"

She swallowed. "I'll be fine."

He nodded grimly. "Well, if you wake up during the night and get scared...I'm only a couple of doors down. That's if you—"

"I don't think so."

The hall light exposed the hard, austere lines of his face and the haunted look in his eyes before he slipped out into the night. She closed and locked the door behind him, but with his departure, Katherine didn't feel any safer. Next, she slid the deadbolt in place. That didn't help either.

She turned away from the door but couldn't forget the expression on Clark's face. He'd looked lost, abandoned, almost as if he'd been pleading silently for her help. Whatever demons chased his heels, it wasn't her problem. She had enough on her plate. Just the same, it didn't stop her from wondering.

She walked over to the living room window and peered outside. The clouds had since broken and moonlight pooled across the yard and the parking lot beyond, painting the patches of snow into blue-silver. Clark had since disappeared.

She couldn't get their conversation out of her mind. And after a while, she gave up trying.

He'd been following her, all because of this so-called interest in her, and if it wasn't because of her mother, then why? She wasn't egotistical enough to think it was her looks and personality alone to warrant such an obsession. She should have pushed more, but she'd been fearful of his anger and his answer. In time, whether or not she wanted it, she had an idea she'd get her answer. Dread banded around her chest. She knew when that time came, she wouldn't be ready for the truth.

It all circled back to one question. Who was Clark Kent?

CHAPTER 7

GASPING FOR AIR, clawing at her throat, Katherine woke with a start. She sat up and kicked at the sheets snarled around her body. Her heart thrashed against her ribs, while a thick layer of sweat chilled her flesh. The curtains hadn't been drawn closed from the previous night, and sunlight, bright and unforgiving, speared into the bedroom. Quiet blanketed the house, which belied the turmoil swirling through her body.

Katherine hated nightmares. She hadn't had any since Miranda's death. This one had been just as vivid and horrifying as those others, but so very different. She'd been clutching her slashed throat, unable to staunch the blood that gushed over her fingers and bathed her shirt. On her back, her body bound to the ground, she'd been alone, dying, crying mutely for help. She'd—

Pushing her tangled hair back from her face, she slipped out of bed and shoved those visions from her mind. Every muscle and bone in her body rebelled when she pulled herself into the bathroom. She had the misfortune of getting an eyeful of herself in the mirror. She not only felt like a wreck but looked it. Her hair appeared as if she'd had a fight with the blow dryer and lost. The bruise on her cheek had turned to an ugly purple and her brown eyes, normally filled with a cheerful sparkle, were dull, listless and dead inside.

"Come on girl, things aren't that bad." Katherine lifted the corners of her lips, and her reflection returned a facsimile of a smile. "How about some coffee? That might do the trick."

Her smiled dipped. Not a good idea. At least not over at The Coffee Company. She didn't want to risk meeting Clark. And anyway, coffee wasn't going to help. She needed more than a jolt of caffeine to drag herself to work today, but staying home with her thoughts didn't appeal—

The ring of the telephone cut off her dark musings. She caught it before the machine answered and found George on the line.

"Are you all right?" George asked. "You usually call if you're not coming in."

"Why? What time is it?" Frowning, she glanced over to the clock on the kitchen wall.

"Almost nine."

"Oh, shoot. I overslept." Did she ever. She'd never done that before. At least not to that extent. "Sorry for worrying you. I'm not feeling up to coming in."

"Flu?"

She grasped at the explanation. "Yeah, it's that time of year."

"Well, get some rest. It's got to be bad for you to miss work. Oh, while I've got you on the phone, your mother called. She sounded ticked that you hadn't come in yet."

Katherine rolled her eyes. She could imagine. Her mother expected things and people to conform to her own time schedule. Katherine glanced down at the answering machine and saw it blinking with a message. The call must have come in while she'd slept. Probably her mother.

"Thanks for the warning," Katherine said and turned her thoughts to Clark and his inordinate "interest" in her. "I was curious... Have you noticed anything odd at the shelter?"

"Not that I can remember. What are you getting at?"

"I don't know. What about some stranger asking questions or hanging around?"

"I've had a couple of phone calls asking about the shelter. More than normal, but nothing strange."

She'd thought for sure... "Okay. Thanks. I'll see you tomorrow."

After Katherine hung up, she checked her messages and heard her mother's abrupt request to call her. Great. Her mother didn't sound like she was in a good mood. She'd call back tonight. By then she might feel up to dealing with her mother.

For the rest of the day, Katherine hung around inside, watched a little television, dusted a little of the house, washed a little of the laundry. She hadn't been lying to Clark. When it came down to it, for years now, she'd focused all her energy on the shelter. She'd lost contact with all her friends from college and had zero social life. Maybe her mother did have a point.

George called back late in the afternoon.

"You know how you were wondering if anyone was asking questions?"

"Yes."

"Someone came by this morning."

"And? What happened?"

"This guy started hanging with a couple of kids who were smoking outside. He asked some weird questions."

"Like what?" She wanted to dive through the phone and prod George, but on some things, he mirrored her mother. He had his own time schedule.

"If they knew anything about Miltronics."

Her heart rate kicked into overdrive. She already knew the answer, but she asked anyway. "This guy. What's he look like?"

"Big. Dark hair. Could have been black or brown. I'm not sure."

"Did he have glasses?"

"I don't know. I didn't pay attention at the time. Charlene's kitten was missing, and she was pretty upset until he turned up at the back door."

"She knows the rules. I thought she said she'd found an owner... It doesn't matter. I'll talk to her about it tomorrow." Katherine rubbed her brow. "Is there anything else I should know about this guy?"

"He came by with an envelope. Said it was for you and the shelter."

"What's in it?"

"I don't know. It was sealed. I put it in your desk drawer."

She debated whether or not to wait until Monday morning to find out, and then realized she couldn't hold off that long. "Can you go to my office and open it?"

"Sure, give me a sec."

While she waited, she paced the length of the kitchen. She didn't know what to think.

"Got it. I'm opening it right now."

"And?" Her hand tightened on the receiver. The continuing silence on the other end drove her nuts. "What is it?"

He whistled, which further rattled her nerves.

"It's cash. Lots of it."

She grabbed a kitchen chair and dropped down in it. "Are you sure?"

After several, long, agonizing seconds, he said, "Oh, yeah. They're all hundreds. We're talking close to ten thousand here."

"It's got to be a joke. That or they're counterfeit."

"Who'd be crazy enough to donate counterfeit money? Doesn't make a whole lot of sense." George laughed. "Anyway, they sure smell real. I'd bet a week's wages they're legit. Whoever he is, he's an angel. You know the shelter's desperate for cash."

"Okay, George. Thanks," she murmured, unable to mask the tremor in her voice. "I'll be down in a bit. I can't leave that type of money there. And especially over the weekend."

"Oh, there's one other thing ..."

She'd been rising to her feet, but she quickly sank back down in her chair. She was almost afraid to ask. "What's that?"

"Well, your question earlier today and this guy got me curious like, so I asked Alex and Scott—they've been around the longest—if they'd seen him before or anyone else that looked kinda suspicious."

"And?"

"They had. But not the guy from today. Someone else. They'd seen him talking to Brian a couple of times."

"And then Brian disappeared." She was not going to get

paranoid here. But just the same… "Maybe we should call the police. Have them look into it for us."

"Don't hold your breath. You need a cattle prod to get them moving. Remember when Steve just up and left?"

"I remember."

But she didn't want to. Steve had been so damaged emotionally. Heroin, his drug of choice, had been his savior from pain and his companion in death. He'd been discovered dead from an overdose a couple of months later by the police, but only after someone called in a complaint about the stench in an alley.

"The way he disappeared like that looked damned suspicious," George insisted, "what with leaving all his clothes at the shelter. And what did the police do? Not a damn thing. Some street kid with a prior and no one who gives a shit isn't going to get a fire up their ass and you know it."

Emotionally drained, she rose to her feet. "I'll see you in a little while."

After a few fumbling attempts, she managed to get the receiver in its cradle. This was getting way out of hand. Clark's 'interest' in her seemed beyond strange. It was darn right frightening. And what in the world was he doing at the shelter asking a bunch of teenagers if they knew anything about Miltronics? What did her uncle's company have to do with the Morning Dove?

Was it some angle on a story? Maybe a story on the Spalding's? No. Clark hadn't made the connection with her or her mother, so why would he go that route? It didn't make sense. Something was really wrong here. And now there were two suspicious figures loitering around the shelter and an envelope of cash she had to worry about.

First, she'd take care of the cash.

Later that day, she deposited the money into the shelter's bank. When she discovered every single bill authentic, she didn't know whether or not to be pleased. Thankfully for the remainder of the day at the shelter, one crisis after another distracted her from the mysterious donation, and she didn't finish up until after dark.

After hearing about last night, George wouldn't let her go back to her car alone, which was fine by her. By the time she stepped through her front door, Katherine, too exhausted to do anything, grabbed some leftovers from the frig for dinner, and hit the bed.

Saturday morning, her head didn't feel any clearer with all the questions and thoughts tumbling inside it.

Until her encounters with Clark, she'd thought of herself as a good judge of character, able to read through a person's B.S. better than some. Clark had never come across as dangerous. Maybe a little strange, yes, but never a threat. Especially when he'd gone beyond the call of duty the other night to help her. And there were his eyes. She'd always believed a person's eyes were the gateway to their soul. Clark's were clear gray, warm and without artifice. But maybe she'd never read them correctly, and they'd been only a buffer, shielding her from a sick, dark mind.

If that were the case, could he have orchestrated the other night to appear as her savior? Was he playing some sick game of cat and mouse? That would be too bizarre. But everything about this situation was bizarre.

Did she dare go over there and start asking questions? And if on the off chance he was home, what could he really do to her in the light of day? Grab her and drag her inside? Kill her? She didn't think so. If he'd wanted her dead, he wouldn't have interfered the other night.

Katherine showered and changed into a wool sweater and khaki pants, and before she lost her nerve, she grabbed a jacket and her pepper spray and went outside on the pretext of getting yesterday's mail. She palmed the canister and hoped to heaven she wouldn't have to use it.

As she walked to the mailbox, Katherine eyed the end townhouse. Clark didn't have a car, so she couldn't tell if he was home unless she knocked. After she pulled out a couple of bills from her box, she stuffed them in her pocket, eased the pepper spray inside her other pocket, and veered in the direction of Clark's townhome.

At his front door, she rang the bell and waited tensely, having no real clue as to what she would say when he opened it. She waited some more, but when she didn't get an answer after the second attempt, she leaned over a prickly hedge, which surrounded the porch, and peered into the large, front window. The blinds and drapes were open, which enabled her to see into the interior of an empty living room. Not even a lamp or a picture on the wall.

Katherine knew he'd told her that he'd rented the place. The rental sign had also been removed. She didn't know what were lies or facts anymore.

Stuffing her hands into her jacket pockets, she trudged around the corner to the side of the house and winced. Snow seeped over and inside her running shoes with each step. Served her right for snooping. She found two other windows that faced the parking lot and street. The opaque one was probably to the bathroom. She walked past it and stopped beside the other window.

Here the blinds were also open. Unlike the living room, this room was partially furnished. A bed, its sheets thrown back, the comforter partially dragging on the carpet, butted up against one wall, and a brass lamp sat on the floor on this side of the bed.

That was it. Not even an end table, book or magazine to identify the owner. Even the bedding, some beige pattern, was nondescript.

Suddenly, Clark stepped into the room with a tiny white towel wrapped low on his hips. His hair, still damp from a shower, looked as if he'd raked it back with both hands. She had a clear impression of his face without his glasses, and it was startling at the dramatic change. His thick-framed glasses had given him an air of intelligence, of reticence, but without them, the hard thrust of his jaw, his prominent cheekbones conveyed a merciless face.

A fine sheen of moisture clung to his body, emphasizing the taut muscles of his arms and the sleek expanse of his chest and stomach. He had long, well-defined legs with a smattering of dark hair across his thighs and calves. He could have easily stepped from a fitness center commercial...or some female's sultry fantasy. He looked like sin personified.

Before she'd recovered from the initial shock of seeing him, he yanked at the towel around his waist and dropped it on the corner of his bed. When he turned and flipped on the light to the closet, she got an eyeful. And what an eyeful. The image was absolutely, irrevocably affixed in her mind. There was no mistaking him for anything other than a man.

"Oh, my!"

She didn't know if he'd heard her. Just the same, he turned toward the window—and saw her. The recognition in his slate, colored eyes was unmistakable. For two, very slow, very agonizing seconds, they stared back at each other. Embarrassment, hot and humiliating, burned up her throat to her face.

Katherine bolted, almost tripping over a mound of snow in her hurry to get away.

CHAPTER 8

The doorbell rang.

In growing dismay, Katherine backed further away from the front door. She'd rushed inside the house, closed and locked the door moments before, but right this second, she stood in the middle of the hall feeling like an idiot for overreacting.

She'd hoped Clark would have let it slide, be the gentleman and pretend he hadn't caught her sneaking a peek at him like some sick voyeur. Talk about mortifying. She paced in front of the door in indecision. Did she dare open it? Maybe if she just ignored him, he'd go away.

The doorbell rang again.

"Katherine! Are you all right?" Clark's words, which sounded muffled yet concerned, penetrated past the door. It looked like he didn't plan on leaving any time soon.

"Go away," she whispered.

When he resorted to pounding the door, she sighed in frustration. If he kept this up, the neighbors were going to call the police.

She grabbed the knob and yanked the door open, and then snapped on the lock to the storm door to keep him from entering. "I'm—"

At the sight of Clark, her train of thought collapsed. He hadn't taken the time to do anything but pull on a pair of faded jeans. He was bare-chested, barefooted—and freezing if she could go by the way he shifted back and forth on the cement porch. He also hadn't bothered with his glasses. His clear, gray eyes, minus the frames, were far too penetrating as he swept his gaze over the length of her.

She'd never be able to look at Clark in the same light again. How could she, with the image of him wet and naked plastered in her mind? He hadn't looked civilized then, and he didn't now.

"What's wrong? You look upset. I didn't come by yesterday because I thought you needed space." He searched her face while visibly shivering and rubbing at his bare arms. "Is it your stomach? Is it still bothering you? Do you want me to take you to the doctor?"

"My stomach couldn't be better." Katherine took a deep breath. Here goes. "Why were you over at the Morning Dove?"

She'd shocked him. Good. Let him get out of this one unscathed.

"What are you talking about?"

She tensed. He was going to deny it. But then, what should she have expected? All she'd gotten from him so far were lies and fabrications. "Someone at the shelter told me you'd been asking questions about Miltronics. You also donated a huge sum of cash. Is it some type of bribe I don't know about?"

"They must have confused me with someone else."

"I don't think so." She started feeling a healthy dose of anger. Good. Maybe then she wouldn't be taken in by a pair of gorgeous, gray eyes and a body more potent than any addictive drug. "Why go behind my back? Why couldn't you have come to me?"

"Come to you? About what? I don't know what you mean."

For a wild moment, doubts assaulted Katherine. Maybe her suspicions were unfounded, driven by her own paranoia.

"Can we talk inside? It's cold out here." Clark nodded to his feet.

"I don't think that's a good idea." If he wanted to run around without his clothes and freeze, that was his problem. "You have me so darn confused. I don't know what to make out of anything anymore. All of a sudden, you and someone else have made the Morning Dove a very popular place."

He grasped both sides of the door frame and leaned closer. "Someone else? Who? The man who attacked you the other night?"

She hadn't thought about that. "I don't know."

"You've got to believe me. I would never hurt you. That's something I *know* more than anything else, and deep down, you know it's the truth."

Katherine swallowed against a suddenly constricted throat. She searched his eyes for the truth. What a mistake. The sincerity in their depths made her waver. Goodness knows, she wanted to believe him. From past actions, Clark never once gave her a reason to believe he was immoral. But before she found herself weakening further, she looked away and glanced over his shoulder.

She inhaled sharply.

Oh, no. Of all people—her mother, walking across the sidewalk and heading this way. Katherine completely forgot to call her back last night, which was probably why her mother decided to show up in person.

Great. Just what Katherine needed. She didn't know what was worse—having her mother discover a strange, shirtless man outside her doorstep or inside her house. Since she couldn't find a lesser of the two evils, she unlocked the storm door and opened it.

"You better come in. My mother's right behind you."

Clark glanced over his shoulder before slipping inside. He tossed her a sheepish smile as he wiped his bare feet on the indoor mat. "I've an idea I'm not going to make the best impression."

"I'm not about to argue with you there."

When Sharon stepped inside, Katherine had to give her mother credit for taking in Clark's appearance with an expressionless face.

"Mom, this is Clark Kent," Katherine said into the silence, keeping her gaze away from Clark's very naked chest. "He's a neighbor who just moved in. Clark, this is my mother, Sharon."

Katherine, among a select few who knew her mother well,

saw the almost indiscernible pause before she shook his hand. Sharon glanced over to Katherine and didn't attempt to conceal her shock.

"What happened to your face?" Sharon glared at Clark. "If this—this man touched—"

Katherine saw Clark's eyes flash with anger, and before he retaliated with some scathing retort, Katherine said, "You've got it all wrong. I was attacked the other night and Clark, here, was the one who saved me from being raped."

As she explained in further detail of her encounter with her assailant, the color leached from her mother's face.

"Did you report it?"

"No. I didn't think it'd be a good idea."

"That was quick thinking on your part," Sharon said in obvious relief. "Goodness knows I have enough publicity without something else being leaked into the papers. With elections this year, it's hard enough trying to keep the media focused on the issues and not on an incumbent's dirty laundry."

"Did it happen here?" Sharon asked. "I can't imagine. You think you're safe in your own home when it's the farthest from the—"

"No. I'd just finished work for the day, and I was walking to my car."

Sharon's lips thinned, and disgust flashed in her eyes. "I should have known. It was only a matter of time before you were hurt at that place. I certainly wouldn't be surprised if you were attacked by some homeless delinquent you befriended. When are you going to give up on this fixation you have with these people? The Morning Dove's a lost cause. Let it go, Katherine. It's draining the life out of you."

"Mother, it's who I am."

"A martyr?" Katherine's mother scoffed.

Clark cleared his throat, his gaze narrowed on her mother with obvious dislike. "Why don't you give your daughter some slack? It's obvious she didn't call the police because she wanted to protect you. The least you could do is return the favor and support her."

Sharon spared him the briefest of glances. "We can discuss this later."

Katherine sighed. "So, why did you come?"

"I was on my way to do some errands, and I thought I'd drop by since I haven't been able to reach you."

Katherine saw her mother's look of reproach and took it for what it was—yet another manipulative move on her mother's part. "I've been a bit busy with my own problems."

"Which is understandable. I actually came by to tell you that David's throwing a birthday party for his father next Saturday. Paul's turning fifty this year, and it would be a shame to ignore such a milestone. And of course, you can invite a friend."

The tight-lipped expression thrown Clark's way told anyone with an ounce of intelligence, Sharon didn't classify him as a "friend". But then, anyone Katherine personally picked was always regarded with suspicion.

"You *will* be able to make it?"

"Of course," Katherine said.

"Good. You may want to call Rachel to see if she needs any help, but from what I gather, she has everything under control."

Realizing her mother intended to go, Katherine stiffened. That would leave her alone with Clark—the last thing she wanted.

"Don't leave yet. How about a bit of breakfast before you're off? Or keep me company while I have mine?" She glanced over at Clark. "Clark was just leaving when you came by. Isn't that right?"

Katherine met his gaze without flinching. For a wild moment, she thought he might argue, but he only raised a mocking brow and said, "That's right."

"I'll talk to you later," he shot back as he strolled out the door.

"Who is he?"

Katherine shrugged. "Just a neighbor."

"The way he's dressed?" her mother asked in disbelief. "Don't take me for a fool. A *neighbor* doesn't run over to a woman's house with only his pants on. I hope you have the sense to know what you're getting yourself into and to use protection. Goodness knows, there are so many diseases being passed around."

At her bald statement, Katherine's face warmed with embarrassment, but she didn't argue. She knew there was little point trying to chip past her mother's point of view, so instead, she listened to her mother during breakfast. Finally, when Sharon disappeared out the front door, Katherine closed and locked it with relief. She was alone.

Over the next couple of days, though, Katherine didn't feel alone. The distinct impression of someone following nagged her. The feeling was nothing she could prove, nothing she could see, but it was there nonetheless. Frightening and aggravating.

And she knew that person was Clark Kent. Even though he hadn't spoken to her since the morning of her mother's visit, she knew he was keeping a close watch on her just the same.

By the third day, she decided she'd had enough and focused on turning Clark's little cat and mouse game around. She just needed the right opportunity.

By the fourth day, Katherine found that opportunity. After coming home from work, she'd just pulled her car into her allotted space, when she spied Clark jumping into a taxi. She decided to follow at a discreet pace in her own car.

The taxi led her to a place both shocking and disconcerting. A block away, she watched as Clark stepped out of the cab and crossed the street toward a large, gray-stoned house.

Paul Spalding.

None other than her uncle's home.

~~*~~

Standing on the sidewalk adjacent to the fence, which encompassed Spalding's estate, Clark angled his watch toward the streetlight. He glanced at the time. Ten before seven. After several days of surveying Spalding's home, Clark had learned that not only Paul but his son and daughter-in-law also resided within the estate. Their housekeeper, on the other hand, left promptly at seven each evening. It didn't give him much time or opportunity to search the place.

He needed to get inside before the housekeeper set the alarm and walked out the front door. Then he had approximately one hour to look around and get out—unless he wanted to cross paths with one of the Spaldings.

Before he started doubting the rationale of what he was doing, Clark jumped, caught the top of the eight-foot, stone wall with both hands, and vaulted over to the other side. Hunched against the ground, he rushed across the snow-covered lawn and paused to listen at the main entrance to the two-story estate. A cough, faint but distinct, came from somewhere upstairs. The acuteness of his senses amazed him. He knew if he focused hard enough, he could track a person through a maze of rooms guided by the mere sound of their breathing.

Assured that he was safe from being detected, at least for the moment, he pressed down on the door latch. Unlocked. He sighed with relief and eased open the door on silent, well-oiled hinges. As for the alarm, he'd worry about that later when the housekeeper left. If he had to trip the alarm on his way out, he'd live with that. By the time security arrived, he'd be long gone.

Two doors down, he found what looked like an office and waited in there until he heard the housekeeper close the front door after her and drive off. When the sound of the car's motor faded, Clark snapped on a floor lamp and flooded the room with a soft halo of light. He then dragged the thick, navy drapes closed. The noise grated against his already taut nerves.

Clark scanned the room, noted a walnut desk and filing cabinet, a matching sofa and chair in maroon and navy stripes, and a globe on a walnut stand at the far corner of the room. Immediately, Clark went to the desk and pulled open the drawers. Nothing there but typical office supplies. Next, he walked over to the filing cabinet. Finding it unlocked, he suspected he wouldn't find anything of importance, but he went ahead and rifled through four drawers of accounting and household files anyway and wasted minutes he couldn't afford.

In frustration, he slammed the bottom drawer closed, rose to his feet and scowled at the rest of the office. He'd wanted to concentrate on this room, because he'd hoped if anything were to be found, it would be here. He looked over the walls, where three pictures, all seascapes, hung.

Clark focused on the first oil, narrowing his gaze, magnifying the painting until he saw each detailed brush stroke and the scrawled signature of D. J. Coleman on the bottom corner. His vision didn't penetrate through the canvas, which left him no choice but to lift each seascape from the wall to look for a hidden safe. On all three, he came up empty.

Driving his fingers through his hair, Clark stood in the middle of the room, not sure what to do next. But he knew he didn't have the time to get indecisive. More importantly, he didn't dare give up. He had his past and future at stake here.

He went back to the desk, and this time, slowly, meticulously combed through the drawers, feeling across the wooden sides and bottoms for hidden compartments. When he swept a hand over the bottom right drawer, he touched something plastic with his fingers. *Finally something.*

"Not too smart after all, Spalding."

Smiling in triumph, he pulled the drawer out and dumped its contents on top of the desk chair. A thin, folded envelope encased in a plastic bag was attached to the bottom. With shaking hands, he tore the package off and slipped the contents into his hand. A ring, a social security card and a driver's license. He glanced at the license but didn't recognize the name or photo. As to the name on the social security card—

A footfall broke into the silence of the house. He froze. What the—

Carefully, silently, he placed all three items on the desk. Because he'd been so focused on Spalding's little stash, he hadn't paid attention to anything beyond his immediate surroundings. Foolish and dangerous on his part. Easing away from the desk, he crept over to the wall and to the left of the door. He pressed up against the wall and listened.

Breathing, quick and agitated, came from the hall. For anyone else, the sound would've gone unnoticed, but Clark's hearing, when utilized, wasn't exactly normal. Another footfall, yet another crept this way. Someone desperately wanted to mask their movements. Either he'd been discovered or someone else had entered the house without permission.

With his back against the wall, Clark waited.

CHAPTER 9

FROM THE HALLWAY, Katherine crept through the doorway into her uncle's office. She couldn't believe she was sneaking around his house like a common thief. If she were caught, she wouldn't even know where to start with an explanation.

Something suddenly moved to her right. Stiffening, she turned as a hulk of a man grabbed her around the waist. She started to scream, but a palm over her mouth turned the cry into a muffle. Squirming, bucking, she jerked her knee up, but missed his groin and ended up flattened against the wall with her hands squashed between both of their bodies.

She glared across the short distance at Clark. Almost immediately she'd known he was her assailant, but that hadn't stopped her from fighting back. She didn't know what motives ran around inside his head.

With Clark's height and build, she'd known he was strong—too strong for her to best in a physical match—but it amazed her how quickly he'd subdued her against the wall. He'd done it in seconds and without hurting her.

"Don't panic," he whispered. "I swear I'm not going to hurt you."

They stood silently, their breathing intermixed, their bodies fused while Katherine tried to mask the fear and anger in her eyes.

"I'll remove my hand, but only if you promise not to scream. Can you do that?"

Katherine nodded. Of course, she'd tell him anything he wanted. A thief, liar, and goodness knew what, Clark didn't deserve anything but lies from her.

Clark slipped his hand from her mouth and eased back, but he still kept her sandwiched against the wall. He probably thought she'd bolt if he let her go. And he'd be right.

Katherine cleared her throat, but her voice still shook with fury. "What are you doing in my uncle's house?"

"I'm the one that should be asking you that question."

"Any *fool* can see I've been following you!"

Katherine wriggled harder and slipped a hand from beneath their bodies. She tried to smack him in the face, but he caught her wrist and lifted it over her head and against the wall.

"Calling me names isn't the smartest thing right now—particularly when I have the upper hand." He rubbed a thumb along her inner wrist. "So why have you been following me?"

"I'm just doing the same thing you've been doing to me for the last couple of weeks."

"I know."

"How?" she asked, unable to keep the disappointment from her voice.

"You're not very good at it."

She narrowed her eyes. "You never answered me. What are you doing sneaking into my uncle's house? Robbing the place?"

He looked offended at the question. "Of course not."

"Then what?"

"Would you believe I'm doing a little sleuthing?"

"Sleuthing? What type of answer's that?"

"I don't expect you to understand. There's something about Miltronics and Spalding that doesn't feel right."

"Oh, I get it. You decided to break into his house for the sake of a story? And all because it doesn't 'feel' right?"

"It's more than that."

"Then by all means, please tell me. I'm waiting with bated breath."

"Cut the sarcasm." Clark stepped back and released her wrist.

A big mistake on his part but a perfect opportunity for Katherine. She rammed a fist into his face. He grunted. She sprang through the doorway. Two steps into the hall, he grabbed her.

She hit, slapped, poked, and elbowed her way down another foot of the hall before he captured her wrists with his hands. Next, she dug her rubber-soled heels against the floor, and her shoes squealed against the wood tile as he half-pulled, half-dragged her into the office.

"Listen to me," Clark muttered. "I'm not going to hurt you, but from the way you're going about it, you're making it damn hard not to."

"Then let me go!"

"Not until you see this."

He pulled her over to her uncle's desk and let go of one of her arms to reach for something on top. She lurched forward and aimed a fist to his head. He ducked. She missed.

"Damn it, Katherine!" He snapped up a document from the desk. "Calm down. I wasn't lying when I said I wasn't going to hurt you."

"My ass!"

Chest heaving, Katherine glared at him for a second before pulling back her fist.

He caught her wrist and shoved a piece of paper in her face. "Here, take this. It's a driver's license. Do you recognize this guy?"

Katherine thought about ignoring it, but something about Clark's face made her pause. "Fine."

Yanking her arm from Clark's grasp, she took the license and stared at the features of a teenage boy—blue eyes, shoulder-length, blond hair, peach fuzz on his chin. She recognized him. She'd talked, laughed and joked with him, and worried when he'd disappeared.

But if Katherine held his I.D. in her hand and he was still missing.… The meaning of it kicked her in the chest. He was dead. For a wild moment, she couldn't swallow, couldn't speak, couldn't catch enough air.

"What is it? What's wrong?"

"Shock," she said in a hollow voice. She closed her eyes, held up a hand, and groped for equilibrium. When she managed to get her breath under control, she reopened her eyes and met Clark's concerned gaze. She lifted the license toward him with a trembling hand. "Where did you get this?"

"It was hidden in your uncle's desk."

"That's impossible."

"See for yourself." He nodded toward the upended drawer on the floor. "It was inside a bag and hidden away in Spalding's desk. So who's the kid?"

She took in a deep, slow breath and exhaled. "A boy at the shelter. He up and disappeared one day, left his clothes, backpack, everything really. I didn't know what to do—other than file a missing person's report and ask around. The only relative he had was a father, but they'd lost touch years ago, and he hadn't seen or heard of Jeffrey and didn't care."

"Is there more?" she felt compelled to ask.

"A ring. A man's probably. The stone's topaz, I think."

He dropped it in her hand. When she saw the crude silver design, she blinked back tears. "That's Joe's ring. I remember it, because it was the one thing he was really proud of. He made it in a lapidary class one summer a couple of years back."

"Another teenage boy missing from the shelter?" he asked softly.

Katherine couldn't speak, so she nodded.

"The social security card's for Carl Mendoza. Also missing?" When she nodded again, he said, "So that's three boys who are missing, and Spalding has their identities hidden away. Why?"

"How should I know? You're the smart one. I'm sure you've got some stupid theory." She shook her head. "Sorry. I'm just having a hard time taking this all in."

Seeing the sympathy in his eyes, Katherine stiffened. She didn't want Clark's pity or the truth he'd revealed. At least not tonight. Maybe tomorrow she might be strong enough to deal with the way he'd blasted into her life and rendered it into something meaningless.

"Someone just drove up. We've got to move." Turning away, Clark grabbed the ring and identifications, put them back in their envelope and re-taped the package to the bottom of the drawer.

Katherine's felt like her heart did a free-fall to her stomach. "I don't hear anything."

"You will." Hurriedly, he stuffed the drawer's contents back inside and slid the drawer into place.

Katherine rushed over to the window, peered through the gap between the drapes and wall and saw the car. "Sheesh. My cousin and his wife are pulling into the garage. They're going to see the light."

"Leave it. If they see it go off now, they'll know someone's inside. Hopefully, they'll think the housekeeper forgot to turn it off. Is there a better way out of here, other than the front door? We've got to hurry, unless you want them finding us?"

She rubbed her damp palms against her jean-clad thighs. The idea of trying to reason her way out of the situation to either David or Rachel wasn't an option. "We'll go through the game room at the back of the house. It's far enough away from the kitchen and the garage door."

He placed a palm against the small of her back and nudged her forward. "And the code? You know it, right? That's how you got in?"

"Yeah." She led Clark from Paul's office, down one hall and through another, until they entered the master bedroom. "Rachel gave it to me. I took the key hidden outside—Forget I said that." She punched the code into the security unit by the French door. "You're liable to come back and steal their silver."

"Funny," he muttered. "Let's go."

Once they slipped outside, Katherine locked the door behind them and replaced the key back in its hiding place.

Crouched low, ducking under windows and weaving around spiked bushes, she followed Clark around the back and side of the house.

"We'll have to hop the fence," Clark whispered from beside her.

She stumbled to a halt and glanced across the snow-covered

lawn to the eight-foot fence in disbelief. "There's no way I can climb that thing. We can go around the side. There's a gate."

"I checked it out a couple of days ago. They keep it locked, and it's too close to the house. Getting over it will make too much noise," Clark argued. "You'll do fine. I'll be right there."

"You'd better be."

"It'll be a piece of cake. You'll see."

Clark grabbed her hand, and they both ran across the lawn and ducked behind a thick spruce by the wall.

Katherine watched in amazement as Clark, his movements fluid and powerful, vaulted to the top of the fence and straddled the thick stone. Leaning over, he grasped her arms and pulled her up after him. He landed on the other side first and caught her in his arms, cushioning her landing with his body and arms.

They reached her car undetected, but once inside and several blocks away from Paul's house, Katherine couldn't calm the wild dance of her pulse. With vise-like hands, she gripped the wheel. The heat of excitement thrummed through her body.

"I think I just lost a couple of years off my life." She laughed, unable to fall off one of the wildest highs she'd rocketed into. "I can't believe I did that!"

"You were wonderful."

When they passed under a street lamp, she glanced over, surprised to see admiration in Clark's gray eyes. "How can you look so relaxed? Do you do this often? Breaking and entering, that is?"

It was his turn to laugh. "Not likely. And I was far from relaxed. The idea of getting caught and thrown in jail for burglary isn't exactly something that gets me all warm and fuzzy."

When Katherine drove into the parking lot of her townhouse, reality set in—hard. As she stepped out and closed her door, she met Clark's gaze over the top of her car. The irrational side of her wanted to blame Clark for forcing her into this situation, but at the same time, honesty with herself made Katherine realize she had to own up to her own responsibilities.

"We need to talk. But not here."

~~*~~

Inside Katherine's townhouse, Clark shrugged out of his jacket and hung it on the coat rack while Katherine snapped on the hall light. She looked pale but composed. When she draped her jacket alongside his own, Clark saw the slight tremor in her hand and realized the sham. He wouldn't be surprised if she was running on pure adrenaline.

He wasn't doing much better, but hopefully, between the two of them, they might be able to form some picture of tonight's jigsaw. Instinct, nothing more, nothing less, had drawn him to Spalding's home. The house itself held no memories, but the person living within those brick walls evoked deep feelings of revulsion—even hatred. Paul Spalding. A link meshed somehow with Clark's past.

"How about a drink?" she asked.

"Sure. After tonight, I think we both need something."

"Hah. Tell me about it. Wine or beer?"

"Beer."

In the kitchen, Clark leaned a hip against a counter and watched Katherine pour a glass of Merlot, pull a frosted mug from the freezer and a bottled beer from the refrigerator. She was amazingly resilient and quick-witted, the way she'd slipped out of Spalding's house without being detected. Each time she got hit by some unforeseen agenda, she pulled herself up without complaint, censure or self-pity. He couldn't help but admire such unwavering strength.

Clark poured his beer into his mug, took a couple of deep swallows and followed her into the living room. As he sank down on the sofa, Katherine placed her wine on top of the mantle, dropped down to one knee and lit the gas fireplace. Orange and yellow flames sprang up and wrapped around the ceramic logs, but their warmth couldn't dispel the chill to his bones. At this point, nothing could.

Rising, Katherine turned and faced him across the coffee table. Color had inched back into her face and softened her once drawn features, but Clark quickly noted the expression in her eyes didn't look the least bit friendly. Naked suspicion glittered in their depths. Just what he needed.

"What were you doing in my Uncle's house?"

Light conversation wasn't an option. She planned on diving right in. Fine. Clark, sick and tired of trying to keep up with the lies, intended to do the same. More importantly, he knew that if he wasn't honest right this minute, he'd lose the tentative alliance he'd found with Katherine. He couldn't afford that. It wasn't just because he believed she could help him unravel his past. It went deeper than that. Call him weak, but at this point, he desperately wanted someone believing in him, because he was having a hard enough time believing in himself. Being thrown into a world of ambiguity, he was weary of questioning his sanity and his competence.

Clark met and held her gaze. "There's no story. Never has been."

"Then why were you at my uncle's house if not for a story? Did you plan on stealing something from the house?"

"Of course not!"

"There's no 'of course not'. For me, everything's possible, because you've told me absolutely nothing." She grabbed her glass from the mantle and took a large swallow. "I want answers. And if you're not going to give them to me, I'll go to my uncle. Because I know as surely as I'm standing that you've got some vendetta against Paul."

Clark banged his mug on the coffee table and stood up. She couldn't go to her uncle. She didn't know what he was capable of. Murder. The word screamed and vibrated through his body. He couldn't prove Paul Spalding was a murderer, couldn't fathom why he knew it, but the knowledge of it was there just the same.

"I won't let you go to your uncle."

"You won't *let* me? I couldn't have heard that right, because that would mean you have this grand delusion of being my boss." She drained the last of her wine. "I don't think so. I'll do what I want, when I want and with whom I want."

"Katherine, you're not thinking." Hell. That hadn't come out like he'd wanted. Nothing was going right. "That's not what—"

"Save it!" Gaze narrowing, she set her glass down on the mantel. "Who are you? Why are you so interested in my family?

If you don't tell me, I swear I'll walk out of here this second and get the answers from someone else!"

"I don't know!" The words, filled with dread and despair, ripped from his lungs. "I don't know who I am!"

75

CHAPTER 10

I DON'T UNDERSTAND. WHAT are you saying?" Katherine asked in obvious confusion.

Clark thrust his fingers through his hair and groped for the right words. "One day I woke up with no memory, no past, no concept of who or what I was." He explained about the car accident, the murdered passenger, fleeing the scene, and the note on the back of a photo that led him to the Morning Dove.

As to his powers and the duffle bag he'd found in the car, he didn't go down either route. His story already sounded far too crazy without adding more twisted elements.

Finally, he pulled his I.D. from his back pocket and tossed it on the coffee table between them. "The only concrete part of my past is my driver's license and the photo. I do have fleeting feelings and images, but none of it significant until I read about Miltronics and Paul Spalding."

She frowned at the license but didn't pick it up. "Do you have the photo?"

"Not on me. But I can show it to you later."

"And you expect me to believe all this?"

"I know I'm asking a lot—probably too much. I don't have any proof. I'm hoping you'll give me the benefit of the doubt like you've done with kids at the shelter." He sighed. "Can you give me that? I know I've nothing to offer you other than my word, but my word's everything to me, because that's all I have." He didn't see any signs of her softening.

"Why me? What's so special about me?" She looked at him as if he'd mutated into some mega-sized reptile. "I've never met you. I would remember if I had."

"In the photo you were standing by the murdered teenager." Clark grabbed his beer and downed the rest from his mug, but the chilled alcohol didn't do a thing to deaden his frustration.

"I don't know what to think. I need another drink. I'll be right back."

A minute later, Katherine returned with another glass of wine for herself and a beer for him. Instead of handing him his drink, she placed it on the coffee table, an obviously effective way of avoiding his touch. Posture rigid, she sat down on the edge of the loveseat. "Can you describe the teenager?"

"I tried not to look at him."

Clark rubbed at his jaw and forced himself to visualize the car accident. The teenage boy slumped in the passenger seat, the blood seeping from the bullet hole to his head. At the images, his stomach rolled.

"He looked Caucasian," he said finally. "He had brown hair. Shoulder length, I think. I didn't look at the color of his eyes, and as to his height—I haven't a clue. He was sitting down."

"That's not enough of a description. There are just too many kids I've met with brown hair. He might have had a haircut when he came through the shelter." She continued to sit on the edge of her seat. "This is way too much to swallow."

"I know."

"Have you thought of going to the police?"

"And tell them what?" Clark shook his head as he sank back down on the sofa. "They'd never take me seriously. How can they, when I don't know who I am? Yeah, granted, I have a name but nothing else. It wouldn't be long before they directed me to the nearest psychiatrist."

"And my uncle? You think he plays a big part in your past?"

"I don't think. I know. I have no proof, but I've been going on instinct since I stepped off the bus in Boston. How our lives are crossed—I'm at a loss. The link could be an indirect tie or something much more."

"You know this is all conjecture—the same with the missing boys from the shelter. Paul might be completely unaware of what's going on. Maybe someone else hid the license and ring."

He knew she was grasping, desperate for her uncle's innocence. "Do you honestly believe that?"

"He's not a killer. He can't be. There's no sense to it."

"Maybe not from your viewpoint. It's possible there's a logical explanation for him hiding those identifications," he admitted. Unable to stomach the anguish etched across her features, Clark focused on the task of pouring his beer into his mug. Once filled, he placed the can on the coffee table, slipped off his glasses and set them down by his mug. "Or someone else might be involved."

"But you don't believe it. You think he killed them, don't you?"

He met her gaze and tried to formulate a reply.

"Don't bother. I can see it in your face."

If Clark denied it now and lied, he'd come across as condescending—something he didn't want. He thought too highly of Katherine. So instead, he asked gently, "How well do you know your uncle?"

"Enough to know that he can't be a murderer. I refuse to believe that. It's not possible! He's family. Something like this doesn't happen in our family. What possible motive could he have?"

"That's what I want to find out."

"Well, you're mistaken if you think I'll sit by and let you slander my uncle."

"Then prove me wrong." Resting both forearms on his knees, Clark leaned forward. "Your uncle's having a birthday party on Saturday. Bring me with you. If he knows me, I'm bound to get a reaction from him. Who knows? The meeting might even jar my memory. And if I'm wrong, I'll leave you alone."

"And what if you're right?" she whispered. "That's what I'm afraid of. Worse yet, you'll put yourself in danger if there's any truth to what you believe."

"I can take care of myself." She didn't know the half of it. "And anyway, don't you want to know the truth?"

Clark didn't like how she shook her head. For a while there, he'd thought he'd managed to get through to her.

"No." Katherine rose to her feet. "I don't like playing games. Why not just be honest? If we went up and talked to my uncle, I'm sure he has a logical explanation. I'll see him tomorrow."

"You can't do that!" Clark jack-knifed to his feet.

Her eyes flared with anger. "Yes, I can. It's only right."

Panic hauled him around the coffee table. "That's if you want to end up with another knife at your throat."

She flinched.

"Oh hell, I'm sorry. I didn't mean that. It just came out."

In two steps he was in front of her and clutching her shoulders. Beneath his hands, Katherine stiffened and looked up. She searched his face, reproach in the depths of her large, brown eyes.

"I'm sorry," he said again in a hoarse whisper. "Whenever you're around me, I can't think—I react." He glanced down at the perfect shape of her mouth and rubbed the pad of his thumb along the full curve of her bottom lip. "You're beautiful—everything about you. You have the most soulful eyes. Every time I look into them, any coherent thought I have crumbles into nothing. I feel like some raw schoolboy with his first crush. I want to..."

"What?"

Clark saw the uncertainty, the desire in her eyes and something clawed not only at his gut but also at his heart.

"I want..."

"To kiss me?" she murmured, inching closer.

"Yeah...and so much more," he breathed, unable to deny himself the feel and taste of her as he replaced his thumb with his mouth. Fearful of her rejection, he tangled his fingers in her hair and cupped the back of her head with his palm, anchoring her so he could deepen the kiss.

But his worries were groundless. Katherine kissed him back, sinking deeper against his body while her hands splayed over his arms and rose to his shoulders. She tasted better than he'd imagined, better than his wildest fantasy. The scent of lemon wrapped around him while the heat of desire rolled inside him.

Clark couldn't have asked for a more responsive woman. Katherine was a contradiction, one moment shy and inquisitive and the next hot and bold, but she was also so much more. As she slipped her hands beneath his shirt to touch his bare back, he caved into the sensuality of her touch, and even if he had the will to stop, he wouldn't, because he wanted this moment, this hunger, this woman.

Craving the feel of naked skin against naked skin, Clark pulled open the buttons of her shirt, then peeled the material to the side. He sucked in one quick, hard breath. A black, mesh bra covered her full, rounded breasts, while the fire's glow turned her skin to warm honey and her hair to molten gold. She was beautiful in his arms.

Bending, he suckled her breast through the material and savored the way she groaned and trembled in his arms, the way her hands clutched at his shoulders, and the way she arched against him, drawing her hips snug against his own. She panted, little erotic puffs that stoked his hunger. With his arm wrapped hard around her waist, Clark drew back. The heat of her gaze caught and held him spellbound. He watched her reaction as he unsnapped the top button of her pants, edged the zipper slowly down and slid a finger along the waistband of her panties. She swallowed and closed her eyes.

Katherine shook her head. "I can't. It's too soon. The wine, the shock of my uncle."

His fingers tensed around the waistband of her pants. "Why? You want this just as much as I do."

"And what if I regret it? I've got too many regrets in my life already."

He brushed his cheek against her temple and the smooth cap of her golden hair. Clark wanted to be selfish and carry her into the bedroom. He wanted her naked, writhing and arching beneath him. He wanted to slide into her, feel her heat, burn with it. If he chose, he could seduce her. One more deep, long kiss and he'd have her.

But because he didn't like to think of himself as selfish or insensitive, he nodded and drew away. That didn't mean it didn't hurt like hell. Tonight, not even submerging himself in the icy Atlantic would deaden the raw, unappeased hunger that gnawed at his insides. "Fine. But this thing between us isn't over."

Katherine didn't deny it, but she didn't look happy about it either.

"Go, Clark. Please." She pulled her shirt together with two, white-knuckled fists.

He grabbed his glasses and jacket and silently left the house. Once outside, he lifted his face to the night sky, never feeling more out of control than that moment.

"What the hell am I doing?"

Of course, no one answered him.

~~*~~

"I don't know how you talked me into this tonight," Katherine said beside Clark as they walked up the car-lined drive to her uncle's estate. Light from every window on the ground floor illuminated the snow-covered grounds.

"Could it be my dazzling personality?"

"More like your pig-headedness."

Actually, Clark's charm and conviction persuaded her, but she wasn't about to tell him that. He might use it later to get what he wanted—just like he'd done a couple of days ago when he'd shown up at her door after work. He'd asked once again, "Can you take a chance on me? You've done it with the kids at the shelter. Can you do the same for me? Bring me along with you to your uncle's house?"

There'd been those guileless gray eyes of his and their silent plea. They'd held more power than mere words. Yes, she'd given many teenagers the benefit of the doubt when society had abandoned them. So would it be so wrong to give Clark that same opportunity?

It hadn't taken long for Katherine to capitulate. When it

came down to it, Clark took her breath away. Masculine, tender, determined, compassionate, dangerous—he possessed all those traits.

Memories of the other night flooded her thoughts. Katherine shivered and remembered the heat of his mouth, the strength and sureness of his hand, the way he'd unsnapped the top button of her pants and how close she'd come to letting—

No. She pulled the collar of her coat up higher against her neck and rubbed her chin against the faux fur lining. She didn't dare delve into such craziness. She needed to focus on this evening.

Katherine eyed the two-story brick house. Plumes of light gray smoke wafted from one of three chimneys, while the scent of burning cedar drifted over the night air. The place looked harmless enough, though somewhat intimidating in size. As a child, she'd grown accustomed to all those rooms. She'd played hide and seek, dove in the pool in the back and been invited for many a dinner within those four walls.

But all that past didn't change the fact her uncle could be involved with the disappearance of several boys and even murder. How was she going to look at or talk to him without her suspicion and unease showing?

"I'm not getting a good feeling," she said.

"You'll do fine. It's a simple birthday party. Nothing you haven't experienced before." Clark placed a reassuring hand against the small of her back and climbed the shallow steps to the front door with her. "And as for me—don't worry. Paul's valuables are safe. I promise I won't pilfer the silver."

At his attempted humor, she laughed half-heartedly. "I see you're throwing my words right back at me."

"And of course, you wouldn't do the same, given the opportunity?" Amusement crinkled the corners of his eyes.

"Never."

"Right.

Katherine reached for the doorknob, but Clark caught her hand and stepped in front of the door. She looked up, surprised at his sudden sober expression.

"Thanks for inviting me," he said. "Most importantly—believing in me. It means a lot."

"Yes, well. It's nothing," she said, distracted at the way he rubbed his thumb over her wrist. Actually, everything about Clark was distracting, particularly when he turned serious on her. Like that night he had her in his arms and—

There she went again. She really did need to focus.

Katherine cleared her throat. "—Anyway, I have my own reason for inviting you. And that's the truth. Something I'm not about to let slide even if nothing comes of tonight. I want answers behind the missing boys at the shelter. They counted on me and the system. We both failed."

Clark tugged at her hand. "Don't blame yourself. It doesn't help anyone."

Katherine sighed. "You're right. I'll try."

"Good." Bending, he skimmed his lips across her temple in a tender yet fleeting kiss.

At the simple gesture and her acute response, Katherine closed her eyes briefly. Given enough time, she could trust Clark, which frightened the heck out of her. To give all that power and control into the hands of one person....

Clark opened the front door. "Tonight, you just might get those answers, but they might not be what you want to hear. Are you ready for that?"

CHAPTER 11

STRAIGHTENING, KATHERINE MET the concern in Clark's eyes. "I really don't have much choice, now do I?"

She then affixed a smile on her face and stepped inside and into a role she'd grown familiar with. Music, laughter, a multitude of varying voices immediately surrounded her, but it was nothing she hadn't experienced. For so long, she'd played the game of a Senator's daughter, always mindful of each and every word that slipped from her mouth. Katherine was tired of it—as far back as her early teens—probably even longer. So she acted.

She'd always felt as if she never belonged, never sparkled, never held her own in an intelligent conversation with the people at these gatherings. They always consisted of a wide range of individuals—politicians, actors, entrepreneurs, scientists—and a Nobel Prize winner thrown in for diversity.

In the cloakroom, she shrugged out of her coat. Clark stood directly behind and helped her slip both arms from their sleeves before he handed their coats to an attendant. His aftershave, a woodsy, clean and distinct male, scent teased her senses.

"You smell nice," Katherine whispered and turned around.

Clark cut a dashing figure in a black tuxedo tailored to his large frame. His thick-framed glasses softened the hard lines of his face and added a keen intelligence to his gray eyes.

"And you look beautiful."

Katherine had curled her hair and left it unbound to fall in waves around her bare shoulders. She knew the formal black, velvet dress, a perfect and unplanned compliment to Clark's tuxedo, accented her curves, and the low heart-shaped neckline exposed more cleavage and skin than she was accustomed to—skin that tingled at Clark's lingering glance.

She saw admiration then something hot in Clark's eyes. Her breath stilled, and then continued in a rapid and unsteady rhythm. When he looked at her like that, it made her feel unique, feminine, and desirable. It made her yearn for the taste and touch of him again.

Everything about him, his large hands and frame, his latent strength and rugged face, made her feel delicate and fragile when she knew she wasn't.

This was crazy. One look from Clark and she turned into a melted marshmallow.

Suddenly feeling awkward and shy, Katherine clasped her hands in front of her. "I guess we better get this over with."

After they left the cloakroom, Clark grabbed two fluted glasses from a passing waiter and handed her one. She took a sip of champagne but didn't give in to the temptation to down the contents. Tonight, she needed a clear head.

"Do you see him anywhere?" Clark whispered by her ear.

Katherine glanced over the crowd. "Not yet."

"Hmm."

Catching Clark's arm, she felt the corded muscles bunch beneath her fingers. She hadn't realized he'd been masking his tension beneath a smooth and relaxed façade. "He'll show. It's not like my uncle's going to miss his own party in his own house."

"Aren't you going to introduce me to the yummy man beside you?" a voice asked from behind Katherine.

Katherine turned and found Rachel in front of her. "Clark, this is my cousin's wife, Rachel Spalding. She's Paul's daughter-in-law. Rachel, Clark's a friend of mine."

"How do you do?" Rachel asked Clark, her lips sliding into a seductive smile.

Katherine watched the two exchange pleasantries and grew uncomfortable watching Rachel flirt with Clark. Unlike Rachel, she'd never been skilled at the art. Almost every time Katherine had tried her hand at it, she'd come across sounding like a moron, so she'd quickly given up.

"No Ethan?" Rachel asked her.

"Not tonight."

"That's a shame. Unlike some people in the family, I really liked him. Such a wonderful sense of humor and he's so comfortable with who he is."

"And David?" Katherine asked in turn. "So far I haven't seen him tonight."

"Oh, the last I saw, he was going off somewhere to talk to Paul. Goodness knows on what. Probably work. I swear that's all David thinks about." She wrinkled her nose and turned to Clark. "At least I hope you have the sense to know when to have fun. Or are you one of the lucky ones with an exciting career? I'm sure with your looks, it's something glamorous."

"Sorry. I'm just a reporter."

"Oh." Rachel waved a hand around the room. "Are you doing a story on—"

"No."

"Too boring, I'm sure." Rachel smiled and looked him over with interest. "Let's see. I would guess you do something dangerous, like a foreign correspondent who travels the world. Maybe someone who goes into third world countries and reports on civil wars or terrorist acts. Am I close?"

"I'm afraid not."

Clark's answering smile didn't fool Katherine. He didn't like the questions. She saw it in the hard line of his jaw and the coolness in his eyes. Either Rachel didn't see it or she had more important things on her mind.

Before her cousin had a chance to ask another leading question, Katherine said, "Clark has a business column."

So it was a lie, Katherine admitted, but it sounded perfectly boring and just the thing to throw Rachel off and drop the subject.

Clark glanced at her sharply, but, thank goodness, was quick enough to catch on and keep silent.

"Well, that's nice." Rachel's smile faltered and the curiosity in her eyes clouded with disinterest. She peered around the room with a vague look on her face. "I guess I should mix a bit. It wouldn't do as hostess to keep to myself." She touched Clark's arm. "I'm sorry I didn't catch your last name?"

"It's Kent."

Nothing showed on Rachel's face. "As in Clark—"

Clark's face tightened. "Yes."

Amusement glittered in Rachel's eyes. "Oh, Katherine. You've got a real, live Superhero with you." Arching one finely drawn brow, Rachel laughed and looked him over in obvious amusement. "I'd hang on to this one. All those special powers— especially in bed. The possibilities sound delicious—absolutely delicious."

Katherine watched her walk away to mingle with the other guests, but her mockery lingered in the air around them. Right this second, she wanted to go after her cousin and give her a good smack.

Clark's voice thickened with frustration. "You know, I never thought I'd say this, but I'm beginning to really hate my name."

"Don't let Rachel get to you. She can be insensitive at times. You have a beautiful name. I can't think of anything better."

The rugged lines of Clark's face softened. "Thank you."

Katherine gave him wry a smile and found herself mesmerized by the admiration and warmth in his gray eyes. "Don't thank me yet. The evening's far from over."

Clark tossed his drink down his throat and grimaced. "I guess if I'm ever going to find your uncle, we need to start circulating."

Katherine's smile dimmed as she took his hand and urged him around a group of impeccably dressed men and women. "I suppose you're right."

Suddenly, Clark pulled her to a halt and whispered in her ear. "Does your uncle have a safe somewhere? Someplace where he'd keep important documents?"

"I think so." Glancing up at Clark's grim expression, she frowned and bit her lip for a second. "When I was really young, I remember David had talked about it. But I'm trying to think where..." Her face cleared. "Oh, yes. I remember. I thought it was so neat at the time. It's in the walk-in closet in my uncle's bedroom. There's a hidden panel in the very back."

"Are you sure?"

"Yes." She eyed him suspiciously. "You're not thinking about doing something crazy tonight? You promised you weren't going to do anything. You said yourself—"

"I didn't exactly say that—"

When Clark stopped speaking and glanced to her left, she turned. "Oh. Hi, Dad."

"Katherine." Her father kissed her raised cheek. "You look beautiful tonight."

"Thank you." She glanced at Clark. "I don't think you've met my father, Alex. And this is—"

"Clark Kent, correct?" Alex pulled back his lips into a smile. "I hear you're a reporter."

"That's right." Clark shook her father's proffered hand.

"What paper?"

"The Globe."

"Interesting." Alex raised a brow, mockery evident in his voice. "I read the paper religiously, and I don't remember your name on any of the bylines."

Clark's eyes narrowed. "I wouldn't be surprised. I just started on their payroll last week."

"Really?"

"Really."

"I'm impressed." But Alex didn't appear impressed. "You must have an extensive background. I wish I did. Or at least my broker did. He hasn't given me the best advice this last year on the market. Do you have any hot tips on stocks?"

Seeing her father's eyes grow as cold and blue as the shore off of Boston on a clear, winter day, Katherine felt the muscles tense across the back of her neck. She stepped closer to Clark and placed a reassuring hand on his shoulder.

"I don't have any leads right now," Clark said. "I'm off of work."

"I see."

"Dad," Katherine cut in. "I don't think tonight's the time to get into the stock market. I know I wouldn't want to talk about work on my night off."

"Of course." Alex conceded.

"Katherine." Clark took her half-filled glass. "It looks like you need another drink. I'll be back in a minute." He nodded coolly to Alex. "It was nice meeting you."

An obvious lie from Clark if she went by his thin-lipped smile and frigid gray eyes, but she decided to let him go without an argument. She suspected Clark was liable to say something nasty to her father if he stayed any longer.

When Clark disappeared into the crowd, she turned to her father and frowned. "You scared him away."

"It seems that way."

"You don't look disappointed."

"Why should I? It's not my problem he's so sensitive. You'd think he'd be the opposite—being in his profession." Alex's gaze slipped to her throat. "Is that the necklace we gave you last Christmas?"

"Yes."

Katherine ran her fingers across the pearl choker. Her father always tended to avoid a topic by changing the subject. Sometimes tactfully. Sometimes not. She suspected he'd learned it as a defense mechanism when her mother latched onto some bone of contention. But Katherine wasn't her mother, and she wasn't going to be sidetracked.

"Why did you do that?"

"Do what?"

"Don't act dumb. I'm not stupid. Clark hadn't said one word, and you were right there ready to pick a fight. You'd already judged him before he even opened his mouth. If I'd behaved that way, you would have been all over me." Katherine shook her head. "I don't understand. What do you have against Clark?"

Alex brushed at a spot on the sleeve of his tailored jacket.

The suit looked like Armani, but Katherine wasn't sure. She hadn't paid attention to designers for years, or at least since she'd moved from home and her mother's vigilant eye. Sharon never liked her daughter to appear seedy in public. Image meant everything. After all, it might affect a vote.

"Your mother's concerned," Alex admitted.

"Why?"

"She thinks Clark isn't appropriate for you."

"If it's because of how she first met him—"

"She hadn't mentioned that part. But I'm sure that's not the reason..."

"Then what?" she asked in frustration.

"It's not important."

Katherine arched a brow and folded her arms.

He sighed. "You're not going to let this drop, are you? Fine. She believes he's somewhat unstable."

"Unstable? What am I supposed to make of that?"

"When someone calls themselves Clark Kent and then claims they're a reporter—it's bound to raise a few eyebrows. After seeing it for myself, I have to agree with her on this. He sounds like he's living in some type of fantasy. He even looks like the damn character."

"Rachel's been talking to Mother, hasn't she?" Katherine asked in a low and angry voice. "I can't believe it. Less than two seconds—and word's gotten around about Clark. No doubt, all of it wrong. What else did Mother say? I'm almost afraid to find out."

Alex laughed without humor. "Sometimes you can be just like Sharon. Stubborn to a fault. Well, if you must know—delusional was one of the words she used."

"Why am I not surprised? She's never liked my friends. You'd think by now she'd know I'm old enough to pick my own company."

"Your mother still has a hard time seeing you as someone other than her little girl. Try to remember that. And as to this guy—this Clark—Sharon's right. Your judgment's way off here. Sharon thinks it's—"

"Spare me. I'm too angry to talk about it."

Her father's voice deepened in warning. "I suggest you don't talk to your mother until you calm down."

"Oh, don't worry. That's the last thing I plan on doing right now." Backing up, Katherine coolly returned, "I'd rather talk to Clark. At least with him, I know he appreciates me and not someone he expects me to be."

Turning, she sidestepped a garishly jeweled, elderly woman and walked away.

Her father didn't follow. Not that she expected him to. After all, he hated conflict.

Her family didn't even know Clark, and they'd already judged him. It was so like them.

They'd always formulated opinions on people before taking the time to know them, which was probably why they'd never understood Katherine's motives to help homeless teens. The adolescences who stepped through the Morning Dove's doors were knocked down again and again by people or circumstances and never given the chance to dream or exhale. Unlike her family, Katherine knew it wasn't too late to turn these kids around. They were still malleable enough to possess the means for growth and change.

If it hadn't been for Miranda, Katherine's life would have turned in a direction filled with triviality, and void of the wonder, hope, pain and frustration her life now entailed. But Katherine wouldn't trade it for anything else.

After weaving through four rooms, being stopped on occasion by a well-wisher, Katherine had yet to find Clark among the crowd. Odd. With his height, he stood a good head over many. When she ventured into the other, unoccupied rooms of the ground floor, she still didn't find him.

Clark had disappeared.

CHAPTER 12

Aⁱⁱ LARM LENGTHENED KATHERINE'S step and quickened her pulse. She suspected—no—she *knew* Clark wasn't getting her a drink. Oh, no. He'd slipped upstairs in search of her uncle's hidden room. Pure insanity. Over a hundred people filled the house. One wrong move or sound by Clark and impending disaster.

Determined to find Clark before anyone else, Katherine weaved through the room congested with guests toward the doorway to the hall and stairs. To her right, the crowd parted, and she saw her mother talking to a man. Katherine's step faltered and then slowed. Jack Kincaid. A key contributor to the shelter—or should she say former contributor? To date, he still hadn't returned her calls. Just then, Sharon turned and caught her gaze across the room, but the crowd merged and swallowed her mother and Kincaid from view.

Katherine glanced to the doorway and back to where she'd seen Kincaid. What to do? She hesitated. Groaning in frustration, Katherine, unable to lose this opportunity, pivoted from the doorway. Unlike her phone calls, Kincaid couldn't dodge her here.

But by the time Katherine shifted through the crowd, she found her mother alone. "Where did he go?"

Sharon frowned. "Who?"

"Kincaid. I saw you talking to him."

Scanning the room, Katherine caught his retreating back. If she didn't hurry, she'd lose him.

"Katherine!" Her mother caught her elbow. "What's going on? You're acting oddly."

Kincaid vanished behind a cluster of elegantly dressed women.

"Katherine!"

She shrugged off her mother's hand. "I need to talk to Kincaid."

"Not tonight." Sharon's voice hardened. "Leave the man alone. He's here to enjoy himself, not talk business."

Katherine opened her mouth to argue but remembered the conversation with her father only moments before. She'd said the same words, or ones very similar, about Clark, so she relented. "Did he mention why he stopped donating to the Morning Dove?"

A fine crease formed between Sharon's brows. "Of course not. The shelter's the last thing on my mind. I'm far more concerned about this *character* you're with tonight. You haven't once mentioned him, then all of a sudden he's everywhere. Who is he?"

"He's a neighbor. He moved into one of the townhouses a couple of weeks ago. Remember, I told you?"

"But you failed to mention he thinks he's a reporter. What type of idiot does he take us for?"

"Mother. Let's not get into this. I've already had a round with Dad."

"Good. I'm glad to see Alex had the good sense to talk to you. Because I find this unacceptable." After Sharon glanced over both shoulders, she leaned over and said in an unpleasant whisper, "Here is not the place to discuss this. Follow me."

Katherine watched her mother, back rigid with displeasure, stride toward the room's exit. She thought about ignoring such a flagrant command. Then she envisioned their next meeting, or more appropriately battle, and how delaying the inevitable confrontation would aggravate her mother that much more.

Deciding on the lesser of two evils, Katherine followed her from the room and into the family library.

As Katherine closed the door, muffling the noise from outside, her mother turned around and glared across the plush maroon carpet. Her mother's mouth, a flat, pale line of disapproval, dipped at the corners.

Katherine's shoulders tightened with tension. Great. Battle might not have been the most appropriate word—World War III seemed more apt. "Okay. Let's get this over with."

"Don't you dare talk to me like that young lady—"

"Then don't treat me like a child."

"Then don't act like one!" Her mother waved a hand at the closed door. "What is it with you? The man's an obvious nut. Who in their right mind calls themselves Clark Kent and claims they're a reporter? He sounds like he's escaped from the mental institute. That, or your homeless shelter. I wouldn't put it past you to drag one of your lost causes here."

"That's low, Mother. Even for you. And as far as Clark is concerned, you're being extremely unfair."

"I might be. But I only have your best interests at heart. If he's a reporter at the Globe as he says—then why hasn't your father heard of him?"

"Because he just started."

"I see."

At her derogatory tone, Katherine struggled to rein in her temper. How typical. She wasn't allowed to act disrespectful, but her mother could act however she liked. "No. You don't see. You've no idea who he is, but you're right there ready to make snap judgments."

"I don't want you bringing him here again. I think he's from the shelter, and you just don't want to admit it."

Katherine lifted her chin. "And what if he were? Would it be that bad? Don't panic. He's not, but he's someone I enjoy being with. He's intelligent and kind—"

"You can save me the résumé. I want someone worthy of you."

"You know, Mother. He might not be from Harvard or

Princeton, but I guess that doesn't matter to you. For someone who claims to sympathize for the subjugated—you sure are a snob. As long as you keep those types out of your yard, that's fine. Goodness knows, you couldn't stand to actually rub shoulders with someone 'beneath' you. Especially if they're useless to your political agenda!"

"Don't start psychoanalyzing me, young woman. If anyone needs it, it would be you and why you like to push me. You've used the shelter to no end. You know I hate it. This cause of yours is something I will never understand. You're wasting your life among a bunch of derelicts. Why?" Sharon asked, looking truly perplexed. "Is it your way of getting back at me?"

The unexpected question robbed the retort from Katherine's tongue. Impossible. Or was it? Could she be using the shelter to retaliate against her parents, knowing how much both of them disliked it?

As far back as Katherine could remember, she'd yielded to their wishes and let them pick the appropriate university, the correct friends, and the suitable extracurricular school activities—for fear of losing their love.

Katherine sighed. "I'm not trying to get back at you."

"Then it's because of Miranda. The shelter, the people you pick. Why do you think you stopped seeing your old friends? Because they didn't need to be fixed."

Katherine stiffened. A slap to the face couldn't have been more shocking. "I don't want to discuss this."

She walked away from her mother, but Sharon followed. "That's exactly what I mean. Miranda's death is a complete taboo. You need to let her go. You've put her ghost between me and everyone else who loves you."

"That's not true!"

Katherine pivoted, the skirt of her dress whirling around her ankles, and stared at her mother in horror. Physically, two feet separated them, but mentally, a broad chasm cut across the floor between them, and right now, Katherine didn't know if either could ever breach the distance—or for that matter, wanted to. Their relationship, which lacked depth as far back as Katherine remembered, would take years and the need to change on both sides to get past the superficial. At this point, she didn't even want to attempt the work.

Katherine shook her head. "And even if it were true, that's my business. I'll deal with it in my own way."

"Well, you're not dealing with it. Period. Someone has to say something since it's been ignored for far too long. Much of it's my own fault. But you've melded your personal life into your professional life until you can't tell the difference between the two. The relationships you create at work are not the type you bring home with you. You need to stop saving people. What happened to Miranda wasn't your fault. Get over her."

Katherine, battling the childish temptation to raise her hands to her ears, turned and strode away. This time, thank goodness, her mother didn't follow. Katherine opened and closed the door behind her and escaped the library and her mother's cuttings words.

In the empty hall, she stopped, leaned her bare shoulder against the wall, and struggled for calm. Her mother wasn't going to make her doubt herself or her motives. Katherine straightened. No. She wouldn't allow it. She was strong, capable, in control and could handle anything thrown her way.

Then Katherine glanced up the stairwell's graceful curve to the second floor, and her determination wavered. She'd forgotten about Clark.

She dragged in a ragged breath and rubbed her damp hands on the velvet of her dress. What a lie. She didn't have control of her life. Not when turmoil loomed at every corner—her uncle, teenage boys disappearing from the shelter, the Morning Dove failing financially, and Clark's shattering appearance. The world as she knew it was fracturing into jagged pieces.

Mindful of her skirt's hem catching against her shoes, she gathered the material in shaky hands and climbed the stairs. A large crystal chandelier, suspended from the vaulted ceiling, illuminated her way to the second-floor landing. As she crept down the hall toward her uncle's bedroom, the lighting, music and voices faded and silence, thick and eerie, descended around her.

Almost afraid of what or who might cross her path, Katherine inched further along the hall. What if her uncle or someone else caught her snooping? What if she'd completely jumped to conclusions, and Clark never thought to come up here?

Well, then, she'd look like a complete idiot.

Suddenly, an arm snaked out from a doorway and yanked her inside. Katherine opened her mouth to scream. A hand clamped over her lips and cut off her cry before it reached her throat.

"We really should stop meeting like this."

Twisting around, she glared at Clark as he slipped his hand from her mouth. "That's not very funny."

"You're right. And neither one of us would be laughing if you'd actually screamed. Even with all the noise from downstairs someone might have come up here and investigated." Clark stepped back and eyed her with concern, his gaze lingering on her breasts. "I didn't hurt you, did I?"

"No, but you scared the heck out of me."

He cleared his throat and nodded. His lips curved into a half-smile. "You may want to fix your dress."

Katherine wondered at his odd smile until she looked down. Her breasts were literally bursting from her heart-shaped, strapless dress. Mortified, she yanked and twisted the bodice back to its original position.

"Thanks," she muttered, far more flustered than she liked to admit.

Clark, on the other hand, looked disgustedly composed. The light from the hall touched a benevolent hand on his tall, sophisticated figure. Not one wrinkle on his tuxedo or hair out of place. A modern-day version of Cary Grant from *To Catch a Thief*. But she was no Grace Kelly. And neither one of them were cat burglars. At least, she hoped Clark's past didn't entail any grand larceny.

"I found something."

Katherine's interest flared. "What?"

"I'll show you."

Katherine followed him into Paul's walk-in-closet. Two columns of clothing lined both sides—everything one would expect in a wealthy man's closet. At the back, Clark swept aside a row of shirts and revealed a beveled wall. He pushed the wood on one side and a panel, from floor to ceiling, slid to the right. Light failed to penetrate into the thick, black opening.

Katherine touched her chest with the palm of one hand. "If there's a dead body in there—"

"Don't worry. Nothing so dramatic."

Stepping inside, Clark pulled on something above his shoulder and a single, bare bulb flooded light into a shallow room. The only item inside was a large, metal safe.

Katherine eyed the safe with disappointment. "There's no way. It has a combination, and I haven't a clue what the numbers are."

Laugh lines crinkled at the corner of Clark's eyes as he smiled. "What's that saying? *Where there's a will...*"

Katherine watched in amazement when Clark moved the knob with agile fingers. He turned it to nineteen, and then back to another number. The combination of both formed the year of her uncle's birth. The third number, Katherine didn't recognize. In all, the combination consisted of three numbers. When Clark grabbed the handle and pressed down, a soft click punctured the silence and the safe's door whispered open. Maybe she shouldn't have compared him to Cary Grant and a thief. Only someone with experience...

"How did you—?"

"It doesn't matter. What matters is what I found inside."

CHAPTER 13

CLARK GLANCED OVER his shoulder and saw the suspicion and doubt in Katherine's eyes. Opening the safe in front of her wasn't the smartest move on his part, but he'd been carried away with his discovery. Now she thought he was some type of criminal. But was it worse than the truth? Would she react any better if she learned he'd broken through the safe by his ability to hear any minute noise? Not likely.

Turning back around, Clark opened the safe door wider and heard Katherine inch up behind him. "There're files and accounts of at least five different companies here." Excitement deepened his voice. "One, in particular, seems to be some type of holding company. Does Harvest and Associates sound familiar?"

"No."

"I'm not an accountant." He laughed harshly. "At least, I don't think so. But something doesn't smell right. I don't know if it's embezzlement or some type of money laundering." He pulled a folder from the safe and leafed through several documents. "What about Kirkwood Incorporated?"

"No. Sorry. Hey, wait a minute. It does sound familiar. Let me see."

When he edged sideways, she shifted closer, brushed a shoulder against his him, and bent over the folder. Several strands of her hair clung to the cloth of his suit.

Clark closed his eyes. She smelled of lemons and flowers, of sunshine and summer breezes. He wished he'd met Katherine under different circumstances. He wished...

"I've heard the name before," Katherine interrupted his thoughts, "but for the life of me, I just can't place it."

Clark opened his eyes and sighed. Hope. He was starting to think of it as a four-letter word.

"Did you see this?"

"I didn't get a chance to go through everything." Frowning, he watched Katherine pull several files aside. "What is it?"

"Money."

She pulled a bundle of bills from the safe. Hundreds. The money in her hand was tied with the same type of strap as the ones he'd found in the duffle bag.

Clark wanted to push the discovery from his mind, to take back the last few seconds, to deny the reality of the situation, but he couldn't as he stared at the money with fear and loathing. The probability of who he was hammered him in the gut.

The gun. The cash. The murdered teen in the car.

Someone must have killed the missing boys. Clark had assumed Paul was that person. But Katherine's uncle wouldn't have dirtied his hands. No. He would have hired someone. Someone capable of killing. Someone with a gun. Someone who expected to get paid for it.

That someone could be him. Clark had the gun. Clark had the cash.

"There's a lot here," Katherine said. "Strange that he'd keep all this hidden away like that, isn't it? Clark? Are you all right?"

Clark struggled to pull himself together. "Yeah. Just surprised at the cash."

"So am I. It's not very smart. All that interest he's losing. Not something my uncle would do unless...it's from something illegal. Oh, my goodness. That's it, isn't it?"

Clark tried to focus on her words, on the room around him.

"Are you sure you're all right?" Katherine touched his shoulder.

"I…"

He grabbed onto the safe door and tried to concentrate. Then he heard something. Over the low murmur from below, Clark deciphered another sound, one separate and different. A footstep. Frowning harder, he focused on the sound. It came from the stairs.

"Someone's coming," he warned.

"I don't hear anyone. You've done this before. I don't understand how you can—"

"I don't know, but trust me on this. Someone's upstairs and coming down the hall."

While Katherine stuffed the money back, rearranged the files and shut the safe, Clark rushed to his feet and closed the panel. He snapped off the overhead light and thrust the small enclosure into a thick, black, claustrophobic blanket.

Over Katherine's shallow breathing, Clark heard light footsteps on the carpet along the hall. He couldn't tell if they'd passed the door to Spalding's room. Katherine shifted and bumped up against him. As he lifted a hand to steady her, his palm touched velvet. Her breast. Swallowing, he moved his hand to the right and grasped the smooth, warmth of her arm. Awareness rushed through his body, and by the sudden rapid change in her breathing, he knew she felt the same.

Clark drew on his exceptional sight, focused and concentrated on the place where he knew she stood. Slowly, shadows formed and separated from the darkness. Katherine's blonde hair, the paleness of her skin became visible—a faded image of how he remembered her in the light, all creamy, ivory skin against black velvet and incredibly sexy with her hair unbound and draped around her bare shoulders.

She was beautiful. And mere inches away. Clark couldn't believe they were hiding in a closet with the possibility of discovery, and all he could think about was how Katherine looked and smelled.

He watched Katherine's lips part and her hand flutter to the place where he'd accidentally touched her. Desire flooded his veins, and he couldn't do anything but react.

Reaching over, he glided a thumb ever so gently along her jaw. She jumped, but when she didn't draw away, Clark inched her chin upward and bent forward. He lightly touched his lips to her own, testing, tasting, savoring the texture of her mouth. She melted toward him. The whisper of her hand skimmed across his chest.

She wanted him.

The knowledge flamed Clark's desire. He curved an arm around her back and fitted her against him as he molded his mouth over her own, deepening the kiss, taking everything she gave and more. But a kiss wasn't enough. Clark wanted to peel back the velvet and touch skin softer than any man-made material.

The gentle sigh of her surrender nearly pulled him under, damning everything but the moment. Clark grappled for self-control. Before he completely lost it, he eased back from the intoxicating feel of her.

"They're gone," he whispered, regret and longing in his voice when he pulled further away.

"Then I guess we better leave while we still have a chance."

The reluctance in her voice matched how he felt. But the timing was off. Hell, it couldn't be worse. What with his suspicions about himself. The sad part was, he'd kiss her again, given the opportunity.

Clark slid the door open and closed behind them. When they reached the landing, Katherine glanced back and paused.

"What's wrong?"

She opened her mouth to say something, but then closed it and shook her head. "It doesn't matter."

"Yes, it does," he replied in a soft but urgent voice. "I've put you into a dangerous situation—even deadly. Something I've no right doing."

She frowned. "I'm at a point where I don't know what to do next. I'll check into Kirkwood Incorporated and find out why it sounds familiar. It'll take me a couple of days. Then maybe the police will need to be called."

Clark stiffened. "You don't need to do anything. I'll take care of it. You're far too involved as it is."

"How can I *not* be involved?" she whispered harshly. "We're talking about my family here!"

Turning, Katherine hurried to the stairs and walked down, and Clark quickly followed.

Things were getting way out of hand. It had been different before when he'd first met Katherine. He'd used her then because of her relationship with her Uncle and Miltronics, but now, he saw her as so much more. She was a living, breathing being, one who didn't deserve the mess he was making of her life.

Hell. Clark knew he needed to put some distance between them, but he couldn't. He needed her. Not just because of her tie to her uncle. It went far deeper. More importantly, he was too damn selfish.

With a tight fist, Clark hit the stair rail in frustration. The balustrade cracked, moaned and splintered. Then the wood shattered and launched into the air. In horror, Clark watched a large chunk break away and spear the stair below, inches from where Katherine had stepped.

Jerking sideways, she grabbed onto the wall with the flat of her hand. She glanced to her feet, and wide-eyed, turned to stare at the large gap between the baluster.

"What in the world! How—?"

"Are you all right?" Clark asked simultaneously.

"Yes. But you? Your hand?"

"It's fine." He didn't want to look. And anyway, the way his body worked, if he was wounded, it wouldn't take long to heal.

Katherine climbed back up the stairs. She bit her lower lip and ran a finger along the ragged edge of one end. "I don't understand how that happened. The baluster isn't flimsy. It's taken years of abuse. But now it looks like someone's put a chainsaw to it. How totally bizarre."

Little did she know, Clark thought darkly to himself. After he checked the floor below and found it empty of witnesses, he relaxed somewhat. "Yeah, but you said yourself, it's taken years of abuse. It's old. The wood's probably rotting from inside. It wouldn't have taken much—like me tripping and falling against it like I did."

Clark laughed and inwardly winced at how false it sounded. Times like now, he felt like a clumsy idiot. One would think with his extraordinary strength he'd be swift and agile. Yeah, right. He'd learned all too quickly that the reality was the opposite. If he didn't continually concentrate, he became a walking disaster.

Katherine sighed. "Wonderful. I don't have a clue what to tell my uncle. We're not even supposed to be up here. These are all private rooms. How am I going to explain this?"

"You don't—"

"But—"

He caught her wrist and pulled it away from the broken wood. Swiftly, Clark glanced down at their hands. No visible wound. At least, this time, he wasn't bleeding all over the place. "It was an accident. And anyway, why do you care if we damage Paul's property? The man might be a murderer."

Clark failed to mention that he might be as bad as her uncle, but he didn't want to consider that possibility right now, and he sure as hell didn't want to inform Katherine of it either.

"You're right. Let's get out of here."

They made it down the remainder of the stairs without any major mishap, probably because Clark made a point of keeping his hands to himself. Once they entered the large living area, she caught at Clark's sleeve and urged him over to the left of the room. He followed Katherine's narrowed gaze.

Sharon Spalding. Great. She stood talking animatedly to some stooped, emaciated man. Probably working the room for all it was worth. She hadn't yet seen the two of them, and Clark wanted to keep it that way.

"How about we find a drink?" Katherine murmured, lengthening the distance between them and her mother. "I think the bar's set up in the kitchen if we don't find a waiter on the way."

"She doesn't like me much, does she?"

When Katherine didn't immediately answer, he thought she was going to pretend she hadn't heard.

Expression hardening, Katherine finally said, "No."

"I can't blame her, really."

"Don't take it personally. She doesn't like too many of the people I associate with."

"Why?"

Katherine blinked and looked away. "No reason I can think of."

Clark sensed the lie. The idea that Katherine had secrets of her own bothered him. It made him realize he'd only scraped through one layer of her personality.

Katherine had so much more depth than he'd expected—unlike her mother. Granted, Clark hadn't spent much time in Sharon's company, but the woman struck him as superficial and self-centered, while Katherine's father... Well, he hadn't seemed much better. "Your father. Tell me about him."

"There's really not much to tell. He's been a rock to my mother, the one person who's always supported her political career. I don't know many men who would put aside their own career like he has. I do admire him for that."

"Strange, but I thought he'd be some silver-haired, stately figure, the perfect foil on your mother's arm. He's younger than I imagined."

Katherine laughed. "It's called plastic surgery. Like I said, my father has some admirable qualities, but he does have his downfalls."

"And that's?"

"Vanity." She grimaced. "He can also be overprotective at times. Like his behavior tonight. Believe it or not, he was trying to look out for me."

"I'd probably do the same if I had a daughter of my own."

"Maybe, but I think he went overboard. He had no right to scare you off."

"Oh, he didn't scare me off. Believe me. If I'd stayed longer, I would have said something I'd later regret."

"Which reminds me. You said you weren't going to do anything crazy tonight. You promised," she accused.

"No. I promised I wouldn't pilfer any of your uncle's silver."

Katherine scowled. "Don't start playing with words. You know what I— Oh, my goodness." Suddenly, she stopped and caught hold of Clark's elbow.

He stiffened. "What?"

"He's right there."

Clark didn't have to ask who 'he' was. "Where?"

"Over in the corner—the one in the black suit."

"That doesn't help. There are a dozen guys in black, including myself."

"He's wearing a paisley tie and talking to a redhead with an ugly looking ruby necklace wrapped around her throat." Katherine's fingers dug deeper into his arm. "There's nothing unusual about him, really. He looks like a typical businessman. Not a..." Her voice lowered as she glanced around. "Well, you know what I mean."

When Clark spotted Spalding, tension ground into the muscles of his neck and back. So this was the man who'd been racing through Clark's mind again and again, keeping him up during endless nights, feeding his thoughts in the light of day.

Katherine was right. There was nothing special about Spalding. Medium height, middle-aged, somewhat overweight, nondescript brown hair. Every inch of him was ordinary and—damn it—unrecognizable.

When he watched Spalding tilt back his head and laugh, Clark felt hatred, pungent and thorough, churn in his gut. The man had no damn right to laugh, not with all the death and pain he'd inflicted.

Why this feeling of overpowering outrage when he didn't even recognize the man? Clark didn't get it.

"So, what do you think?" Katherine asked. "Does he look familiar?"

Clark rubbed the back of his neck. He'd had this crazy idea that if he saw Spalding in the flesh, his past would come flashing back with perfect clarity. Earlier today, Clark would have staked his life on it. Well, he was dead wrong.

A waiter passed by. Perfect timing. He grabbed two fluted glasses, gave one to Katherine and downed the other. Champagne again. Hell. It tasted rancid, but right now he didn't care.

"Familiar? No. There's nothing," Clark said. "Strange. All this time... I thought for sure."

Katherine slipped her hand into his and squeezed gently. Sympathy softened her large, brown eyes. "I'm sorry. I know you were hoping."

He forced a smile, which probably looked more like a grimace. "It was worth a shot."

Suddenly, Katherine's fingers tightened around his hand, and her eyes widened in alarm.

"What's wrong?"

"He's coming over," Katherine said, a distinct tremor in her voice. "I don't think I have the stomach for this."

Feet splayed, the reassurance of Katherine's hand in his, he watched Spalding approach with narrowed eyes. Clark was more than ready for an introduction.

CHAPTER 14

WHEN CLARK GLANCED over at her uncle, Katherine saw something dark and violent flash in Clark's slate colored eyes. Suddenly chilled, she eased her hand from his and stepped away. She'd never seen such rage from Clark in that one, brief glance.

This wasn't the same man from moments before. Gone was the softness, the warmth. In its place, a cold, formidable mask etched across his already austere features. She must have been insane to think Clark was tame and amenable, because right now, he looked anything but.

"Katherine."

She moved her lips into what she hoped looked like a smile. "Uncle Paul! Happy Birthday! Sorry I wasn't able to catch you earlier to give you my best wishes."

"Think nothing of it."

As Paul bent forward and brushed his lips against her cheek, Katherine flinched. She couldn't help it. With what she suspected of her uncle, the idea of having him touch her made her nauseous, and to actually endure it physically, made her shudder all the more.

Paul raised a brow but didn't comment.

Katherine cleared her throat. "Yes, well, you don't look a year older."

"Such tact." His chuckle, low and self-depreciating, scraped against Katherine's nerves. "I wish it were the truth, but, alas, I can't run from getting older. Maybe one day someone will invent a miracle pill to impede the aging process. Wouldn't that be nice?"

"I'm sure," Katherine said. "And if a pill did become available, Miltronics would be the first to create such a wonder drug."

Paul dipped his head. "Thank you for your vote of confidence. I wish it were that simple." He raised a brow and stared at Clark.

She turned and saw Clark's look of polite interest. His expression might fool her uncle but it didn't fool Katherine. "Oh, I'm sorry. Uncle Paul, I'd like you to meet my friend, Clark Kent. Clark, this is Paul Spalding, my father's brother."

Paul sipped his drink. "What an unusual name. You must get many a wisecrack."

"I've had my share."

When her champagne sloshed inside her glass from her wildly trembling hand, Katherine cupped the goblet in both hands. She concentrated on pulling herself together as she warily eyed both men. This wasn't the time for hysterics.

If it came to blows, physically, her uncle didn't have a chance. Clark was fit, incredibly strong and with his latent rage—dangerous. On the other hand, Paul might be the weaker of the two, but Katherine knew behind his urbane demeanor hid an intelligent mind. Also, Paul might not have the power of the fist, but he possessed something far more powerful—money.

"So what do you think?" Paul asked Clark.

"About what?"

"Aging? Mortality? Do you think the search for eternal youth is science fiction or a future reality?"

Clark shrugged a shoulder. "I guess anything's possible, given time. Twenty years ago, no one thought we'd be this close to a cure for cancer. I think the more important question is, would anyone really want to live forever?"

Paul laughed harshly. "I can assure you, over half the people under this roof would give up their first born for just that."

"Then I'd find that appalling. Death's a natural progression.

Without it, the world as we know it would turn into chaos. There'd be overpopulation, a greater battle for natural resources. Land, food. All of it would grow sadly inadequate."

"I find that an alarmist point of view. All you have to do is look at history. Over the centuries the human animal has adapted despite excruciating circumstances and survived."

"But for how long?" Clark quickly refuted.

Paul gave Clark a condescending smile, but anger flared in his eyes. "Now I see where you're coming from. No one of great consequence has died in your life. Otherwise, you might think differently."

Katherine stiffened, this time spilling champagne over the edge of her goblet to drip on her fingers. Jennifer. Her uncle's wife. She'd died quickly and painfully from a ruptured brain aneurysm.

Somehow the topic had latched onto Paul's one passion. She opened her mouth to veer the subject to something less toxic, but Clark's warning touch against the small of her back stilled her tongue.

"That's possible but more likely improbable," Clark argued. "Playing God isn't something anyone has a right to do."

"Really?" Paul's tone softened. "The great debate. Science versus God."

Katherine shifted, disconcerted at the almost zealous look in her uncle's usually placid expression. This whole conversation rang of the bizarre. Something wasn't right.

When the subject changed, and at one point, Paul cracked an inane joke, smiled, and laughed, Katherine tensed. Her uncle didn't joke, didn't carry on a conversation with sophisticated ease or argue with a total stranger. At least not during the time she'd known him. Since the death of Jennifer, he'd grown distant, further detaching himself from the family around him. Her mother had even mentioned the change.

The reason for her uncle's odd behavior bore into her. Paul knew Clark.

Oh, my goodness. Pulse pounding against her ears, Katherine jerked her glass to her lips and swallowed. The sting of alcohol burned against the back of her throat. She blinked back tears.

Somehow, she managed to paste a smile on her face and nod or answer with a suitable rejoinder when needed. Then an enthusiastic female guest pulled Paul away, which left her alone with Clark. She noticed the vitality in his normally sharp, gray eyes had faded. He looked exactly how she felt.

"What do you think?" Katherine asked softly.

"I don't know." Clark shook his head and adjusted his glasses. "Let's get out of here. I think we've both had enough for one night."

Katherine couldn't have agreed more. She'd had enough of her family, the drama, the secrets. She wanted to go home to the safety and tranquility of her townhouse. But, more than anything, she wanted to blot out this evening, which of course, she couldn't.

After getting their coats, they slipped from the house and walked down the driveway to the street, the lighting from a nearby lamp illuminating their way. Music and the myriad of voices from her uncle's house drifted through the damp, winter air and followed them toward Katherine's car. All those people, all that laughter and camaraderie, and Katherine felt so very isolated. The family she thought she knew didn't exist.

Once inside her Mazda with Clark in the passenger seat, she started the car and asked, "Do you remember my uncle?"

"No..."

She steered the car from the side of the road and out of the neighborhood. "But there's something else, isn't there?"

"I felt like I'd had the same conversation."

"With my uncle?"

Clark sighed and leaned back against the headrest. "That's just it. I don't know. It could've been with him or someone else. But the whole concept of mortality and death is a topic I've discussed before."

"I don't think that's unusual. At some point, everyone questions death or dying. I know I've wondered about the purpose of it all."

"But it's more than that..." Clark's irritation came through the dark interior of the car.

"It'll come to you," Katherine said, and then realized how lame she sounded. Clark might never remember. She couldn't fathom the pain and helplessness of losing her past and identity, of just not knowing... Clark deserved honesty if nothing else from her. "And if it doesn't, we'll find the answers. One way or the other."

"I'm likely to argue with you. Yes, we found your uncle's safe, the money, the different accounts, but I'd hoped for more. Some memory or realization of who I am. Or at least someone who recognized me." Clark's voice deepened with sincerity. "Don't get me wrong. I'm grateful for tonight. I don't want you thinking it was for nothing, because it wasn't."

Katherine's grip tightened on the steering wheel. She'd delayed telling Clark, but it had to be said. "But someone did recognize you tonight."

"What are you saying?"

"He knows you," Katherine whispered, hating to admit the truth and what it entailed—the secrets, the lies.

"Who?"

"My uncle."

"How?" Shock coiled around his words. "He would have given himself away."

"But he did. At least to me. He was acting completely out of character. Paul's not a talker, not with someone he hardly knows. He's always been somewhat closed mouthed, the introvert in the family."

"You're sure about this."

She laughed with rancor and guided her Mazda into the complex before parking in her appointed slot. "Oh, yes. Believe me, I wish I wasn't."

"Hell. I'm sorry. All this time I've been so damn self-centered—completely disregarding your feelings and how all this must be affecting you."

Although shadows clung to Clark's face, she heard the sympathy in his voice and recoiled. She didn't want his or anyone else's pity. Hurriedly, she slipped out of the car and slammed the door after her. She blinked back tears and rushed across the parking lot as quickly as her high-heels allowed. She didn't get far before Clark caught up to her.

"It's not your fault," she finally managed while she walked up the sidewalk to her house. "We'll talk more tomorrow. Right now I'm not up to it."

"I don't want to leave you alone. Not the way you're feeling."

"I'll be fine—alone."

With her emotions so volatile, Katherine didn't dare let Clark into her house for fear of asking him to stay. She lifted her key ring toward the porch light and fumbled through far too many keys.

"Do you need help?"

"No. I've got it."

When Clark moved up behind her, Katherine searched for the elusive key with renewed desperation. His scent, woodsy and male, drifted through the air around her. He was temptation personified. No. There was no temptation. She was not tempted. Finally, she managed to get her fingers around her house key and, with the added help from the porch light, unlocked the door.

Clark's urgent whisper floated over her senses. "Invite me in."

CHAPTER 15

THE FRONT DOOR opened on silent hinges, but Katherine didn't move from her spot on the porch. Passion. It filled the husky baritone of his voice. Clark's fingers tangled in her hair and drew the strands from the side of her neck. His breath fanned the vulnerable skin before his lips lightly trailed against the slope of her neck.

Katherine closed her eyes as desire wrapped around her. Clark eased his hands over her shoulders and pressed up against her back. Even through the thickness of her coat, she felt the heat of his body. She opened her mouth to tell him no, but the word caught against her throat. She didn't have any willpower. Not when it came to Clark or the feelings he evoked.

"I don't want to let you go." His whisper feathered the downy strands of her hair behind her ear. On their own, they were mere words, but with the urgency expressed in each syllable, they were so much more.

Katherine turned under the gentle urging of Clark's hands. The porch light illuminated the hard angles of his face, the sensual curve of his mouth and the hunger in his eyes. Oh, my. She wanted him, wanted him in her bed and inside her.

Then he bent toward her, blocking out the light and the night sky, and kissed her. His lips, soft, sensual and with infinite tenderness, traced her upturned mouth.

Sighing with pleasure, Katherine rose on her toes and deepened the kiss. She savored the taste, the texture of him. Their breathing mingled, deepened and quickened as Katharine's hands and mouth matched Clark's own growing urgency. Muscles bunched and contracted beneath her fingers, and the image of how Clark looked naked flashed in her mind's eye. She remembered every male inch of him the day she'd spied him from his bedroom window when he'd stepped from his shower. He'd been all hard muscles and sleek flesh.

Oh, Jesus. She wanted to see him like that again.

With Clark's hands framing her face, his mouth hungry on her own, Katherine backed into the house and stumbled over the threshold. Clark caught her around the waist and followed, closing the door with the heel of his shoe.

Moonlight flowed through the windows, affording enough light to see by. She broke away long enough to shrug out of her coat and toss it against the coat rack. She missed the hook, and Clark didn't do any better. Both jackets landed on the floor.

As Clark reached for her, Katherine shook her head. "No, wait."

She slipped off his glasses. He had a beautiful face, masculine, rugged and filled with such determination and innate strength. And his eyes, now a dark charcoal, spoke of passion and wonder. She could lose herself in their smoky depths.

"Better?"

She nodded.

"Good." He took the glasses from her hand and placed them on a table against the wall beside her. "I want you happy. I want... I want you."

As Clark swept his thumb over her lower lip, and then slid it across her jaw to the lobe of her ear, he looked at her as if he wanted to devour her right then and there. It made her feel beautiful, feminine and oh so very desired. Slowly, ever so slowly, he trailed a finger down the pulse point on the side of her neck and skimmed over the line of her collarbone.

"You have the most beautiful skin," he whispered. "So creamy. So soft."

Undone, Katherine reached up to touch his face, but he captured her hand and pulled it down and around her back, arching her toward him. Her skirt tangled around his legs as he stepped closer, nudging her backward inch by inch until she found herself pressed up against the wall with nowhere to go. Clark's body molded over her own, sandwiching her between him and the wall, while his hands stroked, teased and tormented.

He dipped his head and claimed her mouth in a long, drugging kiss. Wrapping her fingers in the thick strands of his hair, Katherine sighed with pure pleasure at the feel and taste of him.

Clark had her weak, hot and craving the heat of his skin against her own naked flesh. She pulled his tie loose, dragged his jacket over the wide breadth of his shoulders and snapped open the buttons of his shirt, finally able to slip her hands beneath his silk shirt to the unyielding wall of his chest. All the while, Clark's hands were everywhere, stroking, kneading, delving into places that made her heart crash, her stomach quicken and her flesh burn.

Clark unzipped the bodice of her dress and unsnapped her bra. Both garments landed by her feet. She kicked them aside, pulled his shirt apart and pressed up against his chest. A whimper caught against her throat, and she shivered. The feel, the heat of his naked flesh against her bared breasts was pure delight and pure torture.

Clark slid a palm down along the tender side of her breast and her ribs until his fingers caught against the waistband of her nylons. He tugged at the strap of her thong, Her panties dropped to the floor with her other discarded clothing. But Katherine didn't care. Nothing mattered but the moment, the hunger, the man in her arms.

Impatiently, she pulled at his belt, undid the buckle and the top button of his pants, and then traced a line beneath the elastic band of his underwear. She loved how his stomach quivered against her fingers. When she slid her hand lower over the fabric of his briefs to cup him, Clark froze, dragging his mouth from her own, then flexing and pressing his erection against her palm.

"Touch me," Clark demanded in a horse, urgent whisper.

Deeply aroused by the power she had over him, Katherine tugged his pants and underwear over his narrow hips, exposing every single inch of him. She inhaled sharply. Such power. The idea of him thrusting into her made her skin flame and her body quake that much more. She caressed the length of him with a shaky, tentative hand. Then she grew bolder, using both hands to gently massage him.

"Does that feel good?"

"Oh, hell, yes." Clark's breath came out hard and fast against her skin.

"So stiff, but so silky," she marveled.

Clark shuddered and stilled her hand. "Keep doing that, and I'll completely lose it before I've even started."

At his words, she looked up. Clark was absolutely gorgeous with his hair tousled from her fingers, his face taut and flushed with arousal, and his white shirt halfway open revealing a large expanse of smooth skin. Moonlight cast the hard angles of his face in shadow, and without the shield of his glasses, he appeared more dangerous, more male, more...electrifying.

Gently lifting and cupping the weight of her breast in his hand, Clark bent and covered the erect nipple with his mouth, using his tongue, his lips to suckle, to taste, to savor, shooting desire through her veins, into her limbs and every pore of her body.

It felt so good. He felt so good. She wanted him over her, in her. She wanted—

Suddenly, the heat of his palm cupped Katherine between her legs. She cried out and shuddered against his hand. Using his thumb to gently circle and rub her clitoris, Clark eased his middle finger inside her. The feel. God. His mouth, his hands, working both her breasts and between her legs with a hypnotic, savage intensity. She was coming undone, losing herself. She grabbed onto his shoulders, dragged her fingers into the locks of his hair, and shifted her hips in short, quick movements. She couldn't stop. She didn't want to stop.

Clark must have sensed she was near the edge, because he

slowed the rhythm of his fingers and the quick, rapid movement of his mouth on her breast. Straightening, he nipped gently at the lobe of her ear, withdrawing his finger from the moist heat between her legs, only to use both of his hands to gently mold, squeeze, and knead her buttocks. From behind, he swept the tips of his fingers over her inner thighs, opened and readied her for him.

His breath was as heavy, as jagged as her own. "So wet. So hungry. Right now, I could wrap those gorgeous legs around me, slip inside and have you coming around me in seconds."

She sagged against him, aching with anticipation.

"I didn't plan this. I never thought..." His words and voice were rough, urgent. "I don't have a condom."

Katherine, her brain muddled by passion, didn't understand for a moment. "Oh. I've—"

"In your medicine cabinet." He branded her on the mouth with one long, thorough kiss. "Don't go anywhere."

Katherine almost laughed. She didn't think she could even if she'd wanted to. If not for the wall that held her up, she'd be a puddle on the floor. Clark had worked her body into a mass of need. She throbbed with it, hummed with it. Closing her eyes, she touched her swollen mouth with trembling hands.

Suddenly, Clark was back. She smelled his scent, felt the air stir around her as he stepped toward her. She opened her eyes and inhaled sharply. In front of her, Clark stood on strong and corded legs, while the light of the moon touched his narrow hips, flat, ribbed belly, and wide, smooth chest with loving hands. Naked, he looked better than any fantasy.

"I never thought I'd say this to a man," Katherine murmured in wonder, "but you're beautiful."

He lifted his lips into an incredibly sexy, half smile, but his eyes were serious, turbulent and unfathomable when he stepped toward her. He tore the package open and pulled out the condom. As she helped slip it on his penis, her hands started shaking at the feel and size of him.

Clark captured her mouth and molded her body, her lips against his own. Cupping her hips in both of his large hands, he slowly, every so slowly, lifted her up against the wall and the hard length of his body. He was like a drug, and she the addict.

Katherine kissed him back, again and again, massaging the muscles of his shoulder, his upper arms, feeling his tendons flex, his skin shiver against her fingers.

Capturing her wrists, Clark shackled them above her head with one hand and used the other to cup her breast and gently rub the taut tip between his fingers. He broke off the kiss and urged by her ear, "Wrap your legs around me. That's right."

Clark lowered her along the wall until the tip of his shaft nudged the opening between her thighs. She couldn't move, couldn't do anything but feel as he lowered her even further. His erection eased into her, slowly, inch by incredible inch, stretching, filling her with his length. He was hot, hard, inflexible and... pure male.

Trembling against him, she clenched her legs tighter around his flanks. "You feel incredible."

"And you're so tight and hot around me. So wet," he whispered hoarsely. He kissed her temple, her jaw as he gradually withdrew, leaving only the tip of his shaft inside her. "Do you want me deeper?"

She nodded, unable to think clearly enough to find the words.

Flexing, Clark entered her fully and ripped a cry of passion from her lips. Sweat glistened against his brow as he eased in and out of her body, then he stilled.

Katherine turned her head to catch his lips, but he kissed the corner of her mouth, her chin, the pulse point beneath her ear. To her complete frustration, Clark once again edged out until only an inch of him penetrated her.

"Is this better?"

"No—I want...all of it." Her breath came out in short, shaky pants. "All of you."

Whimpering, she jerked her hips to take him in deeper, but Clark eluded her. Her breasts, slick from sweat, slid over his flesh as she writhed against his chest.

Desperate to touch and explore, to feel his muscles bunch and flex beneath her fingers, to drag those same fingers into the silken strands of his hair, Katherine shook her head and pried at his hand around her wrists. He didn't let go. Inflexible and merciless, he bound her to the wall with his body.

"Please... Clark. I..."

Catching her mouth in a kiss that took and devoured, Clark eased deeper into her, his moan mingling with her own. He was teasing her now, his movements slow, shallow and controlled, working her and her body with a rhythm that both taunted and tormented. She bucked, wanting him to move faster and harder, but, relentless and unforgiving, Clark flexed in and out of her with slow, measured strokes.

"I can't take this." Katherine, pinioned against the wall and Clark, shook her head. Completely powerless, she took what he gave, but craved so much more. "I want you deep. Every single inch of you. I want you coming in me."

"Katherine—" Clark pressed his brow against her temple and groaned. "I can't. Damn it. I've got to—"

He drove into her, pulled back and drove into her again. Harder. Faster. Over and over. Oh, God. The pleasure. It crashed into her again and again, pushed her higher, higher, until she thought she'd die with the sensation. Then she was coming, convulsing, crying out as he pumped ever faster, pulling her under, shattering the last of her control. Clark quickly followed, growling low in his throat, shuddering against her.

Shattered, Katherine slumped against Clark. Limbs heavy, body languid and pliant, Katherine had been thoroughly used. He'd made her beg and plead, but Katherine hadn't cared. She would have said or done anything to slake the passion between the two of them.

Clark freed her wrists. She slipped her hands down to his sweat-coated shoulders and felt the muscles beneath his skin tremble as he lowered her down to her feet. Katherine's gaze collided with his. She saw the reverence in their gray depths and melted even further.

"I never thought I could feel like that." Resting a hand against the wall, Clark bent down and gently kissed her.

Katherine smiled against his mouth. "Me neither."

Pushing off the wall, Clark pulled off the condom and grinned. "Let me get rid of this. I'll be right back. The way I'm feeling, I'll grab the whole damn box. I've got a feeling I might need it tonight."

With a matching grin pasted on her face, Katherine bent down and picked up her discarded clothing from the floor. She was going to enjoy making up for all those celibate years. When she rose with a pair of panties in one hand, Clark stepped back into the hall and stilled. At the oddness of his expression, Katherine frowned and followed Clark's stare to a place on the wall to her right. White knuckled, she clutched her clothing against her chest.

A large hole, the size of a fist, punctured the wall to the right of her head. Concrete chips scattered across the floor around them.

In his passion, Clark had pounded his fist against the wall. This particular wall, built for noise and fire protection, separated her townhouse from the other. It consisted of thick solid masonry—not some flimsy layer of drywall. A person didn't smash a hand into a wall like that and create such damage. At least not a normal person.

Katherine looked at Clark's upturned hand—the one he now stared at. The glow of the moon revealed enough. Not even a scratch to his flesh. A sick sensation curled around her stomach as she thought of the baluster earlier tonight and how he'd supposedly bumped into it. Now she knew otherwise. He'd touched it with his hands. If Clark could do either by accident, what could he do when he set his mind to it? Worse yet, what could he do to her in anger? One touch, and he could kill her.

Fear propelled her away from Clark. "Who are you? No. Better yet. What are you?"

"Don't."

"Don't what? Don't be frightened? Don't worry? Well, I am. Unless you can give me a rational explanation. How did you put that hole in the wall?"

"I don't know."

But Clark did. She saw the lie in his face. When he stepped toward her, she warned, "Don't come any closer."

"Katherine, there's no reason to be scared of me."

When he kept coming, she turned and ran down the hall.

"Katherine!"

She didn't stop but rushed into her bedroom, slamming and locking the door behind her. She fumbled for the light switch, found it, snapped it on, and then backed away from the door.

But she quickly found the closed door and lock weren't nearly enough protection.

She watched in horror as the door cracked, groaned, and flew open, the hinges tearing and snapping loose from their moorings. Chest heaving, Clark, naked and terrifying, stood in the doorway.

"Get out! Now! I swear if you don't, I'll scream the bloody walls down!"

When Clark stepped through the room, something in her face or voice must have gotten through to him, because he froze.

"Shit. Katherine. You're really scared of me. I'm sorry." He glanced to the door and flinched. "I honestly don't know what came over me. I'll pay for the damages."

"Go. Just please get out of here."

"This isn't over between us." Clark's voice steadied, then strengthened. "I'll make you see you've nothing to fear from me. That's a promise."

After Clark turned and walked out of the bedroom, Katherine sat down hard on her bed and pushed herself up against the headboard. Bending her legs, she curled her arms around her knees and stared at the doorway, expecting Clark to reappear any second. She didn't relax, didn't hardly breath until she heard him leave. Only then did she scramble off the bed and venture from the room.

Quickly, she locked the front door and almost laughed hysterically at the stupid act. Locked doors weren't going to keep Clark out.

She stood in the hall, her bare feet chilled by the wood floor. She'd had sex, lost complete control with this man—someone she'd thought she was growing to know. But she didn't know Clark.

He could kill a person with the flick of his wrist. He was dangerous. Strange. Frightening.

She wiped her mouth, but the feel of him still lingered.

Heaven help her.

Who was she kidding? If it'd just been sex between the two of them, then why did it feel like her heart was breaking?

CHAPTER 16

So WHAT'S SO important that you needed to see me alone? It's crazy if you ask me—what with over a hundred people running around. If someone sees us together like this, they're going to find it odd."

Paul Spalding checked the hall before he followed the other person into the game room. "No one's going to find out. And even if they do, they'll probably be too drunk to care." He closed the door from the music and crowd. "It's John Davenport. The son-of-a-bitch had the brass balls to show up here tonight."

"What are you talking about? He's dead. The car accident. Everything was set."

"No, he's not *dead*. All this time, I thought we'd covered most of our tracks with the accident and the fire at Miltronics. There was just the shelter to take care of. But now we have *this*. Someone screwed up in Arizona. Right now, he's out there walking around and eating my damn food like he doesn't have a care in the world." Paul strode around the pool table and over to the bar, where he grabbed a bottle of scotch.

"That doesn't make sense. You know, I've never seen him, but I would have known if he was in the house. There's the guest list—"

"He's going under the name of Clark Kent. I'm sure it's his

way of telling us the joke's on us. Talk about the audacity. It's obvious he plans on sticking it to us. I just don't know how."

"You can't be serious. You know, I thought he was another one of Katherine's homeless cases."

"Far from it. Davenport's playing some sick game. If he thinks I'm going to sit back and play, he's got another think coming." Ice cubes rattled as Paul refilled his glass. He needed something with a kick. Tipping back his head, he took a long, deep swallow. It didn't help. "Of all people, Katherine introduced us. Talk about acting. He gave nothing away. It was almost like he'd never seen me before. I swear, I've never met anyone so damn bold."

"How much do you think he's told Katherine?"

"The son-of-a-bitch." Paul thought he was going to be sick. When he thought back, she'd acted strange, even nervous. Shit. He drained his glass. What the hell had he ever done to deserve this? "I don't know what he's said to Katherine. It could be nothing or everything.

"We're up the fucking creek if he has."

"It doesn't matter."

"Why?"

"Because they're both dead."

~~*~~

With a shoulder braced against a no parking sign, Clark stood across the street and, he hoped, far enough from the entrance to the Morning Dove to be unrecognizable. From watching the shelter and Katherine's movements, he'd learned she usually went out for lunch. He glanced down at his watch. Almost twelve-thirty. He didn't have much longer to wait.

Almost a week ago, he'd left Katherine's townhouse after scaring the hell out of her and ruining her door. He'd since hired a handyman to repair her door, and according to the man, he'd completed the job to Katherine's satisfaction. As for Katherine—Clark hadn't heard back from her.

A total of five days of her silence, of feeling like crap, of keeping away from her. Five days of uncovering absolutely nothing new on Katherine, Spalding, Miltronics or his memory. And the sad part—he didn't see that changing any time soon. More importantly, he was afraid to uncover the truth because of what it might reveal about himself. The idea of being a paid killer didn't exactly make him feel all warm and fuzzy.

Two days ago, he'd attempted to break into Miltronics, but its sophisticated security system had blocked his clumsy attempts. Granted, muscle might have gotten him into the building but more than likely gotten him killed or arrested. Clark could live with never stepping foot inside Miltronics; if Spalding hadn't destroyed any important documents or incriminating evidence by now, the fire had. Plus, Clark hated the idea of walking through the building's corridors and various rooms. The whole place stunk of filth and malevolence.

Clark flipped the collar of his jacket up against his neck. As for Katherine, he'd left her alone these last several days, believing in time, she wouldn't see him as a threat. If he'd kept his hands to himself that night, she would be talking to him. But, no. Not him. Unable to stomach the idea of going back to his place with only his thoughts for company, Clark hadn't been able to keep away. After all, what was one more sin, when his past might hold a multitude?

He'd created a hopeless situation. Now Katherine couldn't stand the sight of him and probably thought of him as some sick freak. And could he blame her?

Katherine stepped from the building. Straightening, Clark adjusted his glasses and watched her stride in the opposite direction. When she disappeared around the corner of the next street, Clark crossed the road. Over the last couple of weeks, he'd discovered a number of teenage residents, stomaching the cold snap of winter to smoke by the building's back door.

Today, a girl of about sixteen, with a cigarette affixed to the corner of her mouth, sat on a wood fence that circled the raised porch. Tapping the heel of her boot against the bottom rung, she glanced down at Clark's approach.

"Is Katherine around?"

"No. She went to lunch. She might be awhile. If you want, you can wait inside."

"No. I'm fine."

Clark wanted to question anyone who'd stayed at the shelter for more than a couple of weeks. Hopefully, he might uncover a link to the shelter and Miltronics. But as to how? He didn't know yet.

Pausing at the foot of the stairs to the porch, Clark eyed the girl and wondered what had forced her out on the street. Other than her pierced chin and eyebrow, she looked like any typical teenage girl, with short, black hair and clear skin.

As Clark climbed the shallow stairs and walked over to the opposite side of the fence, the girl sniffed and wiped her eyes with her forearm. That was when Clark noticed the girl's pink nose and red-rimmed eyes, which, he realized, had nothing to do with the cold air.

"Are you all right?"

"Yeah."

But the girl wouldn't glance Clark's way as she dragged hard on her cigarette.

"You sure?"

The girl's chin trembled. She opened her mouth and then closed it.

"Sometimes talking it out can make a big difference."

She rubbed the back of her hand beneath an eye, but another tear reappeared down her cheek. "You wouldn't understand."

Clark realized Katherine's attraction to the shelter. He didn't even know this girl, but her obvious pain tugged at his heart and made him want to ease the hurt. Getting through life as an adult was hard enough, but being thrown a couple of low blows before getting there sure as hell was unfair.

"Try me."

Through narrowed eyes, she stared at him for a long moment while smoke wafted past her face. Finally, she shrugged a shoulder. "Fuck. Why not? It's like everyone else here knows my business." She took another drag from her cigarette. "I just got off the phone with my sister."

"Is she okay?"

"Yeah. That's what she says, but I haven't seen her for over six months." The girl laughed harshly. "But who's counting."

"And you can't go see her?"

"So the bastard can stick his fist in my face again? I don't think so. This place is a hell of a lot better than that shit hole. At least here I don't trip over my old man after one of his drinking binges."

At the image, Clark winced. "Do you think your sister's safe?"

"I thought so. He hasn't ever touched her. But I'm not so sure now." She pulled the cigarette from her mouth and frowned at it in her hand. "I took off and let her deal with him on her own. She's only twelve. He's strong. One punch from him, and he could kill her."

The poor kid. Somehow his problems seemed insignificant. At least Clark, being an adult, could defend himself.

"Is she here in Boston?" he asked gently. "If she is, I can set up a meeting for you. That's if—"

"No! I can't face Amy. Not after I took off and left her to deal with him alone. I was the only one she trusted, and I screwed up. I thought getting high would make it go away, but it didn't. I ran and took the coward's way out."

The coward's way out. The girl's words touched something deep inside Clark. A memory. A feeling. That one word—coward. It filled him with shame and remorse. He'd been fleeing, taking the coward's way out. But what had he been running from? Spalding or himself? Or something more?

"I don't think she'll ever want to see me again."

Hearing the self-loathing in the teenager's voice, Clark couldn't find anything to say other than, "I'm sorry."

"Hey, life's a bitch." The girl's chin lifted, and her eyes narrowed with determination. "But I'm going to make it, and I know one thing—I'm never going to be like my old man. I've been clean for two months, and, unlike my *father,* I plan on staying that way. One way or another, I'm going to help get Amy away from him."

Clark believed her. "You've already made that first step. Taking a look at yourself and changing what you don't like takes a great deal of courage and strength. It's damn hard to do. Even harder to kick an addiction. It's something I'd be proud of."

"Proud? I don't think so."

"Of course you don't right now, but in time." Clark nodded in reassurance. "I think living here is going to be good for you, and ultimately, your sister. You can trust Katherine."

"I know." Her face softened. "Like, she's awesome."

"Yes, she is. With her on your side, you can't go wrong." Clark knew he spoke the truth. There was a strength, an aura about Katherine that soothed a person's soul. Maybe it was her faith in humanity. Or maybe something else, but whatever it was, Clark found himself drawn to it.

Twisting at the waist, the girl flicked her butt over a shoulder, dug into her jacket pocket and pulled out a crumpled pack of cigarettes. She lit another.

"Want one?"

"Sure." Clark eyed the cigarette dubiously but took it anyway. He rolled the filter between his fingers. It didn't feel familiar. "Thanks—?"

"Tracy."

"Thanks, Tracy. My name's Clark."

The back door opened. Clark didn't turn. He didn't have to. Whenever Katherine appeared, Clark knew, would always know. The feel, the sense, the essence of her went deeper than flesh, deeper than bone.

"What are you doing here?" Katherine asked.

"I was in the neighborhood." Clark turned then.

Katherine had closed the door but hadn't moved more than a foot away from it. She'd dropped the sophistication of black velvet from the other night, and today looked as if she'd stepped from some college campus with her thick, blonde braid, faded jeans and black, turtleneck sweater. Damn, but she looked good in black. It drew out her creamy complexion and the vibrant color of her hair. But her expression was anything but warm. Clark never thought brown eyes could look like ice, but somehow Katherine managed it, and then some.

Great. Clark took the lighter the girl offered. Katherine was angry. So what the hell had he expected? A smile of welcome? Not likely. But it was better than fear. Hell. Anything was better than the horror he'd seen in Katherine's face when he'd crashed into her room the other night.

"I thought you were going to lunch," Tracy said, somehow managing to keep her cigarette fastened to the corner of her mouth.

"I decided to pick something up instead. I have far too much paperwork to get through."

Clark put the cigarette in his mouth and lit the tip. Smoke curled into the air and around his face, hitting his nose and stinging his eyes.

"I didn't know you smoked."

Clark ignored the disapproval in Katherine's voice and inhaled. The second the fumes hit his lungs, he convulsed into coughing. Eyes watering, feeling as if he were hacking his lungs out from his ribs, Clark flung the cigarette into the snow where it hissed a protest. Finally, he grabbed enough clean air into his lungs to clear his vision and get a handle on his breathing.

"I don't."

Katherine eyed the spot where he'd tossed the cigarette. "You can clean that up before you leave."

The door slammed shut after her, but not before Clark caught the frigid look on her face.

"Wow. She doesn't like you much."

"Sure seems that way."

"Must have been some fight. I don't think I've ever seen her that angry. I didn't realize she'd hooked up with some guy."

Clark's face warmed. "It's not like that between us."

"Yeah. Sure." Tracy took a long, deep drag and tossed her cigarette into the snow inches from Clark's.

Clark decided not to argue. "So Katherine doesn't normally get angry?"

The girl laughed. "Hell, no. At least not what I'd call angry. Kath can get her point across real well without yelling. Like, everyone listens to her."

"Really?"

"Sure. And if they don't, they can take it up with George. But on the most part, everyone likes her."

Clark's own feelings for Katherine went beyond "like". He just wished she felt the same, but right now she didn't even trust him. Not that he'd given her any reason to.

"You know," Tracy was saying, "when I first saw you, I thought you looked familiar, and I couldn't figure out why. But now I remember."

Clark grabbed the fence's top rung with rigid fingers. The cold wood barely penetrated his senses, because fear, thick and smothering, roped around his throat.

"How so?"

"I saw you talking to Luke a couple of times."

Clark tried to sound casual. "When was that?"

"A couple of months back."

"Is he here now?"

"No. He took off. A couple of days after I saw the two of you talking."

"You sound surprised."

"Well, yeah. I thought we were friends. I could have rated a goodbye or something. But I didn't know he was an asshole."

"Did he act strangely before he disappeared?"

"I don't know, man." She started to pull a cigarette out from the package but stopped and tapped it back inside. "I guess so. He seemed scared for some reason."

Scared of someone or something? Or worse yet, scared of Clark? What he wouldn't give to remember.

"What's with all the questions? You a cop or something?"

"No. I'm just curious."

Tracy grunted. "Well, I got to go inside. It's fucking cold out here."

Clark stood on the porch for several minutes. He thought of going inside and talking to Katherine but decided against it. He didn't think he had a chance to get past her fear and anger. Not when she had the familiarity and reassurance of the Morning Dove and people around her.

Eventually, they would have to talk. Clark knew Katherine

would balk at a confrontation. Too many things still remained unsaid. Damn, but he missed her smile, her big, brown eyes and sense of humor, her dogged determination and plain, good old spunkiness.

Coming here today hadn't resolved anything. His situation appeared bleaker than when he'd first arrived. He'd been seen talking to a teenage boy only days before the kid disappeared. Why would he be talking to a homeless boy, decades younger than himself? Unless Luke had information Clark wanted. If that were the case, had it been important enough to involve murder? And if so, could Clark have been that killer? After all, Clark did have a gun.

Hell. He didn't even want to go there. Unable to look at his hands and wonder what they were capable of, Clark stuffed them in his pockets.

He still didn't understand why he felt this connection between the Morning Dove and Miltronics. Two completely different entities. One a homeless shelter and another a pharmaceuticals company. The only tie between the two was that of Katherine and her uncle. But how the hell could that be a key? A family vendetta? No. That didn't sound plausible. But then, none of it made sense.

A breeze kicked up and urged him from the back porch. The sun, though high over the horizon, didn't diminish the air's bite as it brushed over his exposed skin. Several inches of snow had melted from yesterday's mild weather, but with the drop in temperature, icicles speared down from tree branches and storefront overhangs. His breath fogged out with each exhalation as he reached the sidewalk and avoided a slick ice patch and a woman barreling down the walkway with a shopping cart filled with her ragged belongings. Shoulders hunched against the cold, Clark paused on the edge of the road and checked for oncoming traffic. When both sides of the street cleared, he crossed.

Movement by the corner of his eye caught his attention. Something—a hunch, fate, whatever he wanted to call it—made him turn. A gleaming black and chrome SUV raced down the street toward Clark. He froze. Holy shit. Sunlight bounced off the windshield and camouflaged the driver. It didn't slow but accelerated toward him.

CHAPTER 17

CLARK DOVE FORWARD and onto the sidewalk. But the car veered, hit the curb and locked into his direct path. At the last minute, less than a few feet away from the deadly vehicle, he backpedaled. The car swerved. Tires screamed against the pavement.

The driver overcorrected, missing Clark by inches, but now swerved out of control. The smell of rubber filled the air. Tires ground into a dry patch of road, and then skidded, hitting the slick pavement. The SUV careened, spiraled around and broadsided a compact car moving in the opposite direction. Metal screamed against metal, melding with the cries from pedestrians.

The SUV's impact sent the other vehicle sliding against the icy road. Several bedraggled men fled from the oncoming car and the warmth of a garbage can, its flames from inside keeping the cold at bay. The car hit the can and sent it and its contents flying. Fire and debris shot into the air and landed on the hood and trunk of the car as it fishtailed, slammed into a light post and stilled.

The SUV straightened and hit a snow pile, firing bits of rock and ice in its wake, before plunging forward and speeding off. It jerked around the corner of the next street and disappeared.

A scream crashed over the other cries. A horn blasted from somewhere. The smell of gas and fire wafted in the air. Flaming debris had skated off the car and landed on the ground beside it.

Gas snaked out from beneath the car's belly and confirmed what Clark suspected. A damaged fuel line.

"Look out! It's going to blow!"

People fled, running in the opposite direction from the accident, while braver onlookers rushed to the car. Someone grabbed the driver's door handle and pulled but couldn't get it open. A light post rammed up against the passenger door blocked the only other escape route from the car.

The woman inside banged a fist against the glass. The closed windows muffled her cries but didn't mask the sheer terror on her face.

Clark dodged through the jammed traffic to the wreckage. He elbowed through the crowd rushing in the opposite direction. "Move out of the way. I've got it."

With one hand, Clark grabbed the driver's side door handle and pulled. It snapped apart and came away with his hand. He couldn't open the door. The SUV's impact had crushed the driver's door and jammed the locks.

"Look the other way!" he shouted at the woman behind the wheel. "I'm going to break the window."

When the woman raised her arm to shield her face and slid back against her seat, Clark punched the glass with his bare hand. The window cracked, then shattered, spraying glass pebbles everywhere. Grasping the door with both hands, Clark pulled. Metal groaned and shrieked. He yanked the door from its hinges and dropped it on the ground where it shuddered then stilled. He ripped the seatbelt from its moorings, freeing the woman from inside.

Stumbling out, she collapsed against Clark's chest. He caught her up in his arms and rushed down the street and away from the car. A safe distance away, he set her back down on her feet. The woman looked shaken but unharmed. Then someone took her aside.

He glanced back at the wreckage. Flames flared and swelled, lapping around and beneath the car. He tensed, waiting for the explosion. But nothing happened. The fire, its tendrils caressing steel and metal, faded with each ragged breath Clark took in. It was a damn miracle the car hadn't exploded.

The sound of a siren broke over the noises of traffic and voices, and with each second, grew stronger, louder. Clark looked up and noticed the crowd. He'd heard the woman's cries, smelt the fire and gas, and acted, thinking of nothing but the need to rescue the passenger from inside.

He should have stopped at breaking the window, should have left the door alone, and should have helped the woman crawl out instead. He should have done many things, but he hadn't. He'd reacted without thought. And from the stunned looks and thick silence of the immediate crowd, Clark realized his mistake. Clark had exposed his unnatural powers for all to see. Powers he was beginning to believe were more a curse than any blessing.

Everyone started talking.

"Did you see that?"

"He pulled the door right off as if it was nothing?"

"Look what he did?"

"The guy's a freak!"

"Who is he?"

Clark flinched and backed away. He needed to get out of here. Before the police arrived and started asking questions. Before people were able to pick him out of a crowd.

Amid the chaos, Clark glanced across the street and froze. His gaze caught and held Katherine's. She stood in front of the Morning Dove. The shock stamped on her face told him she'd seen everything. Nausea rolled in his stomach.

Someone grabbed his arm. He shrugged it off and rushed forward, but Katherine bolted back into the shelter.

"Hey! Where are you going?"

Clark didn't turn around and answer. Instead, he veered onto the sidewalk. He couldn't talk to Katherine. Not now. He wouldn't make any sense. His pace quickened until he was running down the street and away from the car accident, the questions and the stares. But he couldn't run from the truth.

Someone wanted him dead.

~~*~~

Katherine rushed back into the Morning Dove. At the sound

of a car accident, she and everyone within hearing distance from inside the shelter had run outside to see. But Katherine hadn't planned on seeing Clark outside, tearing off a car door as if it were nothing. She couldn't fathom the amount of strength a person needed to do something like that. Such lethal power in one person. In the hands of the wrong man... Katherine didn't know if Clark used that power for the right reasons. He'd lied so many times...yet...his actions revealed a man with integrity.

Then from across the street, she'd seen him staring at her. She'd panicked and retreated back inside, unable to face Clark and her feelings.

From the safety of the front window, she watched Clark run from the accident and... Katherine blinked. She searched the crowd and street as an ambulance pulled up behind the wrecked car. Impossible. Clark had disappeared. Almost as if into thin air.

No. There'd been a flash of movement. As if... A shiver raced up her spine, and Katherine hugged herself. Could Clark's powers also entail the ability to run faster than the naked eye could discern? If so—lethal didn't even begin to describe him.

Katherine opened the door and hoped no one else noticed Clark's strange disappearance. "Come on guys. Let's all get back inside. You've got better things to do than stare at someone else's problems."

When no one moved, Katherine threatened, "If I have to ask again, I'm going to be assigning double kitchen duty."

"Not on your life. I hate dishes," one of the girls said as she followed Katherine and the others inside. "But did you see what that guy did?"

"Hell, yeah," Tracy said. "He tore the door off that car. Talk about weird. I was just talking—"

"That's impossible," Katherine cut in. She had no clue why she was protecting Clark. She didn't owe him a thing.

"I wasn't the only one who saw it."

"Yeah," Zack, a mass of dreadlocks sprouting from his head, agreed. "I saw it too. The guy was psycho."

"Okay, people. Let's say he did manage to do that. It doesn't mean he's psycho. There've been documented cases where a person will perform extraordinary feats under a life or death situation. This could very well be one of those cases. After all, it did look as if the woman might get seriously hurt."

"Whatever you say." Tracy glanced out the window where most of the crowd had scattered. "I still think it's fucking weird."

Weird. Is that what Clark thought of himself? Weird? Katherine had never envisioned Clark's thoughts or impressions. But she couldn't forget Clark's expression when their gazes had locked from across the street. For one, brief but shocking moment, she'd seen absolute horror on Clark's face.

This man was terrified of his capabilities. It made her realize he had feelings and failings. Yes, something was deathly different about Clark, but he'd never been unkind, never used what he had to hurt another. At least, from what she'd learned of him.

Katherine realized she might have completely misjudged Clark. Maybe he wasn't the one who'd wronged her, but she him.

"I'd like to talk to you, Tracy. In my office."

"What did I do?"

Leading the way to her office, Katherine laughed. "Nothing."

Katherine didn't sit down but leaned back against the front of her desk. "Earlier you were outside talking to the man who pulled the woman out of the car."

"Yeah. Shit. How weird is that?"

"Tracy."

She rolled her eyes. "Okay. 'Shoot' then."

"That's better."

"Yeah. Your boyfriend seemed nice."

Katherine decided not to argue about the boyfriend bit. Their relationship or lack of was too complicated and too confusing. "Nice? Since when do you describe someone as 'nice'?"

"Because that's the feeling I got from him."

"So you don't get the feeling he's dangerous?" Katherine trusted Tracy's opinion. The girl might be young, but she was far from green. One month on the street had the tendency to add decades to a person's age.

Tracy's brows sprang skyward. "Dangerous? You've got to be kidding, right?"

"Hum, sure," Katherine retracted. The truth was when it came to Clark, she didn't know what to believe. "So what did he have to say?"

"Nothing much."

"Really?" Katherine bit back the urge to volley off several questions.

"Yeah. We talked about my sister and Luke."

"I didn't think you were the type to talk to complete strangers."

"I'm not, but he caught me right after I got off the phone with Amy. And he seemed nice. He didn't act like I was some lowlife. He listened. You know, like he cared."

Many a time Katherine had believed the same. Clark cared, and always appeared to have.

"You know, it was strange. Like we were talking about... what was it? Oh, yeah. We were talking about Luke, and I swear it looked like someone had rammed a pipe up his ass."

On either side of her, Katherine gripped the edge of the desk with both hands. "Luke?"

"Yeah. I'd seen...Clark. Yeah, that's his name— talking to Luke a couple of days before he took off."

"What about?"

"Haven't a clue."

Katherine's growing excitement wilted. The meeting must have taken place before Clark's memory loss. What in the world was he doing talking to Luke? And again talking to Tracy? Only God and Clark knew. Then again, Clark might not even know. He could be going on pure instinct.

Clark. What was she going to do about him? Fear of him and fear of her feelings for him had kept her clear of Clark over the last couple of days. But that didn't mean she didn't obsess over him. Katherine knew she needed to reign in that preoccupation. If she didn't, her work was liable to suffer.

For the moment, she thrust Clark from her mind and focused on her client. "Before you leave, I'd like to know how your talk with your sister went."

Trace shrugged a shoulder, but a telltale shimmer touched her eyes. "Okay, I guess."

Tracy's nonchalant attitude, Katherine knew, shielded a deep vulnerability. Not that Katherine blamed Tracy for putting up a tough front. Life had knocked her around pretty hard. But one person always managed to crack through that façade—Tracy's sister, Amy.

"I just wanted to let you know I haven't given up on her or your situation. I'm going slow, because I want to do this right. No mistakes. I've hired an investigator to compile what he can on your father. Don't worry, we'll get her out of there."

Katherine didn't let on that she'd used her own money for the detective. Tracy didn't need to feel any more obligated than she already did. Also, Katherine could afford it.

There was one advantage of being born into the Spalding family. Money. She'd inherited a trust fund at twenty-five. Not something she advertised, knowing how unfair it seemed when she had so much while others had so little. Yes, she'd never once pulled a cent from the shelter for living expenses, drawing from her inheritance for her monthly salary, but even knowing that didn't stop the guilt from rearing up. She quickly pushed it aside. After all, she'd learned to live with guilt for years now.

"Thanks." Tracy jerked her head into a nod and slipped from the room.

A couple minutes later, Katherine followed Tracy from her office, walked back to the lobby and peered out the front window. A crowd still milled around the street, but several uniformed police had backed them away to make room for the ambulance, which left the scene to merge with traffic. Katherine hoped the lack of lights and siren indicated the driver had minor injuries.

She also noticed a police car parked across the street and an officer talking to several pedestrians. Of course, the officer would have to fill out the necessary paperwork. Katherine wondered what would be in his report and how he'd justify Clark's actions. More importantly, she wondered what Clark was doing at the moment.

CHAPTER 18

WITH THE SUN high on the horizon, Clark stood outside the front entrance of the Spalding estate and listened. A vacuum sounded from one of the rooms upstairs. Probably the housekeeper. As he placed a gloved hand over the door handle, a male voice filtered over the whirr of the vacuum. It came from the back of the house, possibly the kitchen. But even with all the noise, Clark knew that voice.

Spalding.

What the hell was he doing home in the middle of the day? Clark had expected him to be at work, many minutes and miles away. Well, Spalding's unexpected presence didn't matter.

Ignoring the hard, rapid bang of his heart and the sense of foreboding heavy against his chest, Clark glanced over his shoulder one last time before he slipped inside and eased the door closed behind him.

This afternoon, Spalding, the housekeeper—no one—was going to keep him away. Granted, Clark knew walking into an occupied house wasn't the most brilliant move on his part, but, hell, nearly getting mowed down by a car called for desperate acts.

Someone wanted him dead.

Clark should have paid closer attention to the car accident and the reasons behind it. He'd mistakenly focused on uncovering his identity and not on the magnitude of danger around him—until today.

Well, he sure as hell wasn't going to sit back and let someone turn him into a statistic. All the signs pointed to Spalding. But Clark couldn't discount the possibility of someone working at Miltronics or living at the shelter.

Enough. He didn't have time for speculation.

When he started walking down the hall toward the interior of the house, the housekeeper turned off the vacuum. A chair scraped against the floor from another room. Footsteps, heavy and with purpose, moved in Clark's direction.

Spalding again.

Damn it. On silent feet, Clark slipped swiftly into the office and waited, back against the wall. The echo of footsteps grew fainter as Spalding climbed the stairs to the second floor. Voices now. That of Spalding and the housekeeper.

The tension digging into Clark's muscles ebbed. Talk about close. Not waiting around for another near encounter, Clark pushed off the wall and strode to the desk. Quickly, but quietly, he pulled the drawer out. He found the package attached to the bottom. At least something was going right today. With a gloved hand, he yanked the boys' identifications from the bottom, replaced the drawer and stuffed the package inside his jacket.

Evidence. Too valuable to let Spalding keep. Fingerprints on the IDs implicated not only Spalding but also Clark and Katherine. When it came down to it, Clark's prints were everywhere—the desk, safe, doors, everything—too many places to retrace and wipe clean.

He would love to hang around and see Spalding's face when he discovered someone had snatched the identifications from under his nose. Or if Clark was smart, with the boys' items in his hands, he should walk away, this minute, this second, and not look back. Start over in another city, with a new life and forget Boston and his past. Clark had enough cash to do it. After all, he might never remember.

Then he thought of Spalding. By turning his back, Clark

would let a killer walk, allow the deaths of innocent lives to go unpunished and have to live with that knowledge.

He didn't know if he could do it.

There was also Katherine. How could he ensure Spalding didn't turn on her? Being bound by blood didn't guarantee Katherine's protection. Clark would leave her defenseless.

He hated the idea. That and never again seeing the deep brown of her eyes go dark with wonder and excitement or smelling the scent of summer in her thick, glorious hair. She possessed so much power over him...the power to calm yet incite...

He couldn't do it. Damn it. He cared too much.

The sound of a car rolling up the drive cut into his thoughts. Someone else. Great. Just what he needed. A damn airport terminal. He hit a leg against the edge of the desk as he rushed from the office.

A car door slammed. Hurried footsteps. In seconds, they'd be at the door.

Leaving through the front wasn't an option. He'd have to escape through the same door as he'd done earlier with Katherine. Holding his jacket and the package close to his chest, Clark moved down the hall toward the back of the house. He reached the game room when the doorbell rang, and Spalding hastened down the stairs to answer.

Clark paused by the doorway to the game room. Something didn't add up. Since watching the estate, Clark had yet to see Spalding miss a day of work. He had an idea the reason was about to walk through that front door.

"We've got problems," a man said.

Clark didn't recognize the voice.

"Tell me something I don't already know," Spalding retorted snidely. "What is it now, Jason?"

The door closed, and judging by the silence, Clark suspected neither man had moved from the entrance.

"The hit didn't go as planned. He's still walking."

"Son-of-a-bitch!" Spalding lowered his voice to a harsh whisper. "What do I pay you guys for? And keep your voice down. My housekeeper's upstairs."

Realizing they were talking about him as the hit, Clark tensed. So he was still walking. How terribly inconvenient of him. Maybe he should have stood in front of the car and solved all their problems.

And who the hell was this Jason? Neither the name nor the voice sounded familiar. But obviously, he was another low life.

Clark flexed his fingers and choked back the urge to run out and beat the crap out of them. Yeah, he might get some satisfaction by laying a fist or two into Spalding's face but with the housekeeper upstairs and a call away from the police, Clark was more liable to end up on the run. And even if he got the scumbag talking, how would he know Spalding's words weren't all lies?

He'd also expose his one vulnerability—the loss of his memory.

The hell he would.

"I thought you told me this guy was good," Spalding said in a hushed voice.

"You know he is," Jason said just as softly. "He's done fine before."

"But we're dealing with an adult, not some delinquent spaced out on drugs."

"Well, that's all I have. Unless you want to try your hand at finding someone new?" Scorn coated Jason's question and the low laugh that followed. "I didn't think so, and I'm not about to start offing people. That's not my job."

"It could be with what I pay you."

"I don't think so. Not when it comes to this hit. Something's really strange about him," Jason murmured, his voice drawing nearer.

Clark backed away from the doorway, but curiosity kept him from completely retreating. If he could just get one look at Spalding's visitor.

"How strange?"

"Well, I watched the whole thing. Anyone else would've been dead. The car was inches from him, and he did this mind-blowing move."

Again both men stopped talking. Clark couldn't stand it any longer. Easing forward, he peered into the hallway, which intersected the one leading to the front entrance. He found it empty. Frustrated, he inched down the hall until both men came into view.

Spalding's visitor, street post thin and dressed in a navy suit, stood a good foot taller than Spalding. As Jason turned, Clark backed away, but it was enough to catch sight of the man's profile, the weak chin, the hooked nose and slicked-back gray hair.

Clark didn't recognize or remember the face. Damn. But then, what the hell had he expected? A miracle? All his past to come rushing back after looking at some slimy friend of Spalding's? Nothing had altered since finding himself in Arizona with a dead man next to him. Why expect anything to change just because he wanted it?

Pressing the identifications closer to his chest, Clark moved back into the game room and mentally shoved his anger and disappointment to the back of his mind. He didn't dare to let his emotions get in the way. Not with two sick killers feet away.

"It was probably luck more than anything else," Spalding said.

"No. It was more than that. Something's really weird about him."

"How so?"

"Another car got in the way and trapped this lady inside. Well, he goes and rips the door off like it's nothing, and, before anyone thinks to stop him, he takes off. And we're not talking at a run. One second he's there, and the next he's gone. The whole thing's really weird."

As visions of the car accident and the crowd swept through his mind, Clark cringed. He remembered the stares, the fear and shock in everyone's eyes, and how they'd made him feel like some circus freak. The look in Katherine's eyes from across the street hadn't been any better.

He wanted to be normal, go home to a family or work a nine-to-five job—anything other than living with this power—this curse.

Spalding's words, slow and thoughtful, pulled Clark from his dark thoughts. "I wish I'd been there. It would have been interesting to watch."

"Interesting? That's all you've got to say?" A short pause of silence followed. "Is there something you're not telling me?"

"Of course not," Spalding volleyed back, too smoothly, too quickly.

The bastard was lying. Spalding's sharp intake of breath, indiscernible to the normal ear, exposed the lie. That and the rapid beat of his heart, Clark's magnified hearing picked up.

What the hell was going on? Spalding knew about Clark's powers. But why keep it from Jason?

Before Clark had time to take it all in, both men's steps cut the distance between him and them. In seconds, they'd see him.

Clark sped across the game room. He couldn't be discovered. Not when Spalding held a stacked deck and Clark lacked the leverage to protect Katherine. How could he hope to combat Spalding when his past, his personality, the knowledge of who or what he was had been torn from his mind?

He unlocked the back door, stepped outside and closed the door far too loudly. Damn it. He knew he'd just given himself away. As he raced over the snow-covered yard to the fence, he fought against a dark wave of exhaustion and defeat.

~~*~~

"What's that?"

"The back door." Paul rushed into the game room with Jason right behind. Finding the room empty, Paul stumbled to a halt and frowned.

"There's no one here."

He ignored Jason's comment, strode to the back door and stepped outside. Frigid, winter air bit into his face and hands and dug through his suit to the tender skin beneath as he scanned the yard, past the pool, the bushes, the lawn furniture. Then he looked at the snow by his feet. Gaze narrowing, he stared at the trail that led from the porch and disappeared around the side of the house.

"It must have been something else," Paul murmured, keeping the knowledge of fresh footprints to himself as he retreated back into the house's warmth and closed the door.

But when Jason left, those imprints continued to plague Paul until a knot of anxiety twisted his insides. Fisting his hands at his sides, he strode into his office and noticed his desk. Several sheets of paper and a pen littered the carpeted floor by one of the legs.

No. Impossible. Pulling air in and out of his lungs, again and again, Paul fought against the panic as suspicion and dread propelled him across the room. He clasped the top handle and pulled the drawer out, sweeping a hand beneath the bottom, blindly searching for the package taped to the wood.

Nothing.

Son-of-a-bitch. Paul ripped the drawer out, upended it, and spilled file folders, computer cartridges and pencils across the carpet.

The package. Gone.

Shock rolled through his body. Then rage, sharp and bitter, poured through his arms, his legs, every muscle and tendon. He stumbled forward as if someone hit him from behind.

I'll kill you. I swear to God I'll kill you. You son-of-a-bitch.

Paul hurled the drawer across the room. It crashed against the wall, the wood seams cracking at the impact. Then the broken pieces thudded to the carpeted floor. Paul turned away from the mess and glanced over at the portrait of a woman on the other wall.

He stilled.

Jennie.

Paul walked over and stared at his wife seated beneath the umbrella of an oak tree. Sunlight winked through the leaves, dappling the flowing white dress spread out around her. With her legs tucked beneath her, she held a sprig of vibrant spring flowers and smiled back at Paul. She wouldn't be considered beautiful in the normal sense. Her jaw was too strong, her brow too wide and high, but her features held such character and strength. And that smile. He adored the crooked curve at one corner of her mouth and how her smile lit up her green eyes to deep flawless emeralds.

His Jennie. He'd loved everything about her. How she trounced him in cards and gave him as good as she got in a verbal battle.

"Why did you have to die?"

So many times over their marriage he'd always wondered what she'd seen in him. She hadn't stuck it out all these years because of the money. She'd had her own coming into the marriage. No. She'd loved him, not some image or expectation of what she believed him to be.

"I don't understand."

She'd been his sanity, his reason for living. Then Jennie had left, forcing him to turn to work for survival. So he'd submerged himself in Miltronics and found a new meaning to his life. But right now, it felt so damn hollow.

He sighed. A tear slid down his cheek, over the curve his lip and into his mouth. He stood in the house they'd shared. So damn alone.

CHAPTER 19

KATHERINE WALKED THROUGH the front door of her parent's home, shrugged out of her jacket and hung it and her purse up on the coat rack. The murmur of voices and the smell of baking ham drifted from the kitchen.

She had made a point of being on time for dinner tonight, not wanting to fall victim to her mother's disapproval and lose sight of her quarry. Paul Spalding. She'd called earlier in the week and casually learned he was joining her parents for dinner—the very reason she'd invited herself here tonight.

She needed to quiz her uncle. Nothing overt. She wasn't crazy enough to throw some heinous questions his way, and she didn't expect Paul to confess. But maybe, just maybe, if she tripped him up in some way, Katherine might find out something of interest regarding Miltronics, Clark and the missing boys.

Then there was her mother. They hadn't spoken since their quarrel at her uncle's birthday party, but Katherine couldn't avoid her mother any longer with what she'd recently learned—which raised even more pressing questions—ones that she didn't know if she had the guts to ask. Maybe after getting completely drunk on a bottle of wine... Maybe not even then...

Wiping clammy hands on the sides of her navy skirt, Katherine followed the murmur of voices and stepped into the media room. A massive gray, stone fireplace swallowed one wall. Behind the wrought iron fire screen, flames hissed and cackled as they attacked the moisture in the cedar logs. A large, flat-screen television, a prized state-of-the-art device, devoured the other wall.

Her mother didn't curl up with a good book. Oh, no. Sharon preferred CNN by firelight, while her father, he'd be the first to admit he loved watching a good game of basketball.

Tonight, the television, the volume low enough for conversation, broadcasted the local news in a bland and dispassionate flare. A family of five gunned down by their father. No survivors. The lives of three children, a mother and a crazed father destroyed by one single, violent act.

Katherine looked away from the screen, unable to stomach the tormented face of a relative describing the event. So much violence. Unlike many of the teenagers who sought solstice at the Morning Dove from family brutality, she'd always observed from a safe distance. But now she found herself thrust into a world of violence and subterfuge.

On the rust colored, leather sofa that faced the television, her parents sat watching the headlines, while Paul, a drink dangling from one relaxed hand, reclined in a matching, overstuffed chair. He looked so innocent, so normal, so non-threatening sitting there. But beneath that urban veneer lay something apathetic, violent and—

No. She needed to stop thinking like that; otherwise, she'd crack before dinner started.

When Katherine walked further into the room, Sharon turned and smiled. "Hello, dear."

From her mother's pleasant expression, Katherine realized all was forgotten. Katherine quickly revised that. Her mother never "forgot" anything. Goodness knows, her mother would throw their last argument back in Katherine's face sometime in the future.

Urging her lips into a welcoming smile, Katherine bent down and kissed her mother's smooth cheek. She drew away and searched Sharon's face. With what she now knew of her mother, she somehow expected to see a difference. But, like Paul, she looked innocent. How? Katherine didn't understand.

"Is something wrong?" Sharon asked. "You're staring at me in the strangest way."

"No. I'm just thinking how well you're looking," Katherine said in a surprisingly normal voice. "I really like your dress. The dark brown brings out the highlights in your hair."

Looking pleased, Sharon touched a silk sleeve with a discreetly jeweled hand. "Thank you, dear. I couldn't resist buying it last weekend." Sharon tilted her head to one side. "I'm glad to see you're on time tonight."

Katherine ignored the backhanded compliment. "The traffic wasn't as bad as usual."

Diana, the housekeeper, came to the door to announce dinner. As usual, her father took the seat at the head of the table. The place settings worked in Katherine's favor as she sank down in the chair beside her mother and across the table and at an angle to her uncle. The idea of sitting within touching distance from Paul made her want to curl up with revulsion and her skin—well, that didn't define description. But Katherine didn't feel much better sitting beside her mother.

The night of her uncle's birthday party, she hadn't realized why Kirkwood Incorporated had sounded so familiar, but yesterday, the name had clicked. She'd seen a folder on it in her mother's office several weeks ago.

Katherine didn't want to jump to conclusions, but then, she couldn't close her eyes to the truth—a possible bogus company tied her mother and uncle together. The idea made Katherine almost physically sick.

She inhaled deeply. Okay. One thing at a time. She'd worry about Kirkwood after she got through dinner with her uncle. As she draped her napkin across her lap and Diana served, Katherine struggled for a way to broach the topic of Miltronics.

"So how is the Morning Dove doing?"

She glanced over at her father's raised brow. So much for getting prepared. "We did get a donation. Something we desperately needed. It'll keep the doors open that much longer."

"Really?" Paul snapped open his linen napkin and dropped it

onto his lap. "That's good news then. Is it through the government or private sector?"

"Actually, I don't know. It was anonymous."

Alex paused with his wine glass in mid-air. "How strange. Do you have any idea who it could be?"

"No."

The lie came easier than Katherine imagined. Maybe she had more in common with her family, she thought with some disgust. After all, her mother and uncle seemed experts at it.

"I'd just be thankful and not worry about the benefactor." As Sharon leaned forward for her glass of wine, the sharp floral scent of her perfume drifted Katherine's way. "You'll probably find out soon enough. I've never met a person yet who couldn't keep quiet when it comes to donating their time or money. Everyone wants to be recognized."

Thinking of Clark and how closed mouthed he'd been when it came to giving money to the shelter, Katherine tended to disagree. Clark didn't want to be recognized for doing good. He just did it. A characteristic that, Katherine suspected, lay deeply embedded in him.

Unlike her uncle. Paul never offered his time or money unless it benefited him. No. She was being unfair. Miltronics might be a small pharmaceutical company in comparison to others, but in areas of research, they were one of the top in their industry.

Katherine looked down at her plate. She cut a slice of ham, placed a piece in her mouth and chewed, tasting salt and little else. The asparagus tips didn't fare much better. Giving up on dinner, she set her fork down and clutched the napkin on her lap, twisting the corner around her thumb over and over again. She guessed now was as good a time as any.

"Uncle Paul, I've been meaning to ask how Miltronics is doing? Were you able to recover after all the damage the fire did to the building?" Katherine leaned back against her chair, affording Diana enough room to replace Katherine's main course with a dessert of Black Forest Cake. "It must have been terrible for the families involved."

"We're coping, and as to the families—I've seen that they've been amply compensated. I'm sure nothing can replace their loved ones, but money does have a tendency to ease the hurt."

Money. How could Paul say that having survived his wife's death? Had he grown that indifferent? Or had Katherine always been blind to Paul's lack of character?

Then she thought of something Clark had said several weeks back, but at the time she hadn't paid much attention to it. "And the arsonist? He was a janitor, right?"

"That's correct."

"I thought most companies screen their employees."

"They do. We do. He just managed to get through the system."

With a prior record? Katherine thought in disbelief.

Paul placed his fork on his plate and stared across the table at her. "Why this sudden interest in Miltronics?"

"I didn't realize until your birthday party how much I've neglected the family. I've been so focused on the shelter that I've ignored everything and everyone else in my life. I also realized that I've never really expressed enough interest in your work."

Paul laughed. "Why start?"

An awkward silence followed, which Sharon interrupted. "We all tend to focus on our own lives and forget the little things. I'm just as guilty with this gala event coming up at the end of the month. So far, everything's running smoothly, but there's always something that materializes unexpectedly—no matter how much planning's involved. All I know is, without Jason, I'd be floundering. Thank you, Paul, for recommending him to me."

"Think nothing of it."

"Yes, well, without him, I'd be overwhelmed. But I think everything will be well worth it. The event should generate a great deal of publicity. Particularly since a portion of our proceeds is going to breast cancer."

Katherine frowned at her cake. She was not going to get angry. Taking a deep, slow, soothing breath, she waited a minute before asking, "Have you ever thought of partnering with a charity for runaway teenagers?"

"Of course I have, dear. What with it being your pet project—"

"It's not a pet project—"

"Sorry," Sharon retracted, inclining her expertly frosted head. "Pet project wasn't what I meant."

But Katherine knew that's exactly what her mother "meant." Sharon didn't say anything unless carefully thinking it through first.

"The homeless issue isn't on people's minds right now, dear," Sharon explained. "Maybe another time. I'll have someone at the office look into it."

Which meant "forget it." Runaway teens didn't help get the public's vote. My goodness. She sounded too cynical, Katherine realized with some dismay as she placed her napkin by her untouched desert. If she got out of here without a migraine, she'd be happy.

Katherine scraped back her chair and rose. "If you'll excuse me. I'll be right back. I need to check in at the shelter. There's a new client who isn't doing very well. Mother, is it all right if I use your office to make a private call?"

Another lie. But she didn't care. She wanted to get out of the room and away from her uncle, her mother, even her father. And she wanted answers. She just hoped that file on Kirkwood Incorporated was still in her mother's office.

"That's fine. Just don't mind the mess. I haven't had a chance to go through this last week's paperwork, and until today, Jason hasn't been in for days. He's been spending all his time lately at the downtown office."

"Don't worry. I won't touch anything," Katherine reassured, adding another lie to her growing list as she slipped from the room.

When Katherine reached the doorway to her mother's office and snapped on the light, she paused. Every time she walked in here, it took her a moment to adjust. Compared to the wood, brick and masculine feel of the rest of the house, this room couldn't get much different. White, silver and little else spoiled the sterile atmosphere. Even the pictures on the wall lacked warmth or color. Completely modern and completely cold. No doubt, just like her mother.

An unexpected shiver raced across her skin, and Katherine rubbed at her arms as she stepped into the room. She remembered seeing the file on top of the desk, but one quick glance showed someone had removed it. So where else would be the most logical place?

Of course. The filing cabinet. But which one? The credenza by the window or the tall, three-tiered cabinet in the corner? She didn't have much time.

Katherine hurried to the chrome colored cabinet in the corner and opened the top drawer. Rapidly, she thumbed through the alphabetized files, realizing almost immediately the drawer contained only the beginning of the alphabet. In her hurry to readjust the files and close the cabinet, she knocked a set of keys that dangled from an inside hook. With fumbling fingers, she replaced it before moving onto the files in the next drawer. She combed through the Ks with hands that grew shakier with each passing second. She was taking too long.

Kirkwood wasn't anywhere. Then Katherine realized the file must be in Sharon's main, downtown office. She swore under her breath and snapped shut the middle drawer. She couldn't go into the downtown office in the middle of the day. Even if she dropped by while her mother was out to lunch, too many people would find it odd. She'd never spent much time at Sharon's headquarters, only showing up for a quick visit or for lunch with her mother. She'd have to go by after the office closed. But she didn't have a key.

The set in the filing cabinet. Of course. The office key had to be on that ring. Re-opening the top drawer, she wrapped her fingers around the keys.

"Can I help you?"

Katherine froze.

Why now? Why not later? A couple more minutes and she would have been fine. She clutched the keys, digging the metal painfully into the flesh of her palm as she wildly wondered how to hide the blasted things. Her shirt and blouse didn't have pockets. Her bra was out. And she wasn't about to leave them in the drawer, not when she'd gone to all this trouble.

With her back shielding her movements, Katherine closed the drawer with an arm, cupped the keys against her stomach, and folded her other arm across her middle. Hoping her face didn't look as red as it felt, Katherine turned and found Jason McFadden in the doorway, watching her with an unfathomable expression.

"Is there something you wanted?" he asked.

Katherine floundered for a reason why he'd caught her with a hand in Sharon's files. No brilliant comeback came to mind. Absolutely nothing.

"No. I'm fine." She realized she'd let guilt and fear distort her thinking and straightened. So she was in her mother's office. So what? She was family. She'd grown up in this house for God's sake. Why would she think she needed to explain herself to this man? "I didn't realize you worked this late."

"I don't normally, but we've got this black-tie dinner at the end of the month." Tall and gaunt, he reminded Katherine of a gray stork—maybe because of the way he walked away from the doorway with his hands clasped behind his back, his long, spindly legs moving slowly and gracefully out in front of him with each step. "I'm putting in extra time to make sure the evening goes smoothly."

"I see. Well, I'll let you get to work."

She really didn't know Jason even though he'd worked for her mother for over three years. He'd just been there one day, smoothing out her mother's life at home and in the office. Sharon never talked much about her day-to-day life, and frankly, Katherine admitted with some embarrassment, she'd never been interested.

With her arms still folded against her middle, Katherine skirted past Jason and walked from the room. She turned down the hall to the front entrance. After she slipped the keys inside her purse, she found everyone in the media room. Wanting to get out of the house as quickly as possible, Katherine made some excuse about work and said goodbye to her parents and uncle.

By the coat rack, she shrugged on her jacket. Suddenly, she stilled, sensing someone watching her. She glanced over her shoulder. Paul had stepped into the hall with her.

He stood there, silent, unmoving, staring at her in a way that made Katherine draw her coat tighter around her. She wondered if he knew she'd been looking for Kirkland's folder and taken the keys in the filing cabinet. Impossible. But still, something about his expression gave her the creeps.

She grabbed her purse and opened the front door.

"Be careful."

Paul's words, although spoken softly, carried down the hall to slither across the back of her neck. Katherine paused but didn't turn around.

"If I were you, I'd watch your back. You're delving into areas far greater than you can imagine."

His blatant threat followed her as she stepped through the threshold and into the brisk evening air. Shivering, she snapped the door closed behind her. Even outside, and far enough away from Paul, Katherine didn't feel any safer.

She'd be stupid to ignore her uncle's warning or the amount of power he had, but she didn't intend to give up. If he thought a few words would scare her off then he was in for a surprise. Such arrogance. The way he'd looked at her like she wasn't worth his time or energy. Like she was some—some annoying insect that needed to be squashed.

Katherine slipped inside her car and gunned the engine. Lips thinned into a grim line, she pulled the car out of the drive. The tires skidded against the asphalt as she turned into the street. Well, his confidence would be his downfall. She'd make sure of that. Hah. Paul completely underestimated her.

She hadn't learned much tonight. But she'd come close to something. The mention of the fire and Miltronics had sure gotten a reaction from her uncle. So much so that he felt compelled to use threats.

But why? Could Paul have something to do with the fire and not the janitor? If so, Katherine didn't understand the motivation. Greed? A possible insurance scam? None of that made sense. Her uncle had money. There had to be another reason. But what?

Katherine, her anger, sudden to materialize, just as quickly vanished. Her uncle was right. She was way over her head.

CHAPTER 20

CLARK WRAPPED HIS fingers around the cold metal of the gun he'd found inside the duffle bag. He sat slumped on the sofa in his living room. Alone. Night had fallen, and the lamp by his elbow illuminated the few pieces of furniture he'd bought after moving in. A couch, lamp, coffee and end table pretty well did it. All cheap and expendable, since he didn't have a clue where he lived or even if he had a house of his own. Talk about sad.

Clawing his hair back from his brow with his free hand, he stared at the boys' identifications he'd stolen yesterday. They lay on the coffee table along with several comic books he'd bought earlier in the day. Talk about desperate.

Had he really thought he'd get answers beneath the pages of a comic book? Still, something about the character and his story bothered Clark.

Leaning forward, he set the gun on the adjacent cushion and grabbed the top comic. He frowned at the colored picture of a superhero in a cape and tights. He started to open the cover, but instead flung it on the table in self-disgust and watched it slide off and disappear on the floor. He'd searched through every single page a dozen times. Had he gotten any answers?

No.

Would going through it again give him something new?

No.

Clark glanced over to the gun on his right and grasped the handle, the metal still warm from holding it earlier. He tilted the weapon back and forth and noticed how the polished metal gleamed against the lamp's light. The weapon looked simple, efficient and lethal. As to the make or model—he hadn't a clue.

With his free hand, he lifted a long neck beer from the end table and took a deep swallow. What the hell. Flinging back his head, he emptied the rest down his throat and set the bottle on the end table beside the three other empty ones. The way he was going, he'd be drunk within the hour—if he weren't already. Granted, he really shouldn't be drinking the way he felt, but right now he didn't give a rat's ass.

Turning back to the gun, Clark opened the loaded cylinder. With a thumb, he spun the revolving chamber and watched with narrowed eyes as the bullets spun around and around. When the cylinder slowed, he snapped it back into place, flipped off the safety, and aimed the gun at the front door. Clark closed one eye and squinted down the barrel, grasping from some sense of familiarity. Had he looked down this same barrel, aimed at some boy and shot him dead?

He didn't know.

But the more important question—did he have it in him to kill another human being? The idea made him want to throw up. Because he knew, somewhere deep inside him lived a twisted and dark side, one in which, given the right circumstances, he'd do just that.

Unable to look away from the revolver and the way it rested naturally in his hand, he eased back the hammer with one thumb. One shot and he wouldn't have to think, wonder or worry. He had no family he knew of, no job, no past. Clark might never know, and that reality filled him with mind-numbing panic. It wouldn't take much. All he had to do was lift the barrel to his head and pull the trigger.

The doorbell chimed. He jerked, the gun nearly going off in his hand.

Holy shit.

Carefully he eased back the trigger and snapped on the safety, all the while eyeing the door with dislike and suspicion. Tension rolled through his muscles as he rose. He couldn't make out the person's identity on the other side of the door, just agitated breathing.

The bell chimed again.

Holding the gun behind his back, he walked to the door. "Who is it?"

"Katherine."

He inhaled sharply. The muscles across his back and shoulders tensing even further. He'd made a point of keeping away from Katherine, giving her space and time to deal with what she'd seen at the accident. More importantly, he'd kept away because he'd jeopardized her safety and pulled her far too deep into his own nightmare. He flipped on the outside light, unsnapped the lock and opened the door.

The porch light illuminated Katherine's cap of golden hair and her delicate features. He expected to see horror, fear, even repugnance written on her face, but the light touching her deep, brown eyes revealed none of those emotions. Just uncertainty and something else, something Clark didn't know what to make of.

"Do you have a minute?" she asked.

"Sure."

Opening the door wider with a shoulder, Clark stepped aside. As she walked into the house, her scent, reminding him of sunshine and summer breezes, played across his senses. The fragrance evoked images of the night in her apartment. She'd been beautiful, all quivering limbs and hot, silken flesh. For several nights now, alone in bed, with nothing but his thoughts for company, he'd relived those hot, passionate minutes in her arms, the way those incredible legs of hers wrapped around him and how her eyes grew all heavy-lidded with desire—

"Clark?"

He jerked back to the present, feeling his face flush, his chest tighten. "Yes?"

"Are you all right?"

"Of course," he lied and closed the door with the same shoulder. He pulled his hand from behind his back.

~~*~~

When Katherine saw what was in Clark's hand, she stiffened and twisted her fingers around the strap of her purse. "You have a gun. Why?"

"Self-protection?"

"You don't sound too sure."

He shrugged a shoulder.

Katherine took in Clark's disheveled appearance and realized it might not have been such a good idea coming here tonight. His shirt, rolled up at the sleeves, unbuttoned halfway down his chest and pulled from his jeans looked like he'd slept in it, while he'd had some type of battle with his hair and lost. A flush stained his prominent cheekbones and something in his eyes boded of dark, tormented thoughts. Barefoot, he stood tense, almost antagonistic in front of her, over six-feet of muscle and sinew, and filled with such terrifying power.

Katherine swallowed. She'd never seen Clark like this, and she didn't like it or how it made her feel—too darn helpless and uncertain.

"Why are you here?" he asked.

"Would you believe to apologize?"

"Why?"

"For doubting you. For thinking—"

"That I'm some freak."

"No," Katherine denied, maybe too quickly.

Something flickered in his gray eyes, but it was enough. Pain. Clark didn't trust her. He'd incased himself in this thick, defensive wall against her, and she couldn't blame him. Not entirely.

"Really?" he asked in obvious disbelief.

"Yes. Really."

With Clark, the lie tasted sour against her tongue. She'd never been one to hide behind half-truths. At least not until recently.

"That's too harsh a word," she admitted, deciding Clark

deserved the truth. "You have to understand, I was scared. Without any warning, I'm seeing this incredible power from someone else. We're not talking about a person who's worked out every day and pushed their body to normal limits. It goes way beyond that. The whole idea was too foreign and incomprehensible to me—so much so that I couldn't wrap the reality of your powers around my head. I'm still having a hard time of it. And seriously, not many people would take it in stride. Don't you think, given the same situation, you'd have reacted the same way?"

Clark rubbed the back of his neck. "You've got a point. But somehow it's hard to swallow when you're on the receiving end."

"I can imagine." She glanced to the gun in Clark's hand. "You never answered my question. Why the gun? It can't be for protection. Not when you're, well, you know..."

"Just as deadly? Is that what you're trying to say, but being too polite to spell it out?" A half-smile played across his lips. He shook his head, backed up several steps and placed the revolver on top of the coffee table.

Realizing Clark was intentionally avoiding the question, Katherine decided to let it go and focused on her surroundings. She noticed the littered coffee table and—

"You've been drinking."

She pointedly looked at the bottles on the table.

"I've had a few."

She arched a brow.

"Okay. Probably more than a few." He drove his fingers through his hair, standing the shorter strands on end. "And right now, I could use another. Have a seat. I'll be right back."

But Katherine, too tense to sit down in one place, followed him into the kitchen. As Clark flipped on the light switch and strode to the fridge, she noticed he hadn't yet furnished this room. The only things keeping the area from being completely barren were the major appliances—frig, stove, dishwasher—all glossy black to match the charcoal speckled countertops. Face grim, he grabbed two bottles of beer from the fridge, popped the tops and handed her one. After he took a long swallow, Clark wiped his mouth with the back of his hand.

"What's wrong?" Katherine finally decided ignoring Clark's dark mood wasn't going to make it go away. "At first I thought you were just angry with me. But you're wired tighter than someone on amphetamines. Are you drunk?"

Clark laughed without humor. "Not as drunk as I'd like to be."

She frowned, searching Clark's face, the taut lines, the drawn brow, and the hopelessness in his eyes. He'd lost that drive, that force. "Don't—"

"Don't what?"

"Don't do this to yourself."

"I don't know what you mean."

He turned and walked out of the kitchen.

Katherine followed him into the living room. "Oh, yes you do. You're giving up."

"I've nothing to give up on."

"You can't say that. I've seen too many kids at the shelter quit. When that happens, nothing or no one can help them. Hope and faith are so powerful. They can turn a child's life completely around. Given the chance, the future can have so many wonderful possibilities."

She clasped his forearm, but his muscles tensed beneath her hand, and Katherine quickly let go.

"A future with no past? Oh, yeah. That sounds wonderful. Along with my fictitious job and fictitious life."

Her other hand tightened on her beer bottle. She didn't like this new Clark. "Sarcasm doesn't suit you."

"And what does?"

"Not this—this anger. This bitterness."

"How else am I supposed to act?" He shook his head, and a look of disgust crossed his features as he rolled his bottle between his palms. "I'm sorry. You're the last person I should be taking this out on. But you're the only one..."

"Who cares?" she asked softly.

Pain flashed in his eyes. "How can you? I've put you in this terrible situation."

"No one put me anywhere but me. I wouldn't be here if I

didn't think…" She bit her lip, feeling uncomfortable at where she was going with this conversation. But it didn't matter. She'd gone this far. "If I didn't think you were worth it."

And she spoke the truth. Emotionally, Clark touched her beyond any other man she'd met. Her feelings might be confusing, even turbulent but they were genuine.

This time when she grasped his arm, Clark didn't flinch or draw away. Katherine grew bolder, cupping his jaw and rising on her toes to brush her lips against his. Slowly, ever so gently, he kissed her back, a whisper of warm lips, more poignant than any passionate kiss.

Then he touched his brow against the crown of her head and whispered, "Thank you. I don't deserve your friendship. I've taken it for granted, and it's time I put a stop to it."

Abruptly, Katherine drew away. "What are you talking about?"

"I need to keep away from you. Something I should have done long ago. Don't you see, by involving you, I've put your life in jeopardy? It's got to stop. Someone tried to kill me again the other day. You saw it. That woman in the other car might have died! I'm not about to be responsible—"

"You don't see, do you? I'm not your responsibility. I've told you that before. We're talking about my uncle being a murderer. I'm drowning in 'involvement'." Seeing Clark's stubborn jaw and the unyielding look in his eyes, Katherine groaned. "You're not listening."

"Oh, I'm listening. I'm just not agreeing."

Turning away in frustration, Katherine placed her untouched beer on the coffee table and froze. She hadn't paid attention to what littered the table. Identifications—the exact ones she'd seen in her uncle's office.

Which meant only one thing.

CHAPTER 21

With a trembling hand, she picked up Joe Stewart's ring and clasped her fingers around the cool metal. She rounded on Clark. "Tell me you didn't steal these!"

He shifted beneath Katherine's gaze. "Let's just say I borrowed them."

Alarmed, she tightened her hand until the ring cut into her palm. "Do you know how dangerous that was?"

"Katherine, relax. I can take care of myself. No one was hurt. I got in and out without a problem. And without breaking anything," he said the last with a self-deprecating smile. He nodded to the driver's license and social security card. "Our prints are on everything. I wasn't about to let Spalding hold something like that over our heads."

Katherine opened her palm and looked down at the ring. She blinked back tears. So meaningless. Given enough of a chance, Joe could have made something of his life. When he'd had a pencil and paper in his hand, his face would light up with such enthusiasm. Katherine had hoped to turn that enthusiasm for drawing to more practical areas in Joe's life. But now she'd never have that chance.

As she gently placed the ring back on the table, she stepped on something and slipped. Frowning, she glanced down and realized she'd walked on a magazine. She lifted it from the floor and noticed the others on the coffee table. Comic books. The lot of them. Straightening, she stared at them in disbelief.

"Why are you reading these?" Katherine glanced sharply at Clark.

He shrugged a shoulder. "I thought I'd pass some time since I don't have a television."

"But comic books?"

"Why not? They're pretty interesting."

Katherine didn't buy it. The tension in Clark's jaw and the way he kept rolling that beer bottle between his hands belied his pat answers and bland expression.

"But why? Why that comic? Is it because your name is Clark Kent?" Katherine saw a shadow cross his face and realized she'd hit close. "It's more than that, though. Isn't it?"

Clark dragged on the bottle and swallowed. "Hell. It's just a comic book. You're reading far too much into it."

"Am I? Hmm."

Opening the magazine, Katherine flipped through the pages, backed up and sat down on the sofa, all the while feeling Clark's gaze on her as she read the captions. "It's really weird that you have the same powers as a famous superhero. You can twist metal in your bare hands just like him. All I have to do is remember how you took that door off that car."

She flipped another page, growing fascinated with the story and the character.

"Okay, Katherine. You don't have to read the whole damn thing. You've made your point."

She glanced up. Clark, an unmistakable flush to his proximate cheekbones, hadn't moved from his spot, but he'd mutilated the label on his beer bottle. She hadn't realized how truly upset he was. As the silence thickened around them, Katherine stared at him across the coffee table. Finally, she understood.

"You really think you're this character—this superhero."

"Why would I think something like that? That's crazy."

With one hand strangling the neck of his bottle, Clark strode over, and with his other hand, he yanked the magazine from her fingers and tossed it with the others on the table. "How about you just drop it?"

"No. I think you've been seriously thinking it. Why else would you have taken the time to buy all these comics?"

He shook his head, looked up at the ceiling, and then returned her gaze with narrowed eyes. "Are you always this stubborn?"

"My mother seems to think so. At least she used to when I was younger." Half rising, she pulled another comic from the pile, placed it on her lap and sank back down. "But we're not discussing me. I'm more interested in this superhero and the similarities between the two of you," she said the last softly, wiping suddenly damp hands against the side of her jean-clad legs.

"It's just a coincidence." Clark drained the last of his bottle.

"I'm beginning to wonder."

Needing all the help she could get, Katherine leaned over, grabbed her beer and took a deep swallow, feeling her eyes water as the alcohol's sharp malt taste hit the back of her throat. She stared at the comic on her lap but didn't really see it. Then she glanced up at Clark. "My, God. None of this makes sense."

"No, it doesn't." Clark closed his eyes and rubbed the bridge of his nose with two fingers.

"And your powers? Are they the same as the cartoon character?"

Clark opened his eyes and laughed with unmistakable rancor. "Yeah. But there are some differences."

"Like what?"

"I can't see through things or fly," he said the last in obvious disgust.

"And the similarities?" she asked, dread settling low in her stomach.

He sighed. "You've already witnessed a few. Super-human strength. Something I'm still trying to get a handle on. I can also hear through walls and see in the dark if I focus hard enough. My reflexes are pretty fast."

Clark crossed the floor and sat on the sofa beside her, his movements so swift, so unexpected that Katherine jumped, upended the comic onto the floor and almost dropped the bottle in her hand. Biting back a retort, she searched his profile, the hard thrust of his jaw, the clean sweep of his nose. Clark turned and met her gaze. The dark, bleak look in his eyes made her chest tighten with sorrow.

"You hate having this power." Curling a leg beneath her, she turned to rest a shoulder against the back of the sofa and faced him more squarely. "Even if some might consider it a miracle."

"A miracle? But whose miracle? Is it God given or something more malevolent?" He searched her face, the almost desperate need to understand etched across his features.

"I guess," Katherine replied slowly, thoughtfully, "it all depends on a person's inner strength and their sense of morality. To have that type of power. Can you imagine how seductive that is? The ability to steal without ramifications, to overpower another. The possibilities are endless. A weak person could easily break under the pressure of so much temptation." Seeing the doubt in his face, Katherine shook her head. "Don't even think it. You're not weak."

"And how do I know that? When I can't remember a damn thing?"

"*I* would know."

He stared at her in amazement. "Don't you think you're putting a little too much faith in me?"

"Maybe. But if I'm wrong, I'll deal with it when the time comes."

"Then, I hope to hell I don't disappoint you."

"You won't," Katherine insisted, but another part of her, a part she didn't want to delve into, had doubts. It was frightening to put so much faith in one person, but she was willing to take that risk. She'd never been one to watch from the sidelines, to let life go on without actively pursuing every nuance. Otherwise, the Morning Dove never would have gotten off the ground.

~~*~~

Such conviction. It amazed Clark. He wanted to reach over and touch her face and feel the smooth texture of her skin against his palm. He wanted to twine his fingers in the thick, golden strands of her hair, to taste the desire on her lips.

But Clark sat there and did nothing, afraid he wouldn't be able to stop at one touch. But he was more afraid of his infallibility and Katherine's faith in him. What if he couldn't live up to her expectations? The last thing he wanted to do was disappoint her, the one person—no—the only person who meant something to him. Strange as it sounded, she made him want to be the best he could be.

If only he could remember...

He hadn't realized he'd said the words aloud until Katherine replied.

"Your memory—it's still blank?"

He nodded. "I've tried pretty much everything. Nothing seems to have worked."

"What about hypnosis?"

Clark stiffened, disliking the idea of someone delving into his mind. "I don't know. If word leaked out of what I'm capable of, I'd be thrust into a three-ring circus. Every government agency and crack-pot would be after me."

And a part of him, one in which Clark didn't admit to Katherine, might not want to remember. He'd started wondering if he'd eliminated his past for a reason—a reason that involved something dark, tragic or repellent that he didn't want to face.

Katherine sighed in obvious disappointment and sank a shoulder deeper into the sofa's cushion. "You're right. There's no one I know. At least no one I'd trust. But..." She straightened. "I might have something. I've got several photos of the teenagers from the shelter. They were taken over the last couple of months. I even have a picture of Luke—the boy you were seen talking to. I thought you might want to take a look at them. Maybe that might jog your memory. And you can also show me that photo you have of the boy in the car accident. I've been meaning to ask you about it."

"I don't know. Seeing and talking to Spalding didn't work. I don't think anything else is going to make a difference." Not wanting to get his hopes slammed to the ground once again, Clark rubbed at the back of his neck but stilled on seeing the disappointment on Katherine's face. He gave her a tired smile. "Sure. Why not? I'm willing to give it a shot. I don't have anything to lose."

"I brought them home from work to show you. If you want, I'll go grab them in a bit. That's one of the reasons I came by. That and to apologize, but I forgot with everything else."

He didn't like the sudden tension in the delicate lines of her face. "What's wrong?"

She bit the side of her lower lip and ran a finger along the now crumpled comic on her lap. "A couple of days ago, I had dinner over at my parents with my uncle..."

Clark stilled, not liking where this was going.

"Go on."

Katherine cleared her throat. "It looks like I might have gotten in over my head."

"Why do you say that? What happened? You didn't try something—"

"No. Not exactly. Well, maybe." She wouldn't look at him, which made him all the more alarmed. "I was caught going through my mother's files, and my uncle threatened me. Not outright so to speak. But the implication was there just the same."

"Damn it, Katherine!"

Clark's hand convulsed around the beer bottle. The container exploded, shattering glass all over his lap. He jack-knifed to his feet, swearing loudly.

"Are you all right!"

"Yeah," he impatiently wiped at his hand, disgusted at his clumsiness. "It's just glass."

Katherine scrambled from the sofa and reached over to touch him.

He lifted both palms in the air. "Don't. You'll only cut yourself. And I'm fine. Just a couple of scratches. No blood. But I made a damn mess."

After he brushed the last chards from his skin and jeans, he refocused on Katherine's little bombshell. There was no way in hell he was going to let something like that slide.

"What the hell were you thinking—nosing around in your mother's files with everyone around? You're going to get yourself killed. Your uncle isn't some harmless teenager. He's a damn killer. And even if he's your uncle—it doesn't mean you're safe! You're supposed to—"

"What? Lay down and take it?"

"No—no, of course not," he retracted. "But—"

"But nothing." Lifting her chin, Katherine gazed back at him with indignant brown eyes. "Because of my *nosing* around, I found the keys to my mother's downtown office and managed to get into her files after everyone left for the day. I found the tie between my mother and uncle. Remember Kirkwood Incorporated and Harvest and Associates? The company files we found in my uncle's closet? It looks like Kirkwood's a sign company and Harvest is one of the marketing companies she uses for her campaign. I managed to go back three years, but after that I couldn't find anything. She might have the rest in storage. We're talking about a lot of money. Particularly if there're more than these two companies involved."

Clark frowned. "I don't get it. Is your uncle financially unstable?"

"I never thought so until now. The family's always had money—or at least acted like it." She pulled a strand of hair behind her ear and laughed, the sound hollow and unmistakably bitter. "But I'm starting to find out—I don't know anything. When it comes to my family, I don't know what's a lie or the truth anymore."

"I'm sorry."

Clark didn't know what else to say to ease her pain and sense of betrayal. He'd selfishly pushed himself into her life and turned it into chaos, and she was struggling to make sense of it all. Because of him.

"Yes, well..." Katherine cleared her throat, her eyes shimmering with unshed tears. "I'll deal with it. I've dealt with other disappointments. This'll be just another one I'll have to get through."

He hated seeing the sadness in Katherine's eyes. Wanting to touch and hold her, to somehow ease her pain, Clark stepped toward her. Glass cut into his barefoot, and he winced.

"Oh, my goodness! Your feet!"

He felt his face warm with embarrassment. If he kept this up, he'd be nominated as klutz of the year. He forced a smile. "I'm fine. How about I clean this glass up before someone else gets hurt while you go get those photos?"

"You're sure?"

"Yeah."

He brushed off his heel and followed her to the front entrance. As he opened the door for Katherine, Clark looked over her shoulder to the parking lot and snow-covered grounds. No one moved to or from their cars. Somewhere to the right, voices and laughter carried over the evening air, and then was abruptly silenced by the slamming of a front door. A lone car, tires humming against asphalt, sped down the street, its headlights flashing silver against the snow. Across the parking lot and in the shadows of the large oak trees, another shadow, darker than the others, shifted by the thick trunk of a barren oak tree.

A chill—nothing to do with the frigid air—raced across Clark's skin. He stiffened, clasping a protective hand against Katherine's elbow to stop her from leaving.

Something wasn't right.

At his touch, Katherine turned. "What's wrong?"

"Hold on a second."

Gaze narrowing, Clark stared at the spot by the tree. A man, dressed in a dark jacket and slacks stepped from the trunk. From what he could tell, the man was tall and thin, but the cloud filled night camouflaged his features. Through the darkness, Clark focused harder on the face, determined to get a clearer picture. But a flash of light broke past the shadows and caught Clark's eye. The man held something in his hand.

A gun. Silencer attached to the barrel. Pointed right at them.

Holy shit. Clark sucked in air.

Before he had the chance to exhale, shout a warning, move,

the soft ping of a shot broke the night air. The bullet rocketed toward Katherine.

CHAPTER 22

LOOK OUT!"

Katherine didn't have the chance to even blink before Clark lunged. He grabbed her arm and hauled her backward. Astonishment cut off her cry of alarm. She staggered, clutched at but missed the door's threshold for balance. Clark jerked against her. A loud whoosh rushed from his mouth.

Something hit the wall by her head. Katherine ducked, shielding her face with a hand. Bits of wood and cement sprayed into the air. Clark pulled her against his chest. He wrapped an arm around her waist and pushed her head against his shoulder, smothering the air from her lungs and the protest from her lips.

She clawed at his shoulders and turned her head until her cheek rested against the cotton of his shirt. The wild beat of his heart pounded against her ears. When she dragged in air, a strange metallic smell hit her nose.

Katherine tried to think, tried to get her voice to work but fear, stark and vivid, rendered both impossible.

Suddenly, Clark shoved her into the house and slammed the door. Stumbling backward, she gaped at him in utter shock. "Are you crazy?"

Clark slumped against the wall. "Someone was shooting at us."

She inhaled sharply. Katherine didn't want to believe him,

because then all of it—her uncle, her mother, her entire life—would disintegrate into some sick parody. But she had to. She couldn't escape from the look of pain and horror etched across Clark's ashen face, and the blood.

Oh, no. The blood. It ate across the white fabric of Clark's shirt.

"You've been shot—" Panic swarmed up her throat. Then she noticed the blood on her own shirt where she'd pressed up against his chest. Her stomach rolled with sudden nausea.

"I'll be okay."

But Clark didn't look okay as he slid slowly to the floor, smearing a trail of blood against the wall. Terrified of the sudden paleness to his face, she dropped to her knees. This wasn't some superficial wound. Not with all that blood.

Please God. She glanced at his shirt again and quickly looked away. It looked fatal. Any second, and he might take his last breath—

No. Don't think that way!

"Where's your phone?" she asked, her voice hoarse, unsteady and edged with panic. "We need help."

She started to rise from the floor, but Clark caught her wrist. "No."

"No? That's insane! We need to get an ambulance out here. Let me go."

"No—I'll be fine. Give me a minute."

"You're not fine! You've been shot!"

"I know what I'm doing. Trust me. At least on this." Clark took in a couple of short, rapid breathes. "Damn. I might need your help after all. Can—" He dragged in another ragged breath. "Can you see if the bullet went through? If not—I might have a problem."

When she hesitated, Clark ordered between gritted teeth, "Do it. Please."

Jaw clenched, realizing it was pointless to argue with Clark in his current state of mind, Katherine conceded, "Okay."

Right now, she'd humor him. But the second his grip eased, she'd be on her feet and to the phone. She wasn't going to sit back and watch him bleed to death because of some crazy idea of his.

Clark nodded in obvious relief and closed his eyes, the pallid cast to his skin seeming somehow worse than seconds before.

On her knees, she inched to the side of Clark as he leaned forward. More blood stained the back of his shirt. Katherine cringed, while tears sprang to her eyes. She blinked and refocused. Doggedly, she examined the damp shirt until she found a small spot of frayed fabric.

"The bullet went through." Glancing a couple of inches to the right of the exit wound, she found a second one. Katherine sank down hard on her heels. She was not going to flip out. Maybe later when she had the time to take in the horror of everything around her. "You were hit twice. But both bullets went through."

"I guess—that's why I feel so—light-headed."

Katherine wasn't fooled by his smile or weak attempt at humor. Clark didn't look any better, and time was running out. Glancing around the living room, she didn't see a phone. She peered down the hall. The layout looked similar to her own place. Bedrooms to the left and kitchen down the hall and to the right.

"I'm going to get a wet towel and some antiseptic. But you need to let me go. Okay, Clark?"

"Fine." He released her wrist. "But first make sure the front door is locked and the blinds are closed in the living room."

Katherine rose and did as he asked. Then she retreated down the hall and glanced over her shoulder. Clark, eyes closed, deathly still, hadn't moved from his spot by the wall. Assured Clark wouldn't notice, Katherine didn't turn left toward the bathroom but veered to the right and hurried into the kitchen.

She paused in the doorway and frantically hunted around for a phone in the darkened room. She didn't dare turn on the light and alert Clark. Ghostly moonlight speared through the open blinds, illuminating a phone on the counter by the dishwasher.

Easing the headset from its cradle, Katherine pressed her lips together to stifle the sound of her labored breathing. She moved the keypad beneath the moon's rays and punched in nine.

Suddenly, the kitchen light flooded the room. A flash of movement, a blur of color. Clark, all muscle and formidable power, stood at her elbow, towering over her, crowding in on her.

At his appearance, so silent, so unexpected, so darn abrupt, Katherine cried out and jerked back, bumping a hip against the counter and dropping the phone. The receiver clattered to the floor and cracked open. The battery panel flew off and hit a bottom cabinet.

Clark yanked the phone line from the wall, staggered and latched onto the counter with his other hand.

"Stop it, Clark! You're scaring me."

"Sorry, but I'm not going to a hospital. By the time I get there, I'll be fine. Or close enough. And I'm sure as hell not going to let some doctor poke and prod at me as if I were a lab rat."

Katherine edged back along the counter. "You're not making sense."

"Maybe this'll make sense."

He pulled at the front of his shirt. Buttons broke loose and scattered across the floor. He tossed the bloody shirt on the counter and grabbed a kitchen towel draped over the handle of the stove's door and wet it down. The glare of the kitchen light thrust everything into painful detail. More blood. It coated his chest, his stomach, his back. Everywhere.

Lifting a hand to her throat, Katherine smothered down her cry of alarm and backed up until she hit the refrigerator. She watched Clark brush the towel across his skin, staining his fingers and turning the once pale green towel to an ugly red. Finished, Clark tossed the towel on top of his ruined shirt, leaving several stubborn patches of blood smeared across his flesh.

"Does it look like I'm bleeding to death?"

She stared at his taut stomach and muscled chest. Only a few droplets of blood oozed from two small flesh wounds. Somehow she'd expected large, raw and angry lacerations. His injuries seemed days old—not minutes. Which was impossible.

Mesmerized by the strange phenomena, Katherine edged closer.

"Hard to believe, isn't it?" Clark murmured, his voice sounding steadier, his face regaining color.

"That can't be. I know what I saw. You were bleeding to death. Any normal person would either be dead or close to it."

"But then I'm not normal, am I?"

She met his sober gray eyes and realized he'd lost his glasses. The thick frames had masked his beautiful eyes. Clear, gray, rimmed with thick, dark lashes, they stared down at her with such incredible sadness. Sadder still, Katherine didn't have the ability to erase the expression from his eyes.

"This has something to do with your powers, doesn't it?" she asked. "Your body can heal on its own without drugs or surgery?"

"Yeah. I found out about it by accident. Same as with everything else."

"That's amazing. But what about your glasses? I'd think you wouldn't need them then."

"I don't. I came to with them on. I don't know why. They're clear glass. Maybe it was some form of disguise. Hell. Your guess's as good as mine. But it doesn't matter now."

"Why?"

"I stepped on them in my hurry to get into the house."

"Oh. Sorry."

Shrugging a shoulder, he gestured to his stomach. "It's the least of my problems."

Curious, she lifted a hand but paused. "May I?"

"Sure."

As she grazed a finger along the edge of one of his wounds, Clark's flesh quivered beneath her touch. "I'm not hurting you, am I?"

"No."

She stared at the two wounds in wonder. Then she gasped. No. Impossible. For a moment she thought she'd imagined it. But no. Slowly, ever so slowly, the flesh around the fissures meshed, inching closed with each passing second.

Wide eyed, she glanced back up at Clark.

He frowned. "Don't look at me like that."

"Like what?"

"Like I've grown two heads." He was clearly upset. "I'm the same person I was an hour ago."

"I know that."

But she couldn't help looking at him in yet another light. Clark consisted of so many facets. She'd never come across a man like him and knew she never would again. Such shocking power—muscles, vision, and hearing—all enhanced to superhuman proportions. But what awed Katherine more than anything was Clark's refusal to be seduced by that power or waver from his beliefs. He didn't abuse his abilities or use it for personal gain. Clark had ethics, morals. He'd saved that woman in the car, given money to the shelter without any ulterior motive.

Clark's eyes sharpened. "Now you're looking at me as if I'm some damn hero."

"Most superheroes are immune to injury, aren't they?"

"Yes, but—"

"What? You have many of the same characteristics as a stereotypical superhero. But the major difference between the two of you is that you're real."

"I'm not a superhero. I'm not any type of hero. I'm just a regular man with—"

"But you're *not* a regular man. Don't lie to yourself or me. No matter how hard you want to try, you can't get away from who you are, Clark."

"You don't understand. I still have needs like any other man. I still get hungry, tired—I still have urges—"

Without warning, Clark seized her elbows and pulled her against his chest. He caught her mouth, molding his lips over her own, urging her mouth apart, demanding a response.

Katherine stiffened and caught at his shoulders with both hands. Mind-numbing desire hurtled through her body. She sank into his embrace and closed her eyes, kissing him back, using her lips, her tongue with equal fervor. His hands burned into her skin, while his mouth, urgent, unrelenting, took what she willingly gave him.

And Katherine could do no less. One touch from Clark and she forgot everything but the feel and the taste of him. And the need. Oh, how it twisted her insides and shattered her thoughts, leaving only the hunger.

Just as suddenly, Clark broke away. He stared down at her with eyes stormy with desire, and something else. Something equally intense but impossible to read. "Sorry. Getting shot isn't an excuse to jump on you like that."

Dropping her hands to her sides, Katherine stepped back on wobbly legs. Clark's abrupt withdrawal caught her off guard and left her feeling uncertain and self-conscious, though she struggled to hide both as she pulled her muddled thoughts in line.

Clearing her throat, Katherine also struggled for some sane response, but then again, nothing about their situation was sane.

Clark rubbed at his face, sighed and leaned a hip against the kitchen counter. When he pulled his hand away, Katherine realized whatever color he'd regained had vanished.

"Are you all right?"

Clark gave her a pained smile. "I'll be fine in a minute. I'm probably dehydrated."

He walked over to the refrigerator. Opening the door, he pulled a pitcher of water from inside and dropped it immediately. The plastic container bounced against the linoleum and sprayed water against his jeans and the bottom counters. Clark stumbled and slammed the refrigerator door with the back of a shoulder.

Katherine slipped on the water but caught Clark's elbow. She shouldered his weight until he leaned hard against the door.

He grimaced. Using both hands, he shoved back his hair, exposing a hairline damp from sweat. "I guess I'm not as infallible as I thought."

"Well, you're running around like nothing happened. Even with you're body's abilities, it's been put under terrible stress." She grabbed a fresh gallon of water from the pantry. After finding a glass and filling it with water, she handed it to him. "You need to lie down and rest."

While still leaning against the refrigerator door, he downed his water, handed Katherine his glass and wiped his mouth with the back of his hand. "Maybe you're right."

"I'm glad to see we finally agree on something." Then the reality of the situation hit her. They'd both come so close to dying tonight. "We need to call the police."

Clark's face turned cold. "I can't do that."

CHAPTER 23

WHAT DO YOU mean you *can't do that*?" Katherine asked in disbelief. "We've got to call the police. Someone just tried to kill you!"

"And what proof do we have? Yeah, there're probably a couple of bullet slugs somewhere, but that's about it. Do you seriously think the police are going to swallow my story? "Oh, yes, Mr. Police Officer. Someone shot me, but you can't see the wounds because my body healed itself. Right. After they have a good laugh at our expense, they'll threaten to lock me up if I continue bothering them with the same asinine story. That or send me off to the nearest mental institute."

Katherine hated to admit he was right. "There's evidence of something going on between my mother's campaign funds and Miltronics."

"But are you willing to have your mother investigated when we don't know *why* the hell there's that connection between the two?" He searched her face, his voice growing husky. "Once you do that, there's no turning back. You need to think about that."

Katherine groaned in frustration. "I don't know! But something's got to be done."

"You're right. But not the police. Not yet."

Clark rubbed his forearm across his brow. Weariness and self-disgust washed across the taut lines of his face. He opened his mouth then shut it as he leaned a hand against the refrigerator door.

Katherine stiffened. "There's something else you're not telling me, isn't there?" The look he gave her made her tense even further. "Don't you dare keep something from me."

"The less you know—the better off you'll be."

"Don't give me that. I need to know. I'm too deeply involved, and you know it."

"Fine! It's obvious you're going to keep at it." A nerve pulsed alongside his jaw. "I don't know what side I'm on—the good or the bad. My memory only goes back to the accident in Arizona. From there, I woke up behind the wheel of a wrecked car to find a teenage boy in the passenger seat with a bullet hole in his head—obviously murdered. Then I hear sirens, and what can I say—I panicked. I took off. But not before I grabbed something I found in the back seat of the car..."

He swallowed and briefly closed his eyes.

"What was it?"

"A duffle bag. Inside was a gun and over a hundred thousand dollars."

"Do you know why they were there?" When he shook his head, she ignored the wild knock of her heart against her ribs and reasoned, "There's got to be some rational answer—"

"Oh, yeah. I've got an answer." His eyes darkened. "I was paid off to murder someone."

"That's impossible."

"Is it? Your uncle might have hired me to kill those kids at the shelter and the one in the car. And somehow, I double-crossed him."

She didn't turn away from the intensity in his stormy eyes but straightened and lifted her chin. "I thought we went over this before. You're not that type of person. I might be unsure of many things in my life, but that's one I'm not. You're not a killer. It's not in you. Call it gut. Call it instinct. I just know."

His sigh vibrated through his large frame. "I hope to hell you're right."

Clark stepped away from the frig. Pain cut across his face,

and he latched onto the door handle with one hand. Alarmed, Katherine quickly eased his arm around her shoulders. He didn't object, which told her all she needed to know—he felt far worse than he pretended.

They made it to his bedroom without either one of them falling flat on their face. She knew Clark had tried to hold his own, but by the time he eased down on the edge of his bed, her shoulders ached from taking the brunt of his weight.

She rolled her neck back and forth to relieve the tension and walked over to the side of the bedroom window. "I wonder if the gunman is still out there."

"Damn it! Get away from the window."

Katherine glanced over at Clark and found him rising unsteadily to his feet. "Okay! Okay! Just sit back down."

She closed the blinds but managed to get a quick look outside. Nothing unusual. No one lurking in the parking lot or street. Somewhat relieved, she stepped away from the window in time to see Clark wince as he sat back down on the bed.

"Are you in much pain?"

He laughed and winced again. "Let's just say it doesn't tickle."

"Do you want some aspirin?" Katherine asked, and then groaned. Talk about an idiotic question. Like a couple of pills were going to help him. My goodness. Maybe she should ask if he needed a bandage while she was at it.

"More water would be great."

At least Clark had the tact to ignore her runaway mouth. "Sure. I'll get you a glass."

A ghost of a smile touched his lips. "Just promise not to drop it."

She reluctantly smiled back. "I promise."

Katherine hurried into the kitchen, side-stepped the mess on the floor, which she'd clean later, and poured Clark another glass of water. When she walked back into Clark's room, he'd disappeared. Then she heard the shower running from the adjoining bathroom, and realized he'd managed to get himself in there on his own. She looked around for a place to set the glass down on but couldn't find a table.

"Katherine! Are you there? Can you get me a couple of fresh towels in the linen cabinet in the hall?"

"Ah, sure!"

With the glass of water still in her hand, she found several towels in the hall closet. She grabbed two of the thickest and paused at the entrance to the bathroom, feeling decidedly uncomfortable knowing Clark was in there completely naked.

Okay. So he was naked. No big deal. She'd seen him naked before.

"Right," she muttered.

That was the problem.

Straightening her shoulders, Katherine walked inside. The first thing she noticed was the shower curtain. Even though moisture clung to the clear plastic and turned the curtain into an opaque screen, she saw Clark's form and movements through the plastic.

With both hands raised, rinsing his hair beneath the shower, he stood with his back toward her. While staring at the outline of his wide, muscled shoulders, narrow hips, and long, lean legs, all completely symmetric and completely unnerving, Katherine blindly placed the glass of water on the counter. When he turned, Katherine didn't have the willpower to look away from his profile, the tight line of his buttocks, the flat line of his stomach and... She swallowed. The sudden warmth flooding her face had nothing to do with the room's moist heat, but every-thing to do with seeing Clark's naked body and all the memories it generated.

My goodness. How could she forget? The touch, the taste, the feel of him deep inside her, so thick, so hard, so smooth... The way he'd moved.

She'd thought sex with Clark had been incredible because she'd been celibate for so long, but now, seeing Clark and remembering every second, every caress, Katherine recognized the stupidity of such an idea. The need inside of her still gripped her, stronger than ever. All because of this strange and complex man.

Clark didn't kill anyone. She'd stake her life on it. He was far too gentle and compassionate to turn against another in cold-blooded violence.

Clark snapped off the shower and jerked back the curtain.

Katherine bunched the towels between her hands. He pushed back his wet hair with one hand but paused as he caught her gaze. A thick wave of silence wrapped around the room. She looked down. She couldn't help it. It was that darn female curiosity.

He was hard.

She gasped, her breath hissing loudly in the stillness of the room.

"Ah, hell. You've got the most expressive face."

Cheeks getting hotter by the second, Katherine looked away and muttered, "Sorry."

"You've nothing to apologize for." He laughed without humor. "I swear, if I had it in me, I'd have you on your back in two seconds. But right now, I wouldn't do you justice."

After she shoved the towels at him, Katherine stuffed her fingers in the back of her jean pockets. That didn't feel right, so she folded her arms around her middle. Only when she saw him wrap a towel around his waist from the corner of her eye, did she feel comfortable enough to look back at him.

"Are you still in much pain?"

"Nothing like before." He gave her a half-smile. "It feels like I'm getting over a bad case of the stomach flu."

Water droplets glittered off his shoulders and trailed down the corded muscles across his chest and ribs. Katherine glanced to the area where both bullets had ruptured his skin. Her eyes widened. The angry, red welts had disappeared, and only light scar tissue remained.

Clark ran a finger across one of the scars. "Amazing, isn't it?"

"That's an understatement. Do you even get sick?"

"Probably not."

With a hand against the tiled wall, Clark stepped from the shower stall. Katherine moved up to give him a hand, but he shook his head and managed to reach his room and sink down on the bed unaided. Grabbing his glass of water from the counter, she followed.

When he tugged off his towel, another staring fit hit Katherine. Shoving the comforter aside, he slipped in bed and pulled the top sheet up around his waist. He really did have a wonderfully made body. Tight, muscled, but not bulky.

"Thanks."

It took her a second to realize that he was talking about the water in her hand.

"Oh, sure."

Clark took the water she offered, drank down several long swallows, and then rubbed the glass against his forehead.

"Do you think you'll be all right?" she asked, glad to see color back in his face. "I should let you get some rest."

He pulled the glass from his forehead and frowned. "I don't want you going out that front door alone with a killer on the loose. Just give me a minute to rest."

"Sure."

Katherine glanced around the room. When she didn't find a chair, she sank down on the edge of the bed by his hip and curled a leg beneath her, all the while trying not to think of his very naked body beneath that very flimsy sheet. But it was pretty darn hard to focus on anything else when the cloth clung to and outlined his damp legs and...other male parts. His chest, exposed from the waist up, didn't help one iota either.

Clark placed his glass on the carpet by the bed and caught her hand as he eased back against the mattress.

"Talk to me," he said, closing his eyes and twining his fingers with hers.

"About what?"

"Anything. Nothing. It doesn't matter. I just want to hear your voice." He squeezed her hand in encouragement. "What were you like growing up?"

"Hmmm. Just normal." Katherine laughed self-consciously. She couldn't remember a time when someone asked about her life with any real interest. "Did I just say normal? I guess that's not quite true. I had everything I pretty much wanted. Spoiled really. Birthday parties were huge productions. Clowns, ponies, you name it. Nothing was too much for my mother and father's only child.

"When I was young, we'd go down to Florida in the winter. At the time, the family had a condo on the beach. I'd get to bring a friend with me, and we'd spend hours in the water. I even took up surfing for a while."

"Ah." Eyes still closed, Clark smiled and sighed almost whimsically. "I can imagine. Lethal. All tanned, with some killer bikini. I bet you had all the boys wrapped around your little finger."

Katherine laughed. She couldn't help it. "That's got to be some other girl, because I sure the heck didn't have any boys chasing after me."

Clark's eyes snapped open. "Then they must have been blind."

Feeling her cheeks warm at the astonishment in Clark's face, Katherine teased, "Watch out. If you keep that up, I might just get used to all this flattery."

Clark's face turned serious. "It's not flattery. Flattery's a shallow compliment. And nothing about you is shallow."

She froze, suddenly terribly conscious of the way his thumb moved back and forth against her wrist. And his eyes. The way he looked at her. So sincere, so intense.

"And boyfriends. Anyone serious?"

Katherine tensed. "No. Of course not. I wouldn't have done—you know—had sex with you."

Color crept up his neck and into his face. "I meant growing up."

"Oh. Yes. Of course."

She'd embarrassed herself, and, if she could go by Clark's ruddy cheeks, she'd done the same to him.

Strangely, Katherine found his reaction endearing. There was something about a man blushing that touched her, that made her feel feminine, powerful and all warm inside. No. She didn't have that right. It wasn't just any man's blush. It was Clark's.

"So you did have to fight them off."

"Not at all!" Katherine laughed. The man wouldn't give up. "But there was one boy in the first year of college. We were serious for a while. My friends thought he was perfect. He was going into law and had an eye on politics. My mother loved everything about him."

"He sounds perfect. What happened?"

Katherine's slipped her hand from Clark's. "We grew apart."

Clark's brow furrowed as he searched her face. "People don't grow apart. Not really. It's an excuse someone uses when they want out. There's always something more to it."

Katherine frowned at the blank wall above the bed. At times Clark could be too astute.

"What really happened?"

"I grew up," Katherine finally said, unable to conceal the bitterness in her voice.

"Okay. Hint taken. I won't ask again."

Katherine sighed in relief. "And what about you? Any girlfriends I should know about?"

"I don't know."

At Clark's soft-spoken reply and the way he flinched, Katherine wanted to sink into the floor at her insensitive question. Of course he didn't know. He couldn't remember. Katherine seriously needed to start thinking before she opened her mouth—be like her mother at least in that one aspect.

When she'd first met Clark, she'd immediately looked to his left hand and noted his ring-less fingers, which didn't necessarily mean anything. Many married men walked around without wedding bands. The idea of a woman, particularly a wife, in Clark's life hurt. Hurt more than she liked to admit.

She hadn't had sex with Clark for the sake of sex. She'd never been the type to separate the act from her emotions. And Clark had been no exception. Slowly, day-by-day, moment-by-moment, she'd gotten involved, and if she got any more involved, she'd have her heart out there on a platter.

"You could be married," she said softly.

"No."

"How can you be so sure?"

"Because it's something I would know."

Katherine shook her head and decided on this, tact was pointless. "Not necessarily. Not if you can't remember anything."

"If I was in love with someone else, I wouldn't feel the way I do about you."

Heart rate surging into an insane tempo, Katherine straightened. Afraid of the answer, but more fearful of the uncertainty, she asked, "And that is?"

"I'm not sure." He captured her gaze. "Love? I don't know. But I do know that you're always in my thoughts. I know I should keep away from you, but every time I try, I realize I can't. I also know that whenever you're in the same room with me, I get all tongue-tied and twisted inside. What man wouldn't? You're so damn beautiful. I'm not talking about your looks— Hell. Any man can see that. But inside...you've got this soul that's so giving, so gentle, so—I can't describe it. All I know is that I'm drawn to it."

Her throat tightened, and she blinked back the threat of tears. "For someone who says they get all tongue-tied, you're doing an amazing job. I don't know what to say..."

He shook his head against the pillow. "Then don't say anything now. Maybe later. When I can think clearly, and I'm not so tired."

Sighing, Clark closed his eyes. Katherine sat on the edge of the bed and watched as his breathing slowed and deepened, and his brow cleared. When she realized he'd fallen asleep, she uncurled her leg from under her and rose.

Clark jerked awake and caught her wrist. "Don't go."

She sank back down on the mattress. "Okay."

"Promise?"

At the urgency, almost panic in his voice, Katherine stilled.

"I promise."

How could she deny him such a simple request? She couldn't. Then again, when it came to Clark, she didn't have the willpower to say no.

She sat silently on the edge of the bed and watched Clark fall asleep as night pressed against the bedroom window. Light from the bathroom cut across the bed and illuminated the harsh, masculine lines of Clark's face.

Sudden doubts crowded in on Katherine.

The gun. The money.

Of course, there was a rational, innocent explanation for both. Clark wasn't a killer.

Or was he?

CHAPTER 24

So, YOU WANT to tell me what's going on?"

Seated behind her desk, Katherine looked from her computer to George, standing in the doorway to her office.

"You mean Clark?" she asked

"Well, yeah."

"He's not causing any trouble, is he?"

"No. He's out in the kitchen playing poker with Tracy and a couple of others."

Loud laughter carried into her office, backing up George's claim. Katherine dropped the pen in her hand and rose from her chair.

"So who is he?" George asked.

"A friend."

"Really. Since when do you bring 'a friend' to work with you?"

"Since today."

Not that Clark had given her a choice. This morning, he'd shown up at her door, not budging from the porch until she agreed to bring him to work with her. And from the looks of things, he intended to stay glued to her side here on out. Katherine hated to admit she found his presence and special abilities reassuring. Not that she needed his protection, of course. She knew how to take care of herself just fine.

Clark had even insisted she stay at a hotel until he resolved the situation with her uncle and the shelter. And she'd quickly insisted right back that she wanted no part of it. Hole up in some room, while Clark uncovered the mystery behind her uncle and the shelter? Not likely. Too many people depended on her. Plus, it was pretty darn hard to hide from one's family.

As for last night, neither of them had mentioned it or how she'd fallen asleep in his bed. Wrapped in Clark's sheet and strong arms, she'd woken just before dawn. Without a word, she'd slipped from his bed and house. She hadn't dared stay, liable to let her emotions sway her better judgment.

Frowning, George rubbed at his gray beard. "Is something going on I should know about? You've been really jumpy the last couple of days."

She wasn't about to pull anyone into her mess. "I'm okay, George. I've got everything under control."

He muttered under his breath as he followed her from her office and into the kitchen, where Katherine found Clark and three teenagers playing cards. A pile of mini chocolate bars sat in the middle of the kitchen table. Tracy, in the process of anteing up two of hers, clutched her cards close to her chest. A grin curved the young girl's lips, wiping the usual sullen and distrustful expression from her eyes. With each day Katherine saw less and less of that look, which made her job all the more fulfilling.

"So who's winning?" Katherine asked.

Zack, a fifteen-year-old with dreadlocks and a possible nest somewhere in that mass, grunted. "Tracy's killing us. I think she's cheating."

"Yeah, right. You wish, smart-ass. You're just grasping. Can't handle losing, can you?"

He wrinkled his nose. "I still think you're cheating."

"I don't think she's cheating. I think she's just been playing us guys," Clark said with a teasing smile. "She forgot to tell us that she's an expert poker player."

"Expert, eh?" Tracy leaned back and crossed her ankles under the table. "I like the sound of that."

Clark caught Katherine's gaze, and something in his smile changed. Tenderness. It softened the austere lines of his face and made Katherine feel all warm inside. Dressed in faded jeans and a navy sweatshirt, he looked relaxed and strangely at home surrounded by three teenagers.

She smiled back. She couldn't help it. That look in his eyes could curl any girl's toes.

Then there was last night. A new and undeniable bond tied them together. The harrowing events, Clark's injuries, the mind-numbing fear of it all had forced her to see him in yet another new light. He had exposed his frailties and...a secret so profound. For Clark to trust her with something so powerful was humbling.

She glanced over at Tracy and saw the girl's sudden smirk. Katherine made a face at her, knowing exactly what ran through her little head. Clark wasn't her boyfriend. Not that the idea didn't have appeal... With each new day and minute, Katherine found herself steadily falling for Clark, and the scary part—she didn't think she had it in her to stop herself. Or if she even wanted to.

Tracy opened her mouth—no doubt—to spit out some wisecrack remark, but Katherine cut her off. "Not a word. You got that?"

"Fu—" She broke off at Katherine's look and sighed loudly. "Right. Whatever."

Shane, who'd shown up two days ago with nothing but the clothes on his back, stuck five mini bars into his mouth and chewed. Teeth stained an ugly brown, he asked George and Katherine. "Do you want in on the next round?"

"That's disgusting!" Tracy sneered. "Close your mouth. Show Clark we have some manners."

Shane's face turned red, and he glared at Tracy. "At least I can eat without my tongue getting caught on something."

"I like my piercing. And *at least* I don't have a butt hole for a mouth!"

Before it turned ugly, Clark interrupted, "Hey, guys! How about we get back to the game and leave the name calling for another time? Katherine, George, did you want to join us?"

Clark glanced Katherine's way, and a look of understanding and respect crossed his features as if he knew how much she considered these kids her family, warts and all. Strange how Clark's opinion meant more than many people in her life— particularly anyone in her family. Stranger still, for a man she'd only met a couple of weeks ago, he had such a profound effect on her. But then, feelings didn't involve logic.

George pulled up a chair, but Katherine shook her head. "I'd like to, but I'll have to make it another time. I've got an important call to make."

Katherine retreated into her office and stared at her phone with dislike. Sinking down in her chair, she flipped through her Rolodex until she came to Kincaid's number. For a full minute, she stared at the telephone and drummed her fingers against her desk. Okay. Other than going to his office, she didn't see any other option, and since he didn't take any of her calls...

Before she chickened out, Katherine called Kincaid's office and grabbed a pencil to twirl between her fingers.

The receptionist answered. "Can I ask who's calling?"

"Sharon Spalding."

Knuckles rigged from strangling her pencil, she waited.

"Hi, Sharon. How can I help you?"

"Actually...this is her daughter, Katherine."

Complete silence. Not a good sign.

Katherine flipped the pencil between her fingers, and with the heel of her shoe swiveled around until she faced the wall and window. "Sorry for the dishonesty, but I couldn't find any other way to get through. You haven't been returning my calls."

For a moment, she thought he'd hung up, but then Kincaid said, "I've been extremely busy."

"That's all very well, but I want a reason why you've stopped contributing to the shelter after almost two years. I think I deserve some explanation."

"I don't know if it's my place to get into this. Maybe you should talk to your mother."

Her fingers stilled on the pencil. "My mother?"

"Well, yes. She's the one I think you need to talk to. She

recommended that I—Well, what your mother and I discussed is private."

"I guess I'll do that then." She hung up and muttered, "Thanks for nothing."

Katherine shoved her hair back from her face with one hand, uncaring if she looked like Medusa on a bad hair day. After flipping the Rolodex to the next number, she used the same exact tactics on Melrose.

When Melrose dodged one question after another, Katherine asked, "Does this have anything to do with my mother?"

A short pause followed before he prevaricated with, "I really don't want to get into your family business."

Katherine had her answer. She hung up and stared out the window to the world outside. The sky, laden with thick, dark, turbulent clouds, matched her mood. The winter scene blurred as tears filled her eyes.

Why? Katherine didn't understand. She'd always known her mother never approved of her work, though Sharon had hidden it on occasion. But for her mother to pull something like this went beyond Katherine's imagination. Impatiently wiping a balled fist beneath her eyes, Katherine laughed with rancor.

Bitter? Oh, yes. She was bitter. Talk about feeling betrayed and manipulated. Just what type of woman had borne her? Katherine didn't know anymore. If she ever had...

Swinging back around with the help of one foot, she found Clark seated in one of the two chairs in front of her desk. So focused on her own drama, she hadn't heard him come in.

"What's wrong?"

She read the concern in his face and wanted to cry all the more. She didn't need sympathy. Not that she didn't appreciate it from Clark, but it was liable to get her feeling all the more vulnerable and flustered.

Katherine replaced the receiver with trembling fingers. "My mother's decided to make my business hers."

"What do you mean?"

"She's talked two of my contributors out of backing this

shelter. I never understood why they kept dodging my calls and avoiding me. Now I have my answer."

"I'm sorry."

Clark rose from his chair, came around and sat down on her side of the desk. When he caught her hand, she watched his fingers twine with hers. Such large, capable, and powerful hands. Yet gentle and safe. Just like his personality.

"It sounds like your mother wants to shut down the Morning Dove."

She stiffened. Impossible. But was it? Katherine thought back to previous conversations and the active dislike in her mother's words and actions, and Katherine knew, no matter how much she wanted to deny it, Clark spoke the truth.

"If my mother thinks she's going to get away with meddling, she's got another think coming. I've had enough. I'm calling her." Slipping her hand from Clark's, she reached for the phone.

"Wait." He blocked the phone with a hand. "You're way too upset. You need time to cool down."

"I don't know. I can't think. I can't— Why?" Tears burned the back of her eyes. Jaw clenching, Katherine focused on the anger, anything to smother the crazy urge to cry. She looked up, taken aback at the fury in Clark's gray eyes.

"It has something to do with the missing kids from the shelter. Spalding and Miltronics are tied to this place. But I've never been able to understand the why. And now there's your mother."

"So you're saying my mother's involved in the teenager's disappearances." Hearing it aloud made the realization all the more frightening. Then she remembered the last time she'd seen her uncle—the menace in his eyes, the threat in his words. "Oh, my goodness. These kids aren't safe! There's Zack. And—and Tracy. I can't let anything happen to them!"

"Nothing's going to happen to anyone." Leaning forward, Clark cupped the back of her head and forced her to meet his gaze. "Do you understanding? I'm not going to let that happen. We'll figure this out. Don't worry. And we'll do it together."

Zack, with a head full of dreadlocks, popped into the office. "Hey, Kath." Staring at the two of them, he stumbled to halt. "Oh, hey, sorry—"

Katherine stiffened, and Clark pulled away. She started to reply, but she stumbled to a halt. Zack had disappeared.

Obviously frustrated at the interruption, Clark pushed off her desk. "Let's get out of here and grab something to eat. We can't talk here."

"But—"

"No 'buts.' You're taking the afternoon off. I insist. George's here. The guy looks capable of handling things for a while, and as long as everyone sticks together, they'll be fine. And anyway, you're not going to be able to work as it is, are you?"

~~*~~

Clark thought she was going to argue for a minute, but after a long pause, she wrapped a strand of golden hair behind her ear and nodded. He waited as she put away her papers and retrieved her purse from beneath her desk. They grabbed their jackets and found George in the lobby.

He glanced at both of them and frowned. "What's going on?"

"Katherine's taking a break," Clark answered. "But she needs to feel that everyone's safe. Don't let anyone through those front doors you can't trust, and make sure the kids don't go off somewhere alone."

"I knew something was going on," George muttered. He stared at Clark with narrowed eyes but had the sense not to argue or ask questions. "It figures. We've got no security around here. At least I've got a baseball bat if anyone gives us any crap."

Clark eyed the other man and relaxed. George might be hitting his mid-fifties, but he looked like he'd seen and done a hell of a lot in those years. Over six feet of muscle and bone, the guy probably tipped the scales well over two hundred, more than enough weight behind him to do some damage with his bare hands, never mind a baseball bat.

Katherine frowned. "You never told me you had a baseball bat stashed away."

George shrugged a large shoulder. "I keep it around just in case. I haven't had to use it yet."

"I know I've been pretty lax when it comes to security," Katherine admitted. "But I've been looking into getting a guard dog. Goodness knows, the kids have been smuggling any four-legged stray they get their hands on into the shelter."

As Clark opened the door for Katherine and he stepped through the threshold after her, a hand clamped down around his shoulder. Clark turned.

George stood with his feet planted beneath his considerable weight and regarded Clark with dark brown, threatening eyes. Clark didn't flinch or break away from the biting pressure of other man's fingers.

"Take care of her. You got that?"

"I will. With my life."

Which didn't say much with the way Clark was handling his own, but it seemed to be enough for George, because the older man's face cleared, and he nodded, withdrawing his hand from Clark's shoulder.

"Good. She means a lot to us here."

Clark took it for what it was. A warning. He nodded sharply and followed Katherine from the Morning Dove.

When they reached Katherine's car, Clark watched her fumble with her keys. "Here. I'll drive."

Katherine tossed him the keys. After slipping behind the wheel and insuring both their seatbelts were buckled tight, he started the Mazda.

"I think you might've been right about needing a break." From beside him, Katherine pressed her head against the backrest. "I still can't believe George's been carrying around a baseball bat."

"You're far too trusting."

"Mmmm, maybe. But I'd rather be that than too jaded. Anyway, it works with the kids at the shelter. They've had so much distrust in their lives. To actually have someone who trusts and believes in them— Well, it's a balm to their ego and self-esteem and makes them want to achieve so much more."

Clark glanced over and saw the conviction in the gentle lines of her face, the earnestness in her soft brown eyes, and shook his head. "You love what you do, don't you?"

"Very much so."

The soft, husky tone of her voice washed over him. Such feeling, such belief. And beautiful. Inside and out. Today, she'd left her hair loose. It fell, thick and golden over her shoulders.

He remembered how those silken strands had felt between his fingers, how she'd arched, exposing the long, delicate line of her throat for his lips, how her skin had tasted, how hot and responsive—

Damn.

This morning, she'd left without saying goodbye, the scent of her still lingering against his bed sheets. Yeah, he'd been disappointed. He'd hoped...

Sighing, he pulled out of the parking lot and merged with traffic. "So where to?"

"Have you ever had sushi?"

An image of dead fish with slimy scales and open eyes came to mind. "Sushi...I don't know..."

Katherine laughed. All throaty and warm. Completely spontaneous. He loved it when she laughed like that.

"Not a good suggestion, I take it," she teased.

"Let's just say it's not one of your best ones, but I like chili cheese dogs."

"Okay. Hotdogs it is. I know of a great place. You'll like it. I promise. It's a sports bar. It's only about ten minutes away. At the next light, you'll want to turn right."

"Sounds great." He looked over and was glad to see the tension had eased from her face. She worked too hard. Granted, George helped, but Clark knew she shouldered far more responsibility than most women. "So how did you meet George?"

"George...?"

"Yes, George."

"Umm. I don't know... It was so long ago... We just kind of met."

He noticed with one quick glance that she'd grown inordinately interested in her hands folded across her lap. "There's more you're leaving out."

"What makes you think that?"

Now he was convinced she was hiding something. "Because you're a terrible liar."

She sighed. "He answered an employment ad I ran in the paper."

"And you did a background check on him, right?"

"Well, of course!"

"And?"

"Fine!" Her voice turned disgruntled. "He's got a prior. Okay?"

Grinding his teeth to cut off a four-letter word, Clark stopped himself from strangling the steering wheel. Barely. Breaking the thing wouldn't be the smartest move while moving through congested traffic.

"What was he in for?"

"Manslaughter."

"Damn it! What the hell type of people do you have working for you!"

"That's enough! There's nothing wrong with George. He's clean. Has been for years!" She waved a hand toward the windshield. "You're going to want to turn left at the next light."

Clark flicked a glance to the side mirror, and then cut in front of a minivan in the next lane. A car horn blared, but he didn't look back.

"He was in his thirties and going through some personal problems. His wife at the time took off with the kids and didn't leave a forwarding address," Katherine explained. "He'd started drinking. One night he was with a bunch of friends and ran a red light. He avoided hitting another car, but lost control and totaled his car. His friend in the passenger seat died."

Clark muttered under his breath. The story sounded too similar. His own car accident. The dead boy in the passenger seat. The blood. The guilt.

Enough. Swallowing, Clark focused on the road as he turned

into the next street. He glanced in the rearview mirror and saw the SUV right behind them.

"Like I said, George's been clean for over fifteen years. Believe me, he's paid his price, did the time and relived every second of that day again and again."

Clark nodded, not really listening now as he watched the rearview mirror. He'd bet a hundred-to-one the SUV was the same one that tried mowing him down the other day.

"Where to now?"

"You're going to turn left again at the second light."

Beside him, Katherine scanned through the music stations, skipping over a medley of classic, country and rock, as he pulled to a stop at a red light. When the light changed, he turned left, all the while keeping an eye on the SUV. The vehicle continued to follow.

"Damn it!"

"What's wrong?"

Katherine pulled away from the radio. A Bon Jovi song broke into the interior of the Mazda. The rock music drummed through the speakers and across the dashboard to vibrate under Clark's hands locked around the steering wheel. The singer's wail crawled across his skin.

Eyes narrowed, jaw clenched, Clark watched in the mirror. The wild beat of the music matched the pounding of his heart. The SUV shadowed them.

"Someone's following us."

CHAPTER 25

YOU CAN'T BE serious!" Swiveling around, Katherine peered around her seat to look out the rear window.

"I wish I weren't."

"Which car?" Katherine shouted over the music.

"The SUV! Two car lengths down and to the right! I'm pretty sure it's the same one that almost ran me over and caused the accident."

An electric guitar, louder and harsher than before, melded with the loud crash of drums and blasted against Clark's frayed nerves. Unable to take the noise anymore, Clark snapped off the radio. Immediate and deafening silence followed, somehow more nerve-wracking than the rock music.

"Not good. This is not good."

Clark heard the alarm in Katherine's voice. Damn it! He wanted to leap out of the car, grab the driver and strangle the bastard, but he curbed the wild urge. He wasn't about to jeopardize Katherine's life by chasing a possible killer with her nearby.

"Don't worry," he muttered, unable to sound calm. "No one's going to touch you. They'll have to get through me first."

"I can't see the driver." Katherine twisted more in her seat. "The visor's down and the sun's glaring off the windshield."

With his luck right now, Clark wasn't surprised they couldn't get a good look at the driver.

"What do you think we should do?" Katherine asked.

"Nothing."

"But—"

"But nothing. I'm not about to confront the person. If it's the bastard that shot me, he's liable to have a gun on him."

"Maybe it's not the gunman but someone my uncle hired to scare me. Uncle Paul might be following through on that threat he gave me. Maybe if we just talk to the person." Clark sent her a look. "Okay. That was a stupid idea."

"How about we do exactly as planned?" No way in hell was he going to let Katherine near this guy. "We'll be safe in a crowded restaurant. Whoever's in the car isn't stupid enough to try anything in such a public place."

But whoever drove the SUV had nearly run him down in a very public place. Then again, Clark didn't want to think about that.

As he guided the Mazda into the restaurant's lot and parked, he watched the SUV across the intersection. The other vehicle slowed and pulled into a metered parking spot on the adjacent road.

Damn it. The person in the SUV was like a stinking parasite.

The minute Clark stepped from the Mazda, he strode over to the passenger side, all the while keeping an eye on the SUV. Traffic moving from both sides of the street concealed any movement from inside or around the vehicle.

As Katherine slipped from the car, Clark stood, blocking her body from the street and the SUV. He wrapped an arm around her waist. She felt so small and delicate beside him. If anything happened to her because of him... Clark swallowed. He didn't want to think about that either.

"Okay, Clark. You don't have to plaster yourself on me! I'm quite capable of walking the few feet to the restaurant all on my own."

"Yeah, I know—"

But Clark didn't take his arm from around her waist as they moved across the parking lot. Once in the restaurant, the loud monologue of a sportscaster carried over the laughter and drone of voices.

Strange how it seemed so damn normal in here when everything in his life was so damn abnormal.

Clark made a point of getting a table far enough from the window to ensure they weren't visible targets but close enough to view any suspicious behavior from outside. From this vantage point, though, they couldn't see the SUV.

After they shrugged out of their jackets and the hostess gave them their menus, Clark rose, "I'll be right back."

He didn't wait for Katherine to voice a protest but left, weaving through the tables, striding past the lobby and snapping the front door open with a shoulder.

With Katherine safely inside, Clark intended to seize this opportunity. He wanted to end things. Now. He rounded the corner of the restaurant and looked across the street for the SUV.

Gone.

Swearing loudly, Clark curled his fingers into fists at his sides. The driver seemed as elusive as his memory. Talk about anticlimactic. He'd been more than ready for a confrontation.

Empty-handed, he retreated back to the restaurant. When he reached their table, Katherine looked up from her menu and frowned.

"Are you all right?"

"Yeah." He sighed. "We can relax for now. Whoever was following us is gone."

"That's what you were doing?" Katherine regarded him with reproach. "Next time you run off like that, let me know? I thought we were working as a team."

He didn't answer, unable to give her that promise. From the flash in Katherine's brown eyes, she noticed it too. But Clark didn't want to burden her with more problems, not when he suspected she was shouldering enough of her own. Last night she'd tossed and turned, moaning in her sleep. Clark knew her nightmares didn't involve Miltronics or her uncle but someone else.

"Who's Miranda?"

Katherine tightened her hold on her menu as she lowered it

to the table. If he'd shocked her, it didn't show in her eyes or face.

"Miranda?"

"You cried out her name last night. I was about to wake you but thought better of it."

When the waiter came and left with their order, Clark persisted. "So who is she?"

Katherine made a sound at the back of her throat. "She was my best friend—"

"Was? What happened to her?"

Her harsh, derisive laugh was far from reassuring. "I don't want to bore you with the details."

"Impossible. Everything about you matters. I want to know."

Katherine ran a hand back and forth against the table's edge in obvious agitation. "She died of a drug overdose."

"I'm sorry. When did it happen?"

"Seven years ago. We went to university together."

For some reason, Clark had thought her friend's death had happened months ago and not years. "So you were very close?"

"In the beginning." Katherine glanced up and met his gaze, but Clark suspected she saw only the past. "Miranda was on scholarship. She was from a broken home who had little money and even less love. How do I describe her? Sensitive. Smart. And what a crazy sense of humor. Miranda always managed to make me smile, no matter how bad my day was. You wouldn't think it, but underneath, she had such a big heart. I really admired her. She wanted to become a writer..."

"Then what happened?"

"She started hanging out with a crowd that had more money than sense. All the privilege, glamour and wealth these guys had completely seduced her. They didn't care about her. To them, Miranda was a good time and an easy lay." Her voice thickened with loathing, and her lip curled to one side. "My so-called boyfriend and soon-to-be lawyer was one of those 'guys.'"

She shook her head, sadness replacing the flash of anger in her eyes. "I tried to tell her she was being used, but she didn't see it that way. The pretty words and free drugs were blinding her to the truth. By the time they'd gotten tired of her, it was too late. She'd become an addict. But unlike the others, Miranda didn't have a safety net."

"Did she try to get help?"

A tear slid down Katherine's cheek. "She came to me a couple of times, asking for money. I gave it to her until I realized I just encouraged her drug habit. Everything came to a head when I caught her stealing some of my jewelry. We got into a huge fight. A couple days later, she came by, begging me to give her another chance, asking for my help. I never answered the door."

He reached across the table and cupped Katherine's hand. "And you blame yourself."

Sniffing, Katherine jerked her head up and down and grabbed Clark's hand as if it were a lifeline. "Every time I think of her death, I think of my selfishness, of my inability to—" She cleared her throat. "She died in a public restroom. A cleaning crew found her in one of the stalls in the morning. I guess she'd been there since the night before..."

Clark closed his eyes against the image. "Oh, hell. I'm sorry."

"If only I'd been there for her. If I hadn't turned my back like everyone else, she'd be alive."

"You can't know that."

"But don't you see?" she asked as she leaned forward, sorrow and desperation etched starkly across her face. "By doing nothing, I killed her."

"Don't say that. I don't want you ever thinking that. How could you know she'd overdose? You can't blame yourself for someone else's bad choices, Katherine." Clark wanted to reach over the table and wrap his arms around her, hold her, take away her pain and make it his. "You've lived with this guilt all these years, haven't you?"

"I guess."

Clark swallowed with difficulty. Now he understood. The shelter. The kids. Every single one of them was a Miranda walking through the front door of the Morning Dove. For years, Katherine, on a desperate mission to fix these kids, didn't realize she needed fixing herself.

Clark struggled for a way to make Katherine see. "Even if you'd opened that door, do you think Miranda would have stopped the drugs and gotten help? Can you honestly say that? If she needed money for another fix, she would have said or done anything to get it."

Katherine sighed and withdrew her hand from his. "You've got a point."

He saw the skepticism in her face and realized nothing would convince her of the truth until she was ready to see it herself.

When the waiter came with their food, Clark stared down at his plate. No doubt the chili-cheese dog smelled and tasted good, but he'd lost his appetite. And he wasn't the only one from the way Katherine picked at her salad.

Dressed in a simple white cotton blouse and jeans, her thick golden hair cascading past her shoulders, Katherine looked like she hadn't yet graduated from college, but beneath her youthful appearance lay a woman with far more years of experience than many. She'd seen a hell of a lot because of the Morning Dove, but even so, she hadn't become completely disillusioned. Compassionate, stubborn, sincere, honest, and so damn gentle-hearted. Amazing. Hell. Everything about her amazed him.

Clark had yet to thank her for the other night. He'd been so caught up in his own drama, he hadn't thought of what Katherine must have felt at getting nearly shot at or seeing him bleeding all over the damn place.

She'd acted, not reacted, somehow managing to rein in her own fear to take care of the situation. Someone with less character would have left him to deal with everything on his own.

But she had left, another part of him argued. He'd woken that morning, disoriented, disappointed and alone. Clark understood, though, why she'd vanished. The way his body reacted to a couple of bullet holes must have scared the hell out of her.

Clark cleared his throat. "I want to thank you."

She glanced up from her food, a question in her eyes.

He shifted awkwardly in his chair. "Last night...helping me, being there. It meant a lot. I just wanted you to know that," he said the last in a rush.

"Clark, seriously, it was nothing."

"No. You're wrong. It was far more than 'nothing.' I was at a pretty low point. Thanks for being there."

When she nodded, he cleared his throat again. "I can understand why you left. Anyone would have been repulsed."

"Repulsed?" she asked in disbelief. "Never. I left because—just because."

She frowned as if she'd said too much.

"Then why?"

She placed her fork down. "Okay. I left because I was afraid if I stayed something would happen. I didn't want my attraction to you clouding the situation."

"Oh."

As he watched Katherine's face turn a wonderful shade of red, euphoria rolled through him. Katherine saw beyond his oddness. She saw him as a man. His chest expanded, and he bit back a smile as the husky warmth of her laugh washed over him. To the day he died, he'd never get tired of that laugh.

"See?" Katherine made a face. "I knew I shouldn't have said anything. And you can stop smiling like you've got a big bucket of fish in front of you."

"I look that obvious, do I?"

Katherine nodded.

His smile wavered, and then disappeared as an image of her naked in his bed flashed in his mind. "I wish you hadn't left."

Katherine's eyes darkened with awareness. Suddenly, the tension thickened around them, and Clark couldn't stop thinking of sex.

"Let's get out of here." His voice sounded husky and unused, but damn, he felt like being used.

She nodded again, her expression far more serious than moments before. "First, I have to go to the restroom. I'll be right back."

He frowned. "I don't like you being alone."

"Clark, I'll be okay. I'm just going to the bathroom."

"Fine."

"I'll make sure I don't drown in one of the stalls. How's that?" she shot back with an arched brow but didn't wait for a reply.

As Katherine weaved her way through the diners and disappeared down the hall to the restrooms, he watched several men turn in admiration. Katherine didn't notice or didn't seem to care. But then, she was a woman who didn't focus on outer appearance; otherwise she wouldn't be working at the Morning Dove. She saw beyond these kids' coarse exteriors to their broken hearts, and in the process, tried to heal them and rebuild their trust and self-esteem.

If they both got out of this alive, Clark wasn't going to let her go. This wasn't some fling. He knew the element of danger heightened the sexual awareness between them, but Clark's feelings for Katherine went far deeper than surface attraction.

Somehow, he'd convince Katherine they were right for each other. He stilled. Who was he kidding? He didn't have anything to offer Katherine. He had no job, no stability, and no memory. Worse yet—no future.

"Will that be all?" Their waiter interrupted Clark's brooding thoughts. "How about dessert? We have a wonderful selection—"

"No. I'm fine. I'd like the bill now."

When the waiter came back with his tab, Clark slipped two bills between the folder and searched the restaurant for Katherine.

She was taking too long. He didn't like it. Clark should have followed her, and to hell with any protests from Katherine or anyone else he happened on in the restroom. He slowly scanned the diners in the booths on both sides of the wall. The open floor plan didn't afford any room for a person to hide. Except the one hallway that led to the restrooms Katherine had disappeared down.

He didn't like this at all. Another thirty seconds and he didn't care if he caused more than raised brows; he planned on walking into the women's restroom. Frowning, he glanced out the window and caught a brief image of a man and woman before they disappeared from view.

But it was enough. That distinct shade of blonde hair. That slim, youthful frame.

Katherine.

Terror sent Clark's heart free-falling to his stomach. She wouldn't leave her jacket behind unless something was horribly wrong. Right now, this second, she was out there with some strange man—a possible wacko, pervert—killer.

Clark jack-knifed to his feet, shoving his chair back, sending it flying against the carpeted floor.

"Holy shit."

CHAPTER 26

Somehow the person in the SUV had returned and lured or coerced Katherine from the restaurant. While Clark stood gaping at the window like some idiot, that same person might be forcibly dragging her into a car.

He might have a gun.

Already it might be too late—

No.

Clark wheeled around and careened through the restaurant. He hit a leg on a table. Silverware flew. A thick oak table crashed to the floor.

"Hey, watch out!"

But Clark didn't care about the stares, the shouts, the chaos he left behind. He cared only about getting to Katherine.

With the flat of his hand, he smacked the thick wooden door open. Metal hinges groaned and cracked from the force. Clark exploded outside and around the corner of the building to the parking lot. Winded, he paused and searched wildly around for Katherine. An oppressive gray swathe of clouds pressed down from the sky, turning the parking lot, the cars and surrounding buildings and snow into duller, darker facsimiles.

Clark found her standing between two compact cars and only feet from a man in a long, tan, mole-haired jacket—the same person he'd glimpsed in the window. Even though the raised collar of the man's jacket shielded a good part of his face, he looked vaguely familiar. But Clark couldn't place the where and when. It had to be somewhere recent, in Boston. He struggled to remember...

Other than the three of them, no one else moved toward the restaurant's entrance or amid the parked cars. Tires against asphalt sounded from the traffic bordering the parking lot, while the blast of music from a passing vehicle traveled over air tainted with the taste of car exhaust and kitchen grease.

Clark strode across the asphalt. He focused on the man, his dark, almost black hair, the way he pulled open the top two buttons of his coat with a bare hand. Then the man, slowly, ever so slowly slipped his hand inside his coat. Clark's heart rocketed. The bastard was grabbing for a gun.

Had to be.

Clark broke into a run and watched in horror as the man started pulling his hand from inside his jacket.

Holly shit.

Clark leaped. The ground rushed from beneath him; wintry air caught in his hair and dug into his sweater. His breath sounded odd, deep, uneven, and not his own.

He hit the creep, ramming a shoulder into his chest and knocking him off his feet. A grunt. A moan. Clark didn't know from whom as he grasped the bastard's jacket. He reined back the fury boiling within him, knowing his hands possessed the power to kill, to maim, and forever silence the answers to his past.

They smashed against the side of a car, spun and bounced off the driver's window. Glass burst into a firework of jagged fingers. They hit the adjacent car. The force of their bodies connected against the metal and pushed them up, across and over the car's hood to land on the cement on the other side.

Clark got the better deal, landing on flesh instead of unforgiving ground, and he felt just as unforgiving as he glared down at the man lying flat on his back. The creep squirmed beneath him. He reminded Clark of a fish flung from the water, his mouth expanding and contracting wildly for air. The guy didn't look so dangerous now. Pain contorted his face—a face covered in a patchwork of ruddy, ugly red.

Good.

"Clark!"

"Jesus! Get off me!" The man cried. "Tell him to get off me!"

But Clark wasn't finished. He wanted answers, and if it took physical force and a little more pain, then so be it.

"Clark! Stop it."

"My arm! You've broken my arm!"

The man's words barely registered over Clark's pounding heart. He scrambled to his feet and yanked the shorter man up by his jacket's collar. Eyes wide with panic, he looked terrified of Clark.

Good.

"Let go!" Katherine tugged at Clark's arm. "For God's sake, let him go! He's okay! He's my neighbor—a friend. Ethan lives two doors down from my place!"

The word friend cut into Clark's consciousness. Frowning, he released his hands from the friend's jacket and stepped back, realizing now why the man looked familiar. He was Katherine's gay neighbor, Ethan. The one he'd spied the first day he'd followed Katherine home from the Morning Dove.

Reality hit, and with it, mortification. It burned into Clark's face and left him floundering. He'd jumped Katherine's neighbor, pounded the guy's head into the ground and enjoyed it. Clark hadn't waited around to ask questions. No. Not him. Oh, no. He was too much of an idiot to act like a rational human being.

And how fitting. He'd gloated over Ethan's fear and mottled face, but Clark had a good idea his own face looked far redder than Ethan's ever had.

"Hey, I'm sorry—"

Clark lifted an apologetic hand, but Ethan, horror flashing across his face, cupped his arm and stumbled back.

"Get away!" Sniffing, he looked at Katherine in disbelief. "He broke my arm. He actually broke my arm! Since when have you started associating with lunatics?"

"I'm not crazy. And I might not have broken your arm. You could have a torn ligament instead." Clark watched Katherine rub a hand over Ethan's shoulder, slowly, reassuringly.

"Do you think I'm stupid? I know when something breaks!" Ethan, cradling his elbow against his chest, sank against the side of the car—the same one where moments before he and Clark had slid across its hood. "Who is this jerk, Katherine?"

"A friend," Katherine said, her brown eyes dark with concern and lingering shock. "Clark made an honest mistake. He was only trying to protect me."

Clark glanced sharply at Katherine, surprised at how readily she'd backed him up. Stranger still, it looked like she believed every word.

Even so, Clark didn't feel any better by jumping to wild conclusions. He'd just broken some innocent man's arm. What the hell type of person was he? He felt like a damn fool.

"I thought you were someone else." Even to Clark the explanation sounded lame.

"Yeah, who?" Ethan's lip curled with scorn. "Jack the Ripper?"

"I thought you were reaching for a— Forget it. It doesn't matter." He glanced over at Katherine. "Katherine disappeared. She didn't tell me where she was going."

"And who made *you* her keeper?"

Clark ignored Ethan's snide remark. "Why?"

"I didn't think." Katherine, her face just as pale as Ethan's, stared back at Clark. "I saw Ethan and followed him outside. He had the number to a dog breeder I'd wanted. I've been thinking of getting a guard dog for the shelter."

"But what was in his pocket?"

"What are you talking about?" Ethan frowned.

"You were reaching inside your coat for something."

Ethan sniffed in disdain. "I needed my keys. I left the dog breeder's card in my car."

"Your keys?" Clark asked stupidly.

"Yes. My *keys*." The other man glared at him.

Just then, the last of Ethan's color leached from his face, and he crumpled onto the parking lot in a dead faint.

~~*~~

Clark paused by the sidewalk in front of Katherine's townhouse. Daylight had disappeared hours ago, and the moon, somehow brighter and larger than usual, hung in the black sky, inches above the trees and buildings. Its quicksilver glow touched Katherine's face and illuminated her delicate features but also drove shadows below her brow, concealing the expression in her eyes. Hell. He was surprised she was willing to be on the same sidewalk together.

Moments before, Ethan had vanished inside his own townhouse, leaving them with an icy expression and an even icier farewell. Not that Clark could blame Ethan. He didn't know how he'd react if some stranger tackled him to the ground and broke his arm.

At the hospital, Clark did try to alleviate the situation by trying to pay for all medical expenses, but Ethan flatly refused, and, between looks of disgust and dislike, he ignored Clark.

"It wasn't your fault. It could have happened to anyone." Katherine cupped his upper arm, and he tried not to stiffen at the contact.

"Really?"

"Okay. I take that back. But it was a logical conclusion to think Ethan was the person in the SUV. I should have told you I was going outside to talk to him. And since I didn't, I'm just as responsible."

Clark stepped back, which widened the distance between them and forced her to drop her hand to her side. Right now, he couldn't handle having her touch him. "Don't take responsibility for something I did. I'm just lucky Ethan didn't press charges. Not that I'd blame him—what with me acting like a maniac."

"Yes, well..." Katherine trailed off and stuffed both hands into her coat pockets. "We still have no idea who was in the SUV. If only you could—"

"Remember?" He tried to keep the bitterness from his voice, but it came out thick, raw and unmistakable.

"Yes. But there are still those photos I mentioned," she said the last in a more confident voice. "I have a couple of Luke—

the boy you were seen talking to. Did you want to come in and look them over?"

For a moment, Clark thought of refusing, but he nodded instead and followed her up the path to her townhouse. Once inside, Katherine snapped on the hall light and shrugged out of her coat. As she hung it up alongside his, she turned, brushing against his arm. Clark quickly sidestepped.

"What's wrong?"

"I don't know what you mean."

Feeling her gaze on his face, he looked down and brushed imaginary lint off his arm. Here on out, he needed to keep things as impersonal as possible.

"Okay. I'll accept that for now."

Clark caught her frustrated expression before he followed her down the hall and into the kitchen. After she switched on the light, she dug inside the drawer beneath the white ceramic tiled island and pulled out an envelope. When Katherine sat down at the bleached rattan, kitchen table, he picked the chair furthest away and directly across from her.

She didn't touch the envelope but reached across the table and glided her fingers across the back of his fingers and wrist. Clenching his jaw, Clark started to withdraw, but she caught his wrist and turned it until his palm faced outward. Then she used her other hand to draw a delicate pattern over the creases of his fingers and palm.

"Okay," he protested but didn't pull away from her touch. "That's enough."

"No, it isn't."

He lifted a brow, acting unaffected, but in reality, her touch unnerved him. He both loved and dreaded it. Days before he'd used this same hand to caress her breast, her hip, the small of her back. He'd also smashed it into the wall, broken a stair railing, a bedroom door and...broken an innocent man's arm.

"So much power," she whispered with a mixture of awe and fear. "You hate what you're capable of, don't you?"

"I—" Clark sighed. "I hate how I can't control it. It scares the hell out of me. I hurt Ethan enough to send him to the hospital. Next time I might kill someone."

"No," she denied quickly. "You believed Ethan was dangerous. From the questions I heard you ask, I know you thought he was hiding a gun. That says right there you broke his arm because you thought he was going to shoot me. I know you'd never harm anyone. Not unless there was just cause."

"Are you sure about that?"

"Absolutely."

He didn't look away from the intensity of Katherine's gaze as his fingers closed over her hand.

"I could crush your bones so easily."

"But you'd never do it."

Clark closed his eyes against the conviction in her voice and face. Such belief. If only he had the same belief in himself.

"Is that why you've avoided touching me? Because you're afraid of hurting me?"

"Yes," he admitted.

He glanced down at her hand engulfed in his. She had such a small, delicate bone structure. Nothing like Ethan's. Even with Ethan being much bigger and stronger than Katherine, he'd managed to break the man's arm without trying. He could do far worse to Katherine. One simple twist of his wrist and he'd cause her insurmountable pain.

Clark didn't dare touch her.

Abruptly he pulled away and folded his arms across his chest. Hell. He didn't dare touch anything—what with him being a walking disaster and inept at everything he put his hand on. Maybe he should get a sign and staple it to his chest. "Caution. Dangerous when moving."

"You didn't hurt me the other night."

Her low and sexy whisper twisted his gut.

"Then we were both damn lucky."

Clark stared down at the table, not daring a glance at Katherine's huge, brown eyes. If he did, he'd chuck his willpower to keep away from her. Thankfully, he noticed the envelope, which diverted his mangled thoughts.

"Are those the photos of the kids from The Morning Dove?"

"Yes." She pulled several from the envelope and slid one across the table. "Here's a picture of Luke. It was taken by one of the girls. He's the one on the left. Some of the kids used to call him Lucky."

He picked up the photo. Two boys stared back at the camera, but Clark focused on the one to the left. Sun glanced off Luke's shoulder-length, brown hair. The boy's lips lifted at the corner in a semblance of a smile, but his face lacked any humor. Shoulders slumped, thumbs hooked into the front pockets of his jeans, and a hip thrust to one side, Luke stared back at the camera. The kid looked harder than most, and even defiant the way he angled his chin upward. Other than that, Luke seemed like a typical teenage boy. Maybe with a bit more attitude than some, but nothing unusual.

He recognized the teenager. Luke was the same boy as the one in the picture he'd pulled from the dead teenager.

"You said Lucky?" Clark asked.

"He got the nickname because he always seemed to land on his feet."

"Lucky ..." Clark whispered the name, feeling a tightness build inside his body.

Suddenly, a vision of the car accident from Arizona flashed in his mind. The shattered glass, the boy slumped in the passenger seat. The blood dripping from the bullet hole in his head. The face, unlined and young, the hair, caked with blood but inter-mixed with brown strands. Revulsion welled from Clark's stomach. He swallowed, but it clung to the back of his throat.

Clark restudied the face in the photo. The jaw, the length of hair, the thin frame. Luke or Lucky to some.

But why? Why had they been in Arizona, just the two of them? What had they been doing? Had Clark kidnapped the boy? Were they friends? Or did they have some dark, deeper relationship Clark didn't want to remember?

No. He didn't want to remember. Because if he remembered, then that would mean—

No.

Suddenly, Clark pushed away from the kitchen table, scraping the chair's legs against the white tile floor. He stood on rubbery legs and grabbed onto the table's edge as a wave of dizziness assaulted him.

"He's dead," he said. "That's him. The dead boy in the car."

"What?"

"I said he's dead. Killed in a car accident."

"How? I don't understand?"

Katherine's voice, hollow and tin like, sounded from a great distance away. Pictures flashed in Clark's head. His childhood, college, Miltronics, his co-workers and—Spalding.

The teenagers.

Clark gulped in air. His memory, and every agonizing detail of it, hit him. So many images, so many emotions. Gray, and then black edged across his peripheral vision and thickened until Clark thought he'd black out.

Hell. He was in hell.

Pain and panic pressed against his chest. Bending at the waist, Clark grappled for control. Slowly, his vision cleared, but his heart still crashed against his ribs.

"My, God. I dragged Luke away from Boston to save him." With his hands still latched to the side of the table, Clark dragged in a ragged breath, lifted his head and stared back at Katherine in horror. "But instead, I killed him."

"What are you talking about?"

"Not just Luke, but the others. All the missing boys at the shelter. I killed them."

CHAPTER 27

KATHERINE STARED BACK at Clark in matching horror. "That's impossible!"

Clark had to be lying. He didn't have it in him to hurt anyone. All she had to do was remember the car crash in front of the Morning Dove and how he'd risked his own life to save the woman trapped inside.

But seeing the naked emotion glittering from his eyes and etched across every hard line of his face, Katherine realized Clark believed every word.

It didn't make sense.

"You couldn't have killed Luke. You said yourself that it was a car accident."

"Yes, but he counted on me to get him away from Miltronics. I knew Luke was the latest victim. They started working on him, lying and bating him with money. I warned him that he'd end up dead if he continued associating with Spalding. I offered a way out, someplace where he could hide. At first, he didn't believe me, but he must have realized he was in way over his head when he finally came to me."

Katherine stilled. Her breathing grew labored, while the pounding of her pulse thudded over the hum of the refrigerator. The initial shock of Clark's words had blinded her to the real truth. Now she completely understood the ramifications.

"You remember, don't you?"

He shoved his fingers through his hair, thrusting several strands on end. "Hell, yes. Every damn, sick detail."

She'd prayed for Clark's memory to return, but not like this. "I don't understand your connection. What would you know of Luke and my uncle?"

"I worked as a scientist for Miltronics. I was one of several in a classified department on genetic engineering."

"My goodness, Clark."

He closed his eyes as if in deep, physical pain. "My name isn't Clark."

"Then who?"

This was too much to take in.

"John Davenport."

"This is crazy."

She rubbed at her face, vainly trying to comprehend the magnitude of the situation. So many questions, so many frightening scenarios. But one question rose amongst all the others.

"What do the teenage boys at the shelter have to do with Miltronics?"

"They were being experimented on."

"Lab rats," Katherine whispered. A part of her had already guessed, but the idea had been too ludicrous, too evil and perverted to contemplate.

Rising to her feet, she stumbled away from the table and hit her hip against the kitchen counter. She turned and leaned over the sink, struggling to hold down the contents of her stomach. She glanced at the white, tiled counter top, and instead saw red.

The blood of so many innocent boys.

Luke, Brian, Carl—too many. All snuffed out for the sake of some sick scientific experiment.

"And the others? What of them?" Katherine hugged herself. She was so very cold.

"Dead."

Katherine lifted a trembling chin, straightened, and fought against the grief grinding down on her shoulders. In front of the sink, a window revealed her small-enclosed yard. Light from the nearby street lamp partially illuminated the snow-covered ground. At the back corner of the fence, an apple tree, barren of fruit, stood alone. Its limbs, twisted and shriveled from the frigid cold, reminded her of an old, used up woman, with nothing to give and nothing to hope for.

Right this moment, Katherine felt just as aged and useless, and so darn brittle inside.

Some might consider the teenage boys at the shelter throw-aways, but no one deserved the way they'd died, alone, their lives snuffed out so young, without one soul to mourn or vindicate their senseless deaths.

It wasn't fair.

Sudden anger eased the crushing grief from her shoulders. Katherine wasn't going allow their deaths to be dismissed. She'd never been one to let things slide, and she wasn't going to stop just because she felt like giving up.

And what of Clark—or John? She didn't want to believe the worse. But what was she supposed to think when he already admitted to murdering the teenagers at the shelter?

Her whole body recoiled at the idea of Clark—no John—killing anyone—because, well because Katherine knew he didn't do any such thing. She'd seen too many tricks from the kids at Morning Dove. John couldn't hide that much of his character from her.

But what of his guilt?

"And you let it happen?" she asked, staring blindly out the window, her back to Clark as she clutched the counter's edge.

"I didn't know."

She turned. Clark, his hands balled into fists at his sides, stared back at her with an unfathomable expression. But the way he held his body, the tilt of his chin and pale complexion told her something far more. Pain.

"I suspected, but by the time I realized the truth, several boys had already died."

She believed him. Why would he lie now? She didn't see any reason.

"I want to know everything. The beginning. The end. And don't gloss over anything just because my uncle's involved."

"Are you sure?" He searched her face. "You're not going to like what you hear."

"I think I deserve to know it all, don't you?"

"Yeah." John sighed. "I need a drink to get through this. Something with a kick if you have it."

"Beer okay?"

He nodded.

Having a good idea she'd need one for herself, she grabbed two beers from the refrigerator. She didn't bother with glasse but popped the caps off both bottles and set them on the kitchen table.

She sat down and watched Clark—no John—she had to start thinking of him that way—sink down in the chair opposite from her and take a long swallow. A pulse throbbed along his jawline while his face still lacked any hint of color.

John wiped the back of his mouth. "I guess I'll start with Miltronics. The company's far larger in scope than's publicly known, particularly when it comes to their genetic research. I don't know if you knew that from your uncle."

"I'm completely clueless as to what he does or what type of people work for him. I guess I've been too darn self-absorbed with my own problems." Katherine didn't attempt to keep the bitterness or self-disgust from her voice. "But you worked for my uncle as a scientist?"

He rolled his bottle between both palms and nodded. "I was one of several researching immortality by way of the human growth hormone. After several years I was getting very frustrated at how little advancement I'd made. You see, I'd been so fixated on investigating the tie between muscle and adipose-tissue mass and thinning of skin to the human growth hormone—IGF-I axis, that I realized that I might be eliminating something of vital importance. So I refocused my efforts in another direction and decided to manipulate the genetic model. And bingo! That's when I stumbled on something so startling and profound—a way to accelerate and magnify the capabilities of the human animal."

"What are you saying? You can make someone stronger and

more intelligent?" Katherine pushed her beer away. She didn't need alcohol clouding up her mind.

"Intelligence doesn't come into play. It's all physical. But it's nothing like VEGF or erythropoietin, which increases red blood cell count and enhances an athletes' aerobic performance. Both blood boosters don't compare to this new way of gene modification."

Katherine changed her mind, grabbed her beer and took a huge swallow. The malt flavor hit the back of her throat and tongue but didn't do a thing to take the edge off her fear.

"So we're talking steroids."

"It's far more than that."

"But in essence, you've come up with a bionic man without the bionics. And you just happen to be carrying this in your system. That's why you can do what you do."

"Yes." Pain darkened John's eyes to a gray that matched the shores off of Boston on a dark, overcast day. "Spalding started experimenting on humans behind my back, knowing damn well how I'd balk at such unethical practices. These were unsuspecting teenagers at your shelter who were hungry for money either to rebuild a life off the street or to use for illegal drugs. I later learned the first few died by the formula. But then later as the imperfections of the serum diminished, Paul killed them to ensure Miltronic's secret."

"You're right. I can't stomach what I'm hearing. Brian and Carl and the others—they came to me for shelter. I should have done something. I should have known—"

"How *could* you know? Who would think of something so obscene?" The pulse along his jaw throbbed anew. "But I knew, Katherine. I had the chance to go to the authorities, but I didn't. I was terrified. No. I was a damn coward. Don't you see? I selfishly kept silent, because I knew I looked just as dirty as Spalding. All I could think of was my reputation, my career before anything else."

As John paused and grabbed for his drink, Katherine rubbed at her brow with the heel of her hand and glanced at her own beer. At the thought of taking another drink, she felt her stomach twist in protest.

"But even so," she argued, "when you found out what was going on, you didn't sit back and let those kids get murdered."

John downed half his beer. This time he avoided looking at her when he said, "After I finally figured out that the kids were being tested on, I secretly replaced the serum with a harmless glucose. Then I started working around the clock, leading the team in another direction while I worked toward perfecting the formula. I needed answers, and I used myself as a test subject to get to those answer."

Katherine stared back in alarm. "You risked your life by injecting yourself with a possibly deadly formula—all because of science?"

"Not because of science. Because of the kids. And anyway, most of the imperfections had already been corrected. You also have to understand—I wasn't thinking clearly. I was terrified at being found out."

"But my uncle found out. And Luke. What of him?"

John inhaled, and then exhaled in one loud rush. "When I learned about Luke, it took a while to make him see he was in over his head. The money—the same as in the duffle bag— blinded him to the danger. When he finally figured it out, he became irate. He bought himself a gun and planned on taking off with the cash. But more importantly, he wanted to avenge the murder of a friend he'd known from the shelter."

"But you talked him out of it?"

"Barely. I convinced him we needed to get out of Boston until we formatted a plan, and I had the perfect place in the mountains in Arizona for him to hide out. But we didn't make it. I never knew we were being followed. I remember the windshield popping and Luke slumping in his seat. When I finally figured out that someone was shooting at us, they'd put another bullet in one of the tires. I lost complete control and smashed over the side railing. I murdered him. If I'd known we were being watched and followed, I might—"

"Don't!" Katherine clutched at his hand on the table. She hated the tortured look etched across his face. "Remember a while back, you told me I had no control of Miranda's decisions or actions? Well, the same goes with you Clark—I mean John. You had no control of the outcome. Not really. You had Luke's best interests at heart. Do you think he would have lived if you'd left him under my uncle's care?"

She didn't wait for his reply. "No. Of course not. And anyway, how could you know what was to happen? Yes, maybe you didn't do anything at first, but, when it comes down to it, you did try to help. You can't say that about the others, can you? And there have to be others. Just how many know?"

"They all died in the explosion at Miltronics. But there's Spalding. If word got out as to what your uncle has..." John's gray eyes darkened to almost black, and his voice thickened and deepened with urgency. "The demand for it would be astronomical. We're not only talking performance enhancement for professional sports or the Olympics. We're talking warfare in our streets through organized crime or internationally by some crazed dictator or faction. It's a lethal weapon in the wrong hands."

"And my uncle happens to have this in his hands?"

"I'm not sure. I thought I destroyed everything before I left Boston, but I didn't realize how closely I was being watched. Spalding might have had someone copy all my work. Then again, I'm hoping the fire destroyed the lab and everything in it, because Spalding's dangerous. He can't see past its profit potential—the perfect means to fund his research on immortality. He's obsessed. More so since he learned a team in Scotland discovered the key gene that keeps embryonic stem cells in a state of immortality. He's so fixated on prolonging life that he doesn't care about the ramifications or the loss of life."

"I think it has something to do with the death of his wife. I know he was never the same after."

"Well, he's unbalanced and dangerous."

"But he's just a man," Katherine insisted, not knowing whether she was trying to convince John or herself. "Someone the both of us can pull down if we put our minds to it. It's not like he has the same powers as you..."

John must have heard the question in her voice, because he shook his head. "Not at all."

"Thank goodness. At least you've the advantage on that..." Katherine trailed to a halt, realizing John never thought of his powers as an advantage. "But what about you're powers? Do you have them for the rest of your life or are they temporary?"

"I don't know. We'd formulated the serum as a permanent enhancement." He grimaced. "So far, I haven't seen my strength or sight diminish. But I guess only time will really give me the answer on—"

Suddenly, unexpectedly, a loud and sharp bang from outside resounded through the walls of the townhouse and into Katherine's small kitchen. Both of them jumped and stared across the table at each other.

CHAPTER 28

JOHN RUSHED FROM the room, turning off the lights in his wake. Katherine quickly followed, but by the time she ran into the living room, he already stood by the front window. The drapes were pulled back and revealed a moonlit night.

"Do you see anything?"

Katherine's whisper broke into the room's eerie silence. She edged forward, but John raised an arm to stop her from moving closer to the window.

"Be careful," John said in an equally hushed tone. "Someone might have their sights on this townhouse."

She glanced out the window to the snow-covered front yard and the parking lot beyond. Even though the moon and street-lights illuminated many open places, too many shadows clung beneath the trees, by building corners and alongside parked cars. An intruder might easily hide in any one of them. They might even have a gun aimed at the house right this minute.

"The noise was a car backfiring. Completely harmless. But still. I don't think— I've got this feeling. I'll be right back." He closed the drapes. "Don't move. I want you inside and safe."

"Oh, no you don't—"

But Katherine stood talking to a closed front door—John having already disappeared into the night. Frustrated, Katherine grabbed a jacket and slipped out the front door after him.

As she stepped into the shadows alongside her townhouse, a shiver—more from fear than the cold air—raced up her body, and her breath fogged out in front of her. She peered into the dark night for signs of John. Nothing. Or for that matter—no one. The area seemed unnaturally quiet, unnaturally still.

Okay. She was not going to wimp out here. She hadn't caved in yet to all the things thrown her way, and she wasn't going to start now.

With a palm against the brick wall, she edged slowly, carefully along the building only to snag a pant leg on a bush. Swearing silently to herself, Katherine bent down and pulled the jean from a thorn. She rose. Suddenly, a huge, black shadow loomed in front of her. She gulped in a lungful of air to scream.

A hand clamped over her mouth.

"You know, this is becoming a habit I don't like."

At John's baritone, Katherine's body trembled wildly with relief. Before her legs gave out from under her, she grabbed the wall with one hand, and with the other, she yanked off John's hand.

"Will you stop that!" She got the words out on a wobbly whisper. "Just because you can move super fast doesn't mean you have to scare the daylights out of me. I wasn't afraid until you jumped out at me like that," she lied on the last.

"See? That's the problem. On some things being fearless is fine, but on others, it can be damn dangerous. Katherine, we're dealing with killers. Even though he's your uncle, it doesn't mean you're safe."

"I know that." She glanced over the parking lot, the street and surrounding townhouses. Just the idea of having a family member willing to kill—never mind willing to murder his own flesh and blood—made her flesh crawl. "Did you find anything?"

"No. It must have been my imagination."

"Better that than the reality of getting shot at again. I guess we need to be careful about everything we do," Katherine hated to admit as she turned back the way she came and hit a leg against the same bush. This time the thing stabbed through her pant leg, bit into her skin, and wouldn't let go. Muttering, she jerked her leg twice to get the blasted thing off her jeans before walking over to her front porch.

"Careful?" John asked from behind her. Disbelief dripped from the one word. "You weren't acting careful two seconds ago, running over bushes and standing out so much so that even a myopic person could recognize you."

Biting back a snappy retort, Katherine opened the front door to her townhouse and let John inside. She turned on the hall light, locked the door, put her jacket away in the nearby closet, and eyed his rugged good looks only a few feet away. He looked far too cool and controlled, which frustrated her that much more.

"Sorry you're disappointed, but I'm not about to sit around and do nothing while you run off and save the day. I want to help. No. I need to help. Those are my kids at the shelter. I'm responsible for their well-being. And—and you can't stop me."

Katherine knew the last sounded childish, but at the same time, she meant every single word. No one was going to stand in the way of her protecting her kids.

"But I can try," John argued. A flush stained his prominent cheekbones, while the stubborn thrust of his jaw looked suddenly darn right mulish. John didn't look so coolly in control now. "I don't want anyone near you unless I know they're safe. One funny look from anyone—friend, family member, you name it—and they're history. I'm not going to ask questions, and I don't care if I break someone else's arm. Yes, I'm sorry about Ethan, but I'm not going to take any risks when your welfare comes into play. You're too important to me. Don't you see? I can't have anything happen to you. There's no way I can handle—"

"It's okay." Katherine saw how truly upset he was and softened. "Nothing's going to happen to me."

She ran the tips of her fingers over the rough skin of his jaw and met the intensity in his gaze. He had beautiful gray eyes, filled with such strength and passion.

Yes, John made mistakes, some of which she knew he was deeply ashamed of, but what she found admirable was that he had every intention of making amends for those same mistakes.

Inching closer, Katherine trailed a thumb along his lower lip. She heard and felt his quick intake of breath and saw his eyes darken with a different passion, one of longing and desire. Her body instantly reacted with a need of her own.

"You have no idea what you do to me," she whispered, the sudden fear of moments ago stoked a craving for the feel of his lips on her own, and so much more.

Suddenly the expression in his eyes shifted and changed. The look of hunger dissolved into a dark gray, expressionless void. With sure, abrupt movements, he pushed her hand away and stepped back.

Katherine hitched her chin upward. Okay. That hurt. "You're doing it again. Avoiding my touch."

"I don't know what you mean."

Katherine snorted. "Don't play dumb. Every time I lay a finger on you..." To prove her point, she reached over to place a hand on his chest, which he predictably dodged. "...you jump."

"It's your imagination."

"Come off it. Don't treat me like I'm stupid." Then a new idea formed. And she hated it. "Are you married? Is that it?"

He laughed but the sound lacked any humor. "No. Never even came close. Work was my be-all and end-all. Real stupid when I think about it now."

Relieved John didn't have anyone waiting for him in another city or state, Katherine grabbed onto his sweater and tugged. When he didn't budge, she dug her fingers deeper into the wool and edged closer. John didn't say a word, but she felt the tension in the corded muscles of his chest, sensed it in the way he held his body, and saw it in the ridged cast of his jaw.

"Was the sex between us that bad?"

Katherine didn't know how she managed to voice the question when she absolutely loathed the possible answer.

John closed his eyes briefly as if the question hurt. This time when he looked down at her, he didn't shield the expression in his eyes. Anguish, stark and vivid, lay exposed for her to read. Katherine's hold on his sweater tightened. She swallowed, the pressure against her chest almost unbearable.

"Don't ever think that." He lifted a hand as if to touch her face but dropped it back to his side. "I can't get over this fear of hurting you. One wrong move on my part and I can cause you irreparable damage. I can't risk that."

Katherine exhaled. Until now, she never realized how crushed she'd be by John's rejection. Because in all honesty, she hadn't been asking about their sexual compatibility; she'd been thinking beyond the physical act to a far deeper emotional tie.

John still avoided her touch for fear of physically hurting her. Which was so like John. And why she loved every blessed facet of him.

She seized his hand and rubbed his knuckles against her cheek. "I thought you understood these fears of yours are groundless and pure conjecture." She opened his hand and placed a light kiss on his palm. "We made love the other night, and in the heat of passion you lost control—we both did—and you didn't hurt me. That surely says something."

Katherine let go of his hand and rose on her toes to cup his face in both of her palms. She brushed her lips over his unmoving mouth again and again, urging a response from him. She felt his body shudder before his lips parted on a sigh.

"Don't," John whispered against her mouth as he rubbed a thumb along the line of her jaw. "I can't think when you—"

"Then don't think."

Katherine eased back on her heels and searched his face. The look of longing and mind-shattering hunger in his eyes gave her the courage to take his hand and urge it lower, over her neck and collar bone. The heat of his palm, fingers splayed, burned through the fabric of her blouse. Awareness flamed across her skin, her breasts, her belly, while her breathing turned shallow and ragged.

Her gaze locked with John's, she continued to slowly, ever so slowly lower his palm until she pressed his hand against her breast. "I won't break. You can touch me."

Katherine heard his quick intake of breath while his hand shook beneath her own. At the feel of his fingers, strong and masculine, cupping her breast, she felt equally rattled. Her legs barely managed to keep her upright, while desire, almost painful in its intensity, clenched at her belly.

She watched John's pupils dilate yet further as he rubbed a thumb over the tip of her breast and lowered his head until their lips were mere centimeters from touching.

"Do something, John." Her lips grazed his as their breath merged into one deep sigh of anticipation and hunger. "Do something, before I go stark raving mad. That, or use every trick I can think of to get you in my bed—naked."

~~*~~

Stunned, he looked down at Katherine. Her words sent his blood roaring and evoked the wild image of her naked, astride his hips and riding him mercilessly. But it was the passion and love in her large, brown eyes that did him in.

With his memory restored, John understood why he found Katherine's face familiar. While asking questions at the shelter and aiding Luke's escape, he'd spotted her numerous times— always from a distance. But because of his inordinate sight, he'd caught and captured her features and found himself mesmerized by her beauty. The flawless skin, the huge brown eyes, the inner warmth, and energy that radiated from her every movement. He'd wanted to walk up to her, capture her attention...touch her.

The urge to touch her had only intensified after coming to know and love her. He'd tried hard to keep his hands off her, but now John didn't care. Not when Katherine pulled his head down and nipped gently on his lower lip, not when she arched against him and pushed her breast deeper into his palm, not when her feminine scent wrapped around him and—

Katherine's fingers burned through the fabric of his jeans as she pressed a hand against his erection.

"Jesus!"

He jerked against her palm. Swallowing, John closed his eyes while sweat formed on his brow. He grappled for control. But by sliding both of her hands under his sweater to explore his stomach, his chest, she sure as hell wasn't making it easier.

Okay. Enough. He needed to focus. Slow and gentle. Calm

but with purpose. If he got rough, he was liable to hurt her. Plus, he wasn't that big of an ass. Katherine deserved better than a quick fuck.

Ever so gently, he kissed her upturned mouth, skimmed lightly over her full lower lip and the delicate line of her jaw. He glided a finger along her hairline, from her temple to her ear, and followed the same path with his mouth. He loved how she shivered in his arms as he nibbled her lobe and ran his tongue along its outer curve. Conscious of the power in his hands, he trailed them over the indentation of her spine, the curve along the small of her back. John found himself returning to the petal softness of her mouth, unable to keep away from the taste and feel of those luscious lips.

Abruptly, Katherine turned her head aside, and he kissed her cheek instead.

"Stop it!"

John lurched backward. "What's wrong? Did I hurt you?"

"Of course not!" Katherine looked completely frustrated.

John straightened. "Then what's wrong?"

"You're holding back and treating me like glass. I told you I won't break. Do you know how completely frustrating that is sexually?" She bit her lip. "Sorry. I'm just— It's just that I want you so much."

Suddenly she stepped back, unbuttoned her blouse and shrugged out of the sleeves until the garment dropped to the floor. The hall light illuminated skin so silken, so beautiful. Her perfectly sized breasts, covered in a little lacy, red bra, begged for his touch.

"I know exactly what to do so you won't worry about being too rough."

"And what's that?"

Katherine gave him a seductive little smile, which sent his blood pounding that much more. "Now that's something I'll have to show you."

She turned around, fiddled with her bra and tossed it behind her shoulder. Catching it in midair, he watched the sway of her hips and butt in her tight jeans and followed her into her bedroom. She disappeared into the adjoining bathroom and reappeared with several condom packages in her hands. With a smile more wicked than the last, she fanned them in the air and tossed them on the bed.

While John pulled off his sweater, she slipped into her walk-in closet and two seconds later came out with a belt in each hand. He stopped abruptly and took in her lithe frame. There was something mind-blowing about a woman in tight, faded jeans, with a mane of long tousled hair and naked from the waist up.

She ran a hand along the length of one thick, black belt. "It's really simple. We'll tie you up."

CHAPTER 29

KATHERINE SAW JOHN swallow. She'd shocked him. Actually, she'd shocked herself. But the idea was perfect.

John raised a brow. "I don't think so."

"Oh, I beg to differ." She gave him a confident smile. "I think it's a perfect idea. You can't get very physical this way. If you struggle to get loose, you're forewarned."

"Then you'll be the one with all the power."

"But I'll be gentle."

He chucked his pants and underwear and tossed them on the floor with her bra and his sweater. "Is that a promise?"

When he straightened and she got an eyeful of his hard, naked body, Katherine lost her smile along with her ability to think of a coherent reply. To her dismay, she realized John was actually the one with all the control.

"You're beautiful," she whispered, sounding as hungry as he looked.

Growling deep in his throat, John caught her up in his arms and kissed her, deeply, slowly. By the time he drew away, she was panting. Next, he unsnapped her jeans and peeled them from her hips, thighs and legs. As she bent down to help him get them off from around her ankles, he ran a hand over butt, then trailed his fingers lower to dip between her legs.

Oh, God.

Someone groaned. Then Katherine realized it was herself as John dropped to his knees and nudged her legs apart. He ran both thumbs along the seams of her legs, and then brushed the crotch of her panties to one side to play with her clitoris. Katherine latched onto his shoulders with both hands.

"John, please . . ."

He tugged the wisp of lace from around her hips and let it fall to the carpet. She kicked it aside as he edged deeper between her legs.

Right then and there, she thought she was going to die from anticipation.

"Please what?" he whispered, inches away from her skin.

"Please..."

John dipped his head between her legs and lapped, then suckled her clitoris. She inhaled sharply and dug her nails into his shoulders. Ever so slowly, he eased away while he kneaded and squeezed her buttocks.

"What..." He kissed her inner thigh. "...was that you said?"

"Please don't..." She gasped as he slipped a finger inside. "...stop."

The last word was ripped from her lips, but John didn't let up. He relentlessly used his mouth, his hands, his tongue.

Katherine's body tensed from the inside out. Then the pleasure hit, powerful and mind-numbing, and she was shuddering, crying out his name, and climaxing against his mouth. Before her legs buckled from under her, John rose, swept her up in his arms and carried her to the bed where he laid her tenderly down on the mattress.

With her body still shaky and weak, Katherine rose on one elbow. John stood with a knee on the edge of the mattress. Raw sexual awareness smoldered within his slate dark as she rolled onto her hands and knees and prowled toward him.

"It's your turn," she whispered in a husky voice.

Katherine wasn't going to play around. She wanted him as excited as she'd been moments before. She opened her mouth and wrapped her lips around his engorged penis. When her hand glided over his balls, he jerked into her mouth and caught her head in his hands.

"My, God, Katherine. You're tongue—"

She loved the way his voice shook with desire and urgency, the way his hands trembled in her hair, and the way his flesh quivered beneath her touch. To have this much power over a man, to have John shaking with such need sent a new wave of desire rolling through her body.

Slowly, she slipped her mouth from around his erection and kissed the tip. "Lie down."

"No. We should stop."

"You won't hurt me. We'll use the belts."

She ran a hand over the hard line of his hip and looked up into his heated gaze. When it seemed like he wasn't going to give in, she bent and licked slowly up the base to the tip of his penis.

This time John didn't argue but sank onto the pillows. When she found both belts, she lifted his hands above his head and tied a belt to each wrist and thick wooden bedpost. With each click and tug of the leather, Katherine's own excitement rose.

She eased back on her heels. She ran a hungry gaze over the taut lines of John's body, finding it incredibly sexy having him tied up on her bed and—from appearances at least—completely in her power. He was perfectly formed, from his lean and tight muscled chest and flat stomach to his long, powerful legs and... erection, which thrust out from the dark hair at his groin.

Katherine swallowed, suddenly intimidated. She wasn't exactly the most experienced woman around and might even be considered inept at sex by some. But more than anything, this wasn't some sexual game where she'd leave this encounter with her emotions intact.

She loved John.

Even all her uncertainty and fear, though, didn't stop the compulsion to reach over and skim her fingers over the thick, length of him. His flesh, fiery hot against her palm, quivered and hardened even more beneath her touch.

At John's harsh intake of breath, Katherine looked up and met his heavy-lidded gaze. Beyond the heat of sexual awareness in his slate-gray eyes lay something that went far deeper. A new wave of emotion, intense and painful, seized her.

Until now, she'd never realized this was just as serious to John. Nor had she understood just what power she had over him.

Holding his gaze, she straddled his hips and slid on the condom. She watched the corded muscles along his neck tense, the tendons across his chest, forearms and shoulders strain as she slowly, ever so slowly took him inside her, inch by incredible inch. He lifted his buttocks off the mattress and pressed deeper.

She cried out at the sheer pleasure, and her knees clamped harder against his hips.

"Touch yourself."

At his urgent command, she cupped and caressed her breasts and watched John's eyes darken with hunger and his chest shudder. She was turning him on. But even though it thrilled her, she craved the touch of his hand, his lips, the warmth of his arms around her. She closed her eyes and slid her hands over her stomach, her hips and between her legs, imagining they were John's hands on her instead.

"You're beautiful."

John's husky baritone washed over her as she flung back her head and let desire take over every thought and action. She closed her eyes and slowly, surely rode him, barely aware of the creak or movement of the mattress beneath their weight.

At the sound of cracking and tearing, Katherine paused and opened her eyes. John had pulled the leather belts from the bedposts. With the leather still wrapped around his wrists, John sat up, caught her around the waist and wrapped her legs around his hips. Katherine whimpered and grabbed his shoulders. Thighs splayed, she arched into his thrust. Stretching her even wider than before, he twisted his hips in a way that rubbed against her clitoris and pulled a cry of pleasure from her lips.

"I tried. I just couldn't keep away," he whispered, brushing the damp strands of her hair from her neck before sliding his hand lower to trail an imaginary line around the curve and underside of her breast. He lowered his hand yet further. "I love how you're so sensitive, the way your stomach quivers from my touch."

She looked down to his hand, fingers spread out against her pale skin, and how her stomach trembled beneath his palm. The way they were joined so intimately, the feel of him inside her, the touch of his mouth against the curve of her neck—everything—made her simply melt.

Closing her eyes, Katherine reveled in the feel of his mouth, his tongue, of his hard body against her softer curves, of how he whispered those little love words in her hair. His lips were incredibly gentle against her neck, her shoulder as he used strong, capable hands on her back, her flank, her hip, kneading, stroking, urging her faster, harder.

With each incredible thrust of his hips, Katherine cried out in pleasure. She clutched at his sweat-coated shoulders and back. The tempo quickened, pushed her on, closer, closer until she was coming, shattering in his arms. Then John was right behind her, clasping her hips, shuddering, calling out her name.

Groaning, John sank back on the mattress and pulled her down along with him. Katherine sprawled on top of his chest, tangled her legs with his, and sighed with pure contentment. She rested a cheek against his very big, very hard shoulder.

"I told you so," she said with a smile, feeling completely wicked as she watched John tug off the broken belts from around his wrists. "You didn't hurt me a bit. All your fears were groundless."

"You know, I don't like getting the standard 'I told you so'."

Katherine pulled away and gaped at John's grim expression. Suddenly grabbing her at the waist, he flipped her on her back, propped his head up with a hand and he glared down at her.

"I won't stand for it."

The guy was nuts. Katherine's mouth gaped wider before she snapped it shut. "If you think you can talk to me in that—"

"Nope. No talking back. You've been rude and now you need to be punished."

Then John struck. He moved in on her ribs with lightning speed. His fingers, gentle but relentless, tickled her sides.

The moment he found the spot beneath her armpits,

Katherine broke into uncontrollable laughter and squirmed wildly around on the bed.

"Stop—" Another fit of giggles hit. "Stop!"

He stopped—for the moment. This time, it was John who had the decidedly wicked smile. "Promise me you'll never tell me 'I told you so' again?"

"I promise!" She gulped in a mouthful of air.

"Good." He had the audacity to tweak her nose. "Now that I've got you thoroughly breathless, I'll leave you to rest up for a bit. I need to clean up and have a shower before I use another one of your condoms. I think we'll try one of the flavored ones."

"You wish!" Rising on an elbow, she flung a pillow at his back before he disappeared into the bathroom, while his deep, throaty chuckle drifted back to her.

Smiling, Katherine plopped her head back against her pillow and stared up at the ceiling. She needed to take a shower, but she wanted to savor this feeling of pure, inundated happiness. With John she felt feminine, incredibly sexy, smart—she could go on and on. And with all that latent strength, John still managed to be incredibly tender.

Far too quickly the muffled noise of a door closing from another townhouse forced Katherine to acknowledge the reality of the outside world, and with that reality, happiness, fleeting yet extraordinary, withered. They could only stay in her apartment and ignore the danger from her uncle for so long.

When she heard the water turn on, she slipped from the bed. As she stepped into the bathroom, she watched John showering in the cubical. Memories rushed back of how she'd walked in on him in another bathroom. Since then, everything and nothing had changed.

John's life and the lives of the kids at the shelter were still at risk. She also had a new love and an unexpected glimpse of happiness, which terrified her, because both could be ripped away before she even had the opportunity to appreciate either.

When she slipped inside and closed the shower door, John, rinsing his hair, stepped from under the water.

"What's wrong?" he asked.

"Everything. For a moment, I managed to forget the shelter, my uncle, all of it. Being with you was perfect, but now——"

"I know."

"And I still have so many questions. I got completely distracted when that car backfired and you ran outside." She trailed a finger along his temple. "Like the name you used. Clark Kent. Why that name? It's almost like a joke when you think of what you can do and the resemblance to the character."

John's lips lifted into a wry smile. "It was a running joke at work. At one point, I thought 'what the heck.' If everyone thought I looked so much like Clark Kent, I'd give them a show. I replaced my wire-rimmed glasses with a pair of black, thick-framed ones, slicked back my hair and wore these god-awful polyester suits for a while."

"So that explains those ugly glasses you had."

John raised a brow and tweaked her nose. "I didn't think they were so ugly. The hair and the suit—now that was ugly. But anyway, my co-workers had to do one better by getting me a fake driver's license with the name of Clark Kent. I'd annoy the hell out of them when they'd be having a particularly difficult time reading an X-ray. I'd run into their department, all smiles, wearing my glasses and flashing my fake license, and tell them I'd save their sorry asses, because I was a superhero, ready to save the day."

John's smile turned sad, and his eyes darkened to smoky gray. "But that's the past. They're all gone now."

"I'm sorry," Katherine whispered, edging closer and sliding a palm tenderly against his damp cheek as the shower's warm mist hung in the air around them.

Briefly, he closed his eyes. "Yes, well..." He cleared his throat and blinked twice. ""Anyway... I got rid of the suit and the slicked hair, but I kept the license and glasses. After the experiments on myself, I didn't need a prescription, but I changed the lenses to glass and continued wearing them. I didn't want anyone suspecting what I was up to."

"All this time you've had no one to turn to or trust." Katherine shook her head in amazement. "You've gone through so much——"

"No more than you," John said, his voice rough with emotion, his expression intense. "But you're wrong about not having anyone to trust. There's always been you."

This time it was Katherine who blinked several times. It wasn't the shower's steam that made her eyes mist over but John's unfailing belief in her.

"And we'll come out of this on top." John brushed his lips across her brow. "That's a promise."

"I hope so."

"I know so."

Katherine wished she could sound and look as confident, but the future held too many uncertainties.

"It'll be okay, you'll see," John assured her one last time before he gathered her into his arms and held her under the water's warm spray.

With slow and incredibly soothing hands, he first shampooed and conditioned her hair, and then washed her body. After he grabbed a towel from the rack and dried the moisture from her torso and limbs, he swept her up in his arms and carried her to bed.

John turned off all the lights, double checked the locks, closed all the blinds and finally joined her. Beneath a cocoon of darkness, Katherine snuggled under the covers and against the comforting, warmth of John's body.

"I don't want you leaving my side tomorrow," John's whisper ruffled the fine hairs by her brow.

Even though John's face and body melded into shadow, she heard the fear in his voice.

"I have that gala event for my mother. That's something I can't miss. Everyone would get suspicious if I didn't make an appearance. I always show my support by going to my mother's events."

John sighed, but after a moment, he said, "Actually, that'll probably be the safest place for you. I'll meet up with you later in the evening after I get into your mother's headquarters and pull those files. You've already found sufficient evidence to incriminate your mother, but we need leverage against your uncle. There's got to be something more. But with what you've found—if any of it gets out and the police are notified, a criminal investigation will result."

At the hesitation in his voice, Katherine realized the implication and how her mother would be ruined politically and personally. Panic twisted her stomach into a tight knot. "I need to know the truth."

"And if it's worse than you imagined?"

Feeling torn, Katherine struggled for an answer. "I guess I'll have to deal with it then."

"You might know everything by tomorrow." John's husky warning hung in the air as he slid a reassuring hand along her arm. "But we'll get through this. Together. I'll always be there for you. I love you."

His last words whispered against her brow as he tenderly kissed her temple. Katherine closed her eyes and pressed deeper into the crook of his arm.

"I love you, too. And you're right. We'll get through this..."

But how would she feel tomorrow in the harsh light of day? No longer a little girl who believed in fairy tales, Katherine knew real life rarely involved happy endings.

She dreaded the morning. With the death of Miranda, she'd thought she'd lost her innocence, but now she wasn't so sure. Within twenty-four hours, she might lose far more...

CHAPTER 30

HUNCHED OVER SHARON Spalding's desk, John slowly closed her top drawer. A noise, short and faint, carried through the building and into the office. John snapped off his penlight, straightened and glanced over his shoulder at the blackened doorway leading into the hall.

Must be the wind hitting the shattered window and damaged wall.

Earlier, using the cloud filled night as camouflage, he'd searched the outside premises of Sharon's political headquarters for a way to bypass the building's security system. Suspecting the window at the back of the building, too small for a human body to slip through, lacked an alarm, John had broken the glass. He'd used the gap as leverage and pulled the brick and cement from the wall. Then careful of his formal dinner suit and winter jacket he wore for later in the evening, he'd slipped through the opening and found himself in a restroom.

Another sound.

John froze. A scrape. A small shuffle. No. Not the wind. Something far different.

Glancing to the files on Sharon's desk, John decided to leave them for now. He crept across the carpeted floor and listened over the pounding of his heart.

Breathing. A footstep.

John moved into the hall, which led to the back of the building. Up ahead lay a doorway and deeper shadows, but John remembered walking through a luncheon area. Alert now, he peered into the darkness and focused past the doorway. Separating and deciphering the shadows from each other, he made out a counter across the wall, a microwave and the edge of a chrome table and chair.

But no movement.

Yet.

He inched further down the hall, hearing the rustle of clothing, a harsh whisper, quick, agitated breathing. A person stood behind the partially opened back door.

"Someone's broken in."

John froze. He'd heard that voice before.

"You should see the wall," the man whispered. "It looks like someone took a chainsaw to the thing. It's got to be him. Who else? I'm not going inside—"

The person must be on a cell phone; John didn't detect anyone else as he moved across the lunchroom. And that voice...

"Well, what if it's him?" The man swore under his breath. "Yeah, okay, okay. You've made your point."

John edged along the wall and closer to the back entrance.

"All right, already." The man muttered another four-letter word. "I'll deal with everything here, but you said yourself that you'd take care of your end tonight. We all know the scientist's hard to kill off, but she isn't."

Each word, each syllable whispered into the room but screamed into John's brain. John clutched the wall. Horror slammed into him, splintering his thoughts, numbing his limbs, and crushing his chest with the sheer weight of it.

They planned on killing Katherine tonight.

The door eased open. A man stepped inside.

Still off-balance at the man's words, John reacted slowly, awkwardly. He pushed off the wall with the heel of his hand.

The intruder turned. John instantly recognized him as the man in Spalding's house the day he'd stolen inside the estate. Jason, he recalled—Spalding's weak-chinned, hooked-nosed henchman, a tall, bony man, who didn't look like he'd be physically capable of harming a microorganism, never mind a person.

John glanced down and sucked in air.

The other man held a gun. John quickly changed his mind. The creep looked very capable of harming someone.

Jason fired. A flash of light. The smell of gunpowder. The bullet arrowed toward John.

Twisting, John pivoted to the side, dodging the bullet by mere centimeters. Then he lunged toward the other man.

In alarm, Jason's mouth gaped open. John hit him in the face with a fist. The man's mouth sagged wider, and the gun flew out of his hand. John caught the weapon in mid-air and watched Jason crumble into an ungainly heap on the floor.

After John set the gun down on the counter behind him, he glanced back to Spalding's henchman. Jason hadn't moved. John nudged him with a toe, but the man still didn't stir. Realizing he might have actually killed him, John hunched down by the body and checked for a pulse.

Yes. Definitely there.

John exhaled. He didn't want murder on his conscious, but he *did* want the creep alive and awake. The bastard knew tonight's plans. John needed that information.

Hunching down, mindful of the power in his hand, he gently slapped the man's cheek. Head lulling to one side, Jason remained unconscious.

"Damn it."

John sprang to his feet, grabbed a glass in one of the cabinets and filled it with tap water. He tossed the contents into the creep's face. Not even a flicker of movement.

Glaring down at Jason, he brushed his hair back from his brow. He was wasting time. He couldn't stay here indefinitely with Katherine across town with a killer.

He rummaged through the drawers, found some thick, durable packing tape, and bound Jason's ankles and wrists behind his back. John thought of tying him even more securely in case Jason managed to get free and go running to Spalding, but he didn't dare waste another minute.

John dropped the tape's empty cardboard ring by the discarded cell phone. Something—a hunch, instinct, gut feeling—whatever—made him pick up the phone and scroll down its menu. He punched the button to retrieve the last received call and then dialed the number.

He waited tensely. On the third ring, someone answered.

"Hello?"

John frowned. The person on the other end wasn't Spalding.

"Jason, is that you?"

He didn't answer—even if he wanted to. Shock affixed the words to his throat.

"Jason?"

A long, thick pause of silence followed. Then the connection died.

But John heard enough to recognize the person. And it scared the hell out of him.

He and Katherine never suspected. Never would have. They'd been so damn clueless, and now Katherine was in that house, vulnerable, unsuspecting, and blind to the truth.

Holy Shit.

~~*~~

Katherine stood tensely along the edge of the room and watched the dance floor in the midst of over two dozen tables slowly filling with people. Waiters impeccably dressed in black and white uniforms cleared the last course. Chandeliers glittered from above, while candlelight glowed on tables draped in crisp, white linen, highlighting centerpieces of fresh cut flowers in wispy shades of pink and lavender. Their floral scent teased the air while the slow beat of music played over the hum of voices and laughter.

The setting, romantic, expensive and surprisingly unpretentious considering the $10,000 per person contribution needed for the evening, contradicted the storm of emotions raging within Katherine.

So far she'd managed to avoid her uncle, but she'd caught him watching her over the course of the evening. And each time their gazes clashed, she'd been the first to glance away, finding his look too threatening, too disturbing to hold his gaze for long.

Rolling tense shoulders, Katherine glanced over to the doorway, which led to the front entrance of the house, and searched the crowded room. No sign of John. She thought he'd be here sooner.

Unless something happened...

No. Impossible. John wouldn't let anyone get in his way. He stood by his promises, an anchor of stability and strength Katherine desperately needed. All too quickly, he'd entangled himself into her life so thoroughly that she didn't see a future or a possibility of happiness without him.

When she glanced back at the doorway, she thought of the hidden closet in her uncle's bedroom. For hours she'd been battling the urge to sneak upstairs and pull the company paperwork on Kirkwood and Harvest Associates. She remembered the combination but hadn't yet had the opportunity. That is, until now. She hadn't seen her uncle for the last fifteen minutes and everyone else seemed occupied long enough for her to slip away for a couple of minutes.

"Hey, Katherine. You can relax. The evening's almost over."

When she turned around and found David, she hid her disappointment with a smile. "I didn't realize I was that obvious."

"God, no. Probably the only reason I can tell is because I feel the same way. You'd think we'd both be used to it by now." He shrugged a shoulder. "Oh, well. Here. This should help."

He held two glasses and offered her the fluted one. At her questioning look, he explained. "Champagne. I, on the other hand, prefer something a bit stronger—like a good, expensive glass of scotch. Especially when my father's footing the bill."

"Thanks."

Katherine sipped her drink and watched David's profile as he looked out over the huge hall. She'd never been particularly close to David. Probably because their interests were far too diverse to have anything in common. Articulate, always immaculately groomed, a trial lawyer in pursuit of fame and his own fortune, he possessed the characteristics her mother fawned over and found sadly lacking in her daughter. With a perfect nephew like David, no wonder her mother considered Katherine a disappointment.

"Cheers. To a successful evening." Her cousin lifted his glass in a toast.

"It's not over yet."

"Close enough."

After taking a long, deep swallow of champagne, she nodded at her half-empty glass. "I think I needed this."

"I'd like to take the credit, but it was my father's idea. He got sidetracked by a guest and asked me to do him the favor. He thought you could use a drink."

Before she had a chance to work out David's words or her uncle's motives, a man materialized by her other side.

She turned. Standing inches from her elbow, Paul Spalding smiled down at her. She couldn't smile back, couldn't do anything for several seconds but stare back as she grappled for self-control.

All evening she'd managed to avoid the man so why did her luck have to run out now?

"Oh, I better go," David said.

No. This couldn't be happening. Her luck hadn't just run out—it had crashed and burned.

"I see my wife, and I can't ignore that look on her face. She's in desperate need of rescuing." David touched Katherine's elbow in parting before he left her alone to deal with his father.

Panic. The sheer force of it momentarily cut off her breath.

Get a hold of yourself.

She grasped her glass, started to take a drink, but decided against it. Her uncle might have put something in it. He had every opportunity. As to motive—

Her panic escalated to new heights.

No. You will not give him the satisfaction of seeing how frightened you are.

"As always, you're looking good tonight, Katherine."

Nodding, slowly dragging in a lungful of fortifying air, she turned and met Paul's cold gaze.

~~*~~

"Can't you move this thing faster?"

Sitting in the back seat of a taxi, John, in mounting frustration and anger, watched the vehicle inch through traffic.

"Hey, Buddy. Give me a break. I'm not some friggin' superhero. Take a look around," the driver tossed over his shoulder, disgust evident in his voice. "There's obviously an accident up ahead. Hell. It's not like I can take the sidewalk."

He muttered something else John didn't catch, but he didn't care. All he cared about was the man's driving. And his driving wasn't getting John anywhere any time soon.

Irritated, John shifted on the vinyl seat and watched the lane of traffic to the left move forward.

Even with his powers—characteristics admired in any fictionalized superhero—John was helpless, unable to get to Katherine's side fast enough.

What type of hero did that make him?

John grunted in self-disgust. He was far from a hero. He'd let his superior abilities inflate his ego and blind him to reality.

But he'd always been a self-important fool. His parents, both from the scientific community, encouraged his every move when they learned of his interest in the sciences. They'd left his sister, Margot, to flounder while they'd praised and fawned over him, their darling little boy. Faculty and then co-workers considered him gifted, and he let their praise encourage his self-absorption.

Then his world had been ripped savagely from beneath his feet because of Miltronics. Those teenage boys... They'd never stood a chance—

John blinked rapidly, rubbed at the bridge of his nose, and cleared his throat. Guilt. Years wouldn't be enough to get it out of his system.

How Katherine saw him in such a favorable light amazed him. She'd always believed in him, and he found her complete faith humbling, because he knew he'd never done anything to warrant it.

No, he wasn't some hero, and he sure as hell wasn't in some comic strip with a fictitious villain. The danger to Katherine was far too genuine.

John couldn't—no—wouldn't fail her.

Somehow he'd get across town and to Spalding's estate in time. He'd thought the quickest way was by cab through the freeway system and surface roads. He'd never tried running for any length of time or thought he'd hold the same speed as a car, but at this point, John was liable to try anything.

He glanced down to Jason's cell phone in his hand. Hitting the menu button, he illuminated its face and the time. Just over thirty minutes since he'd left Sharon's headquarters. Too much time. Too many possibilities of something going wrong.

Fear. He tasted it against the back of his throat, experienced it in every tendon of his body—actually felt ill from it.

The traffic on his left moved ahead two car lengths. Frowning, he glanced down at the cell again. Another minute.

"Get in the left lane," John ordered. "It's going faster."

"Bud, how about you keep that trap closed and save your opinions for someone else. Or better yet, if you're in such a damn hurry, why don't you walk?"

"Good idea."

John grabbed the handle and opened the door.

"Hey, what are you doing? You gotta wait until I pull to the side—You crazy fool!" The cab jerked to a stop as John placed a foot on the pavement. "You haven't even paid me! Take another step, and I'll call the cops!"

"Oh. Sorry."

John slapped at his coat pockets until he found his wallet. He threw a couple of twenties into the driver's area but didn't wait around to see where they landed.

"Idiot. What a—"

John didn't pay attention to the cabby's last words as he slammed the taxi door. Metal groaned. He cringed, knowing he'd broken something. The cabbie started screaming. Any second and the driver would get out and start pointing at him. The police would get involved. Time would be wasted.

He grabbed his wallet, took the last of the cash, reopened the cab door and threw the bills inside. Another minute wasted.

More screaming, but John didn't care as he pivoted around.

He needed to get to Katherine. A horn blasted. A car came at him from the other direction. He sucked in his breath, twisted and pulled himself away from the car's grill. Metal nicked his hip. The car swept past, the heat from its engine smacking his exposed skin.

Another round of screaming. This time from someone else. Too much noise. Too much chaos.

Breathing heavily, chest pounding, he leaped to the other side of the road. Unharmed.

Another minute wasted.

Then John ran. Ran across busy intersections, dark alleys, snow-covered yards and dirt packed parking lots. Minutes relentlessly ticked by. Minutes, which brought the future perilously closer. At this very moment, John never felt more powerless.

CHAPTER 31

HER UNCLE MIGHT think she looked good tonight, but Katherine couldn't say the same for him. He appeared haggard—his band of brown hair dull, his face and bald patch sallow. Even his cheekbones seemed sunken.

Good.

He deserved sleepless nights. No. He deserved so much more. He deserved to feel Jeffrey and Brian's pain, to experience their horror right before their deaths. She stared at Paul and wondered how he could be so immoral and such a—

"Sick bastard."

Her words, unconsciously spoken aloud, hung in the air between them. Paul grabbed her wrist. Eyes narrowed with fury, he flexed the fingers of his other hand. She hitched her chin up. He wouldn't dare hit her here.

Katherine yanked at her arm, but Paul didn't let go. He dug his fingers deeper into her flesh, pressing yet harder when she didn't react.

"Is anything wrong?"

Her father appeared at her side. Katherine didn't answer as she stared at Paul. This time she didn't intend to be the first to look away.

"No. Of course not." Paul released her arm, stepped back and glanced over to her father.

Katherine ignored the urge to cradle her arm against her stomach; she wasn't about to give her uncle the satisfaction of showing how much he'd hurt her.

"Are you sure?"

She turned and met her father's questioning gaze. "Positive."

"Well, you seemed upset. I hope it wasn't because you were trying to get Paul to contribute to the Morning Dove."

"Of course not!" Katherine denied.

"Good. I know how much that shelter's been consuming your life. You know, you tend to force it on everyone in the family."

At her father's uncalled for taunt, she lifted her brows. "It never seemed to bother you before."

"A person can take only so much."

Katherine stiffened. She hadn't expected this from her father. "You should have said something."

"I guess my patience's finally run out from your continued obsession with the Morning Dove," her father retorted, his voice loud and fierce. "You've ignored your friends and family because of it. Now it's hurting you financially, and still, you continue. You know, you're letting this shelter distort your judgment."

"My judgment?"

"Yes," Spalding interrupted. "You're so fixated with the Morning Dove that you're letting it affect your health. It's not worth ruining your life," he insisted, raising his voice even louder than her father and causing several heads to turn in their way. "Just don't do anything drastic. Come to us first."

Katherine frowned. Her uncle's behavior was all wrong. When she met his bland expression, she realized then that he was orchestrating something—something that involved her. Fear, raw and unmistakable, scraped up her spine, and she stepped back from both men.

Suddenly, nausea surged into her stomach. Katherine clutched her middle with her free hand, willing the sensation away as she slowly inhaled and exhaled. Now was not the time to let her nerves get the better of her.

"Are you all right?"

Katherine didn't believe her uncle's look of concern.

Gently, her father rubbed her upper back. "What's wrong? Are you feeling ill?"

"It's my stomach." Abruptly, the queasiness vanished as quickly as it materialized. Her nerves were obviously a mess. She dropped her hand to her side and shook her head. "It's nothing. I'll be fine."

"Good." Her father offered her his elbow. "How about we forget the Morning Dove, and you give your old man a dance around the floor. You know, they're playing something slow and old-fashioned."

"Sure." Anything to put some distance between Paul and herself. She looked around for a place to set her drink.

"Here. Give your glass to Paul. He'll have one of the waiters take care of it. Isn't that right?"

"Of course."

Katherine gave Paul her glass. His hand, cool and dry, brushed against her fingers. Smothering the urge to shake off the feel of his touch from her hand, she clasped her father's arm and let him lead her through the tables to the center of the room.

Unable to relax, she circled the dance floor with her father. As other couples flowed and ebbed around them, she caught a glimpse of her uncle standing where they'd left him, her drink still in his hand. Then he disappeared when more dancers merged onto the floor. Somehow Katherine found his departure more threatening than if he'd continued watching her.

Someone nudged her elbow. A woman's high, piercing laugh hit her ears. Bodies edged closer, trapping her, shrinking the little space they had on the floor. Arms, shoulders, heads of the crowd swayed and shimmered. She blinked as the strong tang of cologne mixed with the sweet, cloying scent of perfume wafted across her nose. Her stomach twisted and rolled with nausea.

Stumbling, Katherine clutched her father's shoulder. He clasped her elbow and pulled back.

"Are you sure you're okay?"

She grimaced, embarrassed. Even though she'd only had two glasses of champagne, she felt drunk. She should never have had alcohol on a nervous and empty stomach.

"I don't know."

Katherine staggered to an abrupt stop. Someone collided against her back, but her father steadied her.

"Here. We need to get you outside and into some fresh air. You look pale and clammy. We'll go through the game room. That way, we'll avoid anyone asking questions."

With the help of her father's much-needed arm for support, Katherine focused on getting her feet to move in front of her and ignored how the walls in the hall tilted back and forth. Somehow they slipped into the game room and away from the public without any embarrassing mishaps.

Then she realized something frightening. Maybe it wasn't a nervous stomach or too much to drink that made her feel like passing out. Maybe it was because of something in her drink.

Uncle Paul.

He'd given her the drink through his son. But he'd have to be crazy. All those people around. All those witnesses...

Katherine tried to open her mouth to speak, to warn her father as he opened the door to the back yard and ushered her outside. The moment the frigid air touched her face, Katherine's legs collapsed from under her. Blinding light slashed across her vision. At the last minute, she flung a hand out to protect her head from taking the brunt of her fall against the cement.

Then nothing.

~~*~~

Lungs screaming in protest, John slowed to a walk when he reached the perimeter of the Spalding property. He strode up the drive with legs weak from running what must have been close to a damn marathon. He forcibly tapped down his ragged breathing—and the fear, which, if he let it, would corrode any clear thinking, and right now he desperately needed to count on his wits.

With a trembling hand, he raked back his hair and cleared his throat. He passed a valet dressed in a formal black and white uniform. Windows from the ground floor blazed out onto the snow-crusted lawn, while the porch light, a miniature version of the huge chandelier in the foyer, illuminated a man stationed at the front door. On the bottom step of the broad, shallow steps stood a couple, no doubt, waiting for the valet to retrieve their car.

As John reached the porch, a six-foot wall of muscle and man stepped forward and blocked the front door.

"Your invitation?"

The guy's face consisted of one large slab of flesh. The flat nose, cheeks and brow looked as if they'd received a brutal fist pounding.

"I don't have one."

"Then I need your name."

Impatiently, John watched the hulk glanced down at the clipboard in his hand. He had no intention of giving this guy his name. No doubt, Spalding had already pre-warned security of his possible appearance. "It's not going to be there. But if you let Katherine Spalding know Clark's here, you'll see I'm more than welcome."

The man's eyes narrowed. From the dull glimmer in their depths, it looked like the many whacks to his head had reduced his I.Q.

Grunting, the hulk grabbed for his radio at his belt but stopped. "Hey, wait a sec."

John stiffened and watched the guard shuffle through the clipboard's pages and stop. Right there. Smack in the middle of the page and perfectly illuminated by the chandelier's light was a picture of John's face. He didn't need to see the words written beside the photo, because from the way the hulk's face twisted into a frown, John guessed they weren't complimentary.

John sighed, not seeing any other option. He glanced over his shoulder. Squinting into the darkness, separating and clarifying the shadows around him, he searched for the valet and anyone within sight. Finding no one, he turned back around just as the hulk glanced up. John tapped a fist into the brute's face. With the look of recognition still stamped on his flat face, the man crumpled, shaking the cement beneath John's feet.

~~*~~

Katherine became aware of the floor, hard and cold, beneath her and the purr of a car's engine. Pain throbbed into her right shoulder and her hip while gas and oil fumes assailed her. Flat on her back, she opened her eyes and blinked, trying to focus. The light. It burned into her eyes and forced her lids closed. But she'd seen and smelled enough.

Her uncle's garage.

"She's coming too."

She tried to lift a hand, a leg. Nothing. Her limbs lay paralyzed and useless at her side.

"That can't be. You said she wouldn't wake up."

"Don't worry. She'll be out of it again in a minute."

The slap of flesh against flesh carried over the car's engine. Pain cut into her cheek as her head snapped to the side. Katherine opened her eyes and found her uncle peering down at her.

"That's for calling me a bastard." He sneered. "How's it feel to be on the receiving end this time?"

"My, God! What the hell are you doing! Don't mark her. This is supposed to look like a suicide."

Katherine closed her eyes. That voice. No. She didn't want to believe it.

"I know what I'm doing," Paul retorted. "She's not going to bruise. I slapped her just hard enough for her to feel it. She deserves it. I've always hated how she looks at me. She's not any better than me."

"You better be right. I'm not going to prison. I'd rather die."

"Shut up and help me here."

Hands clasped Katherine beneath her arms and around her ankles. She felt the sway of her body, the air against her back as she was lifted and twisted around. Then something cool pressed against her back and legs.

Again she managed to open her eyes. She was being set inside the front seat of her car. A different face wavered in front of her. Katherine stared back in horror. Her protest came out as a strangled whimper.

"Ah. You're surprised." Her father smiled somewhat sadly. "But you didn't give me any choice. I tried everything to shut down the Morning Dove, but you were blocking me every step of the way."

He hit a button on the side of the driver's door, and the window whispered open. "Don't worry. This will be completely painless. The GHB Paul put in your drink will do its work and the carbon monoxide will do the rest. By the time you're found, the drug will be undetectable in your system. People will assume a suicide. After all, you were deeply depressed over the shelter."

Katherine shut her eyes, not wanting to see or believe. But she couldn't shut her ears to his words.

"I know. How could I kill my own daughter?" Her father's breath floated sinuously into her ear. "But you see, you're not my daughter. Your dear mother screwed around when we were first married. I didn't know about it until years later. By then, I didn't care. I'd been doing the same. What man wouldn't? You can't get much colder than her. But I decided to stick it out anyway. Money can be a great motivator."

Katherine heard the words, but didn't respond, didn't feel the horror or shock, because she was slumping sideways and spiraling back into unconsciousness. One fleeting thought registered before her mind completely shut down.

She was going to die, and strangely, it didn't seem to matter.

CHAPTER 32

A FTER CHECKING THE security guard's pulse and pulling him behind several bushes alongside the house, John brushed flecks of snow and dirt from his sleeves. He started back to the front door but backed up and shrugged out of his winter jacket. He placed it over the guard. Maybe a stupid move, but John didn't want another innocent death on his hand. Or maybe the guard wasn't so innocent.

Well, it didn't matter. What mattered was finding and getting Katherine out of this place.

Once inside, he casually walked down the hall toward the heavy drone of voices and past yet another flat faced guard who'd been hired for his bulk rather than his brain. At least John blended in with the other contributors, having the forethought to dress in formal wear before arriving at Sharon's office.

He paused beneath an arched doorway, which led into a huge hall—possibly a ballroom at one time—and searched the tables for Katherine's golden hair. He didn't see her anywhere, but he did see the man dressed in elegant black and white behind a podium and to the side of a small orchestra.

Spalding.

"As will anyone attest who knows me," Spalding was saying, "I'm completely inept at public speeches, so I will quickly step aside and give the floor over to a person, who I consider not only a family member, but more importantly a friend, Sharon Spalding."

An enthusiastic wave of applause swept through the room. Spalding stepped from the podium, wiped his hands down the sides of his dinner jacket, and folded them behind his back. John frowned. Spalding's movements seemed stilted. Gaze narrowing, magnifying the distance between them, John focused.

Sweat glistened off the man's brow, and his fingers shook when he brushed at his jacket. Nerves from talking in front of a crowd? John didn't think so as he watched Spalding walk to his table and glanced repeatedly at another doorway to the left of John. The way Spalding kept peering at that empty doorway seemed odd.

Something was going on.

More alarmed than ever, John, careful to keep out of Spalding's line of vision, again searched the large, banquet room while moving along its perimeter. Still unable to find Katherine, he focused on the voices and attempted to distinguish Katherine's from all the others. When he came up empty, he closed his eyes. Blocking out Sharon Spalding's voice and the murmured encouragement from the audience, he listened to any discernible sound from beyond the huge hall.

The tick of a grandfather clock, the whirl of a toilet flushing, a woman's snide comment on her husband's Botox treatment, the throb of a car's engine and possibly a dishwashing machine, the caterer's in the kitchen arguing—

Damn it. Still nothing. There were far too many background noises and voices to distinguish one from the other accurately.

He was wasting too much time. Quickly, methodically, and as inconspicuously as possible, John searched the ground floor. When he found nothing unusual, he rushed up the stairs, past the repaired handrail, down the empty hallway and into the east wing of the second floor. He forced himself to slow down and use his senses to their optimum capacity. He didn't encounter anyone, which was good, because he didn't have a plausible excuse to be roaming around in this part of the house.

When he still didn't find any sign of Katherine on the second floor, he started to panic.

Control yourself. Now. Think.

Then John heard it. He froze, standing in one of the bedrooms in the west wing, and listened closer.

There. A cry, faint but distinct. He focused harder. Someone yelling. Another voice. Angry. Softly spoken. Deadly.

Spalding.

John sped down the hall, grabbed the stair railing and hurtled over the top. Knees bent, hands outstretched on either side for balance, he landed on the marble tile on steady, sure feet. Rising, he turned. And froze.

John stared back at the same security guard he'd hit in the face. Standing feet away, the man looked fully conscious...and fully angry.

"Holy shit."

~~*~~

Katherine woke up. Something dug into her ribs as she lay slumped on her side. Varying shades of gray pressed down around her. With muscles weak and unsteady, she pushed herself up on one elbow and glanced down. Despite the shadows, she recognized the console between the two seats of her car.

She pushed herself completely up. Sudden nausea flared and rolled through her stomach. She gasped, clutching the steering column as her vision tilted and danced wildly. Pain dug into her temples and brow. Taking slow, shallow breaths, she didn't move for several long and uncomfortable moments.

Eventually, the queasiness receded, and she carefully eased around at the waist and glanced over her shoulder. Artificial light seeped in through small, arched windows along the top of one wall. No. It wasn't a wall, but a garage door.

She was in her uncle's garage and in her car. Fleeting, fog coated memories stirred in her head. Something about her uncle, but more importantly her father. She tried to wade through the disturbing visions but couldn't grasp their meaning.

Then Katherine became aware of the rumble of the car,

the sealed garage and the danger. When their meaning sank in, her memory sharpened with terrifying clarity. Her father, her uncle—both wanted her dead. With each breath, each moment of inaction, the carbon monoxide cut off more oxygen to her brain, slowly, surely suffocating her.

She fumbled with the key in the ignition for several long, agonizing minutes. Finally after the third attempt, she wrapped her fingers around the metal. She turned and pulled the key from the ignition and immediately dropped it. She watched the key land on the floor by her feet, which seemed near impossible to reach from her position with her motor skills near to zilch.

Exhausted from the entire experience, and even knowing she needed to get out of the car and garage before she passed out again, Katherine, slumped deeper into her seat. The feat of getting out of the garage seemed inordinately difficult. If she rested her head against the seat and closed her eyes, everything would be just fine. All she had to—

No. Deadly gas fumes still permeated the air. If she lost consciousness now, she'd never wake up.

She thought of hitting the horn to get someone's attention but realized the stupidity of it. The odds of attracting her uncle or father's attention far outweighed the chance of getting some unsuspecting guest. If either man came out, they were liable to kill her in a far more gruesome manner.

Struggling to focus, Katherine blinked and stared out the windshield. She noticed the small, rectangular panel, darker than the rest of the wall, but it took a moment for her brain to grasp the simple idea.

The switch to the garage door. She needed to hit the button to open the garage door for air—and focus long enough to actually do it.

With the aid of a shoulder, she opened the door. The second she stepped onto the pavement, her legs buckled and her peripheral vision darkened and thickened. Feeling herself about to pass out, she latched onto the open door. Please. She couldn't faint. She just needed a little longer. Hanging onto the car for a long, woozy moment, she managed to remain conscious.

She blinked again and grappled for strength. When it felt like she'd regained some control over her muscles, she surged from the car's hood to the wall and slammed a palm against the rectangular panel. She hit the garage button and then flipped on the light switch beside it.

Lightheaded, nauseous, Katherine floundered and caught a hand against the ladder hanging the length of one wall. The metal clanged against the wall. She winced at the noise and the sudden glare from the garage's harsh fluorescent lighting. The garage door rumbled opened, and Katherine, too exhausted to be relieved, sank to the cement to rest against the wall.

Cold air caught against the film of sweat across her brow, neck and spine and sent a chill racing up her back. She shivered. Blessed air, frigid and oh, so beautiful rushed into the garage, dispersing car exhaust and sweeping into her lungs. Loving the texture, the crisp feel of the winter air, she inhaled again and again, and with each inhalation, her mind grew lucid and her dizziness subsided.

But with the fog easing, images of the past took on more substance and with it a horrifying reality. Her father. Involved all this time. Katherine raised her knees and clamped her arms around her legs. She wanted to be dumb and blind to her father's betrayal, wanted to pretend the drug in her system had turned her delusional. Ducking, she brushed a cheek against her knee to wipe away the tears.

And what of John? What had they done to him? He should have shown up. Had her father and uncle killed him? A thick, painful lump caught at her throat.

She couldn't think that. The thought of losing John after just finding a man like him was unspeakable.

Ernest. Compassionate. Unique. A rare man of principle. John possessed all those traits and so much more. He was too strong, too filled with life to have it all come to an end.

Well, it wasn't going to happen. She was going to make sure neither man touched John. Using the wall for aid, she rose. Her legs quivered beneath the strain, and the floor and walls tilted right, then left. Afraid of falling, she placed a palm against the car's hood for support. Standing, between the wall and the car, she took another fortifying breath of night air and edged toward the door.

Was she nuts? How could she hope to help John if she couldn't even walk right?

Just then, the knob on the door leading from the garage to the house turned. Not knowing whether the person on the other side was an ally or enemy, Katherine froze. The door eased open. She took a step back. Her father slipped into the garage. As she met his gaze across the short distance, fear roared into her head.

By the look of shock on his face, he probably thought she'd be dead by now, Katherine realized, sickened by the idea.

As her father moved toward her, Katherine moved backward, using a hand against the car for support. He blocked the door, the only entrance to the house from the garage. As for a possible witness, there were none. The garage, used solely for family, sat at such an angle that anyone standing by the front entrance or driving up toward the house couldn't possibly see inside. Since her father blocked the only means into the house, Katherine's other option was to back up and race down the opposite side of the car and outside.

That is if she could outrun him. The way her legs felt, though, she doubted she'd get out of the garage, never mind reach the front door. Of course, there was the other option she hadn't thought of until now.

"Take another step, and I'll scream."

Her father stopped. He lifted his hands until both palms faced her. "No one's trying to hurt you, Katherine. You're the one doing it to yourself. You know, suicide isn't an answer..."

For one wild, irrational second, she doubted herself. Then she realized the drug and carbon monoxide must be toying with her head.

"...because all you needed to do was come to us for help and we'd—"

"Stop it! I'm not stupid!"

"Fine! Okay. No games. You're right. You're not stupid. But you're too damn stubborn. If you'd just let the shelter close down like we wanted, its tie to Miltronics would have died. Everything would have been fine then."

He sounded calm, assured, but Katherine saw the sheen of sweat across his brow.

"Fine for who? You and Paul? And Mother? What of her? Is she involved?"

"Of course not. She's too wrapped up in her politics to understand what's going on."

"And what about Jason?"

"She has no idea that he's really working for my brother. She hired him because of Paul's recommendations. My brother wanted him for the position as her assistant. The man's brilliant at eliminating paper trails."

"So no one would guess he used bogus vendors to steal from mother's campaign funds." Katherine didn't even try to camouflage the disgust and bitterness from her voice. Even so, it didn't seem to bother her father.

"You don't understand. There wasn't enough money. Not Miltronic's liquid assets or all of Paul's private contributors were enough. We had no choice but to look somewhere else. This project's been like some sick black hole, sucking every available dollar."

"Eventually she'll figure out what you're doing," Katherine insisted.

"Don't hold your breath. She can be so damn clueless at times." His voice turned snide. "Just like those kids."

""Those kids didn't deserve to die."

"Come off it. They were felons, taking up space. I did the world a favor."

At his complete disregard, Katherine felt her chest swell with outrage. "How can you say that? They were kids in need of a guiding hand—someone who cared. They were beautiful, living, breathing beings. And that "shelter" was a place they could stay to feel safe. And you ruined it all. For what? Some genetic experiment?"

"It's more than that. You can't imagine the amount of power and wealth I'd have with a monopoly on such a discovery. I've had enough of living in Sharon's shadow day in and day out. Without this, I'll always be 'Senator Spalding's husband', a lackey and nothing more."

Katherine couldn't believe how blind he was. With Paul, he'd still be in someone else's shadow. He was too weak to be anything more. God. She'd grown up with a man she'd never known, a man she couldn't even stomach looking at.

The door silently eased open from behind Alex. Katherine fought to keep her face expressionless. Please. Please let it be John.

A man slipped into the room. Katherine's hope shattered. She should have expected this.

Paul stood mere feet from behind her father. His features devoid of expression, his silence, more threatening than any words, sent Katherine's pulse crashing.

"And Uncle Paul?" Katherine managed to ask without her voice cracking. "Is he in it for the power?"

"Hell, no. Paul's off his rocker. He's hoping the money on this human enhancement drug will fund his immortality project. God knows, the outlay's astronomical. But he doesn't see the complete waste. Oh, no. He's too obsessed—has been since Jennifer's death. And you know what? I don't know what the attraction was, because I never particularly liked her."

A soft bark of sound punctuated her father's last words. Blood and brain matter splattered into her face and hair. She saw the frayed hole in her father's forehead and his eyes, blind and frozen, as he tumbled toward her. Her uncle had shot him in the head. Without warning, without hesitation.

"The son-of-a-bitch. I knew I couldn't trust him."

Her father's body struck her shoulder on the way down, and she stumbled against the car. A wild keening cry erupted from her throat as Alex thudded to the cement, brushing against her legs, staining the folds of her dress. Almost climbing the hood of the car in her hurry to get away, she hysterically wiped at the blood from her face and hair.

Another shot cracked inside the garage, hitting the wall by her head. Ducking, she hunched behind the passenger side of the car. Paul stepped over Alex's body and held a gun in each hand. She backed up along the side of the car. Paul followed.

"You're crazy. You can't get away with this."

"Oh, I beg to differ. Two guns. One from your father, and one from the burglar he interrupted. You both were in the wrong place at the wrong time. It's a tragedy that the thief got away." Katherine watched in horror as Paul rounded the side of the car, lifted the gun he'd shot Alex with and aimed it at her chest. "I've never liked you, so I'm actually going to enjoy this."

Moments earlier, Katherine had cheated death, but this time she knew she'd not only lost the deal but the game. She turned and ran, waiting for the bullet in her back.

CHAPTER 33

THE LAST PERSON John expected to see was the security guard he'd punched. He suspected the feeling was mutual by the shock and anger on the man's flat face.

Grunting, the guard reached for the gun strapped to his waist. "You're coming with me."

"I don't think so. I'm—"

The loud crack of a gun went off, stuffing the words back in John's throat. The guard hadn't cleared his gun from its holster. No, the shot had come from somewhere on the ground floor in the direction of the east wing.

Which meant— Panic caught at John's chest. "No…"

"What's your problem!" The guard grabbed for his arm.

John dodged his hand just as a woman's cry cut across the distance. Katherine. Of course the guard hadn't heard. He didn't have the capacity to hear like John. "Move! I've got to get to Katherine. She's in danger!"

"You're not going anywhere!"

The guard snapped the gun from its leather case. John lost patience. Before the gun cleared its holder, he rushed forward and shoved a shoulder into the other man. The guard went flying and hit the wall with a loud thud. John winced but didn't stop. He raced from the foyer, past several startled individuals in the hall and into the kitchen crowded with a half-dozen catering employees.

As John stumbled to a halt, he hit a platter on the edge of a counter. The metal disk launched into the air, flinging lettuce and chunks of fish onto the floor, countertops and into the face of a gap-mouthed caterer.

Over the shouts of the workers, John heard another gunshot. His stomach knotted and twisted. Panic swelled inside his chest. If he lost Katherine—

Think. Wrap your mind around the noise.

It was closer. Beyond the kitchen and still further east on the estate. There was also an oddness to it, almost a hollow sound following the initial shot. But that didn't make sense. Unless—

Then he had it. Of course. The garage. She'd been there the entire time. If he'd just—

No. There wasn't time for suppositions. John launched himself across the room. The garage had to be down this way. If not, he'd tear the wall apart to get it.

In her hurry to get out of his way, a woman stumbled into his path. Inches before colliding, John pivoted, caught the kitchen island with one hand and swiveled up and around the counter. He knocked silverware, glasses and utensils with his feet and legs as he brought his body up, over and down on the other side of the island.

When he ran down another hall, past several closed interior doors, he heard Katherine's voice.

"You're crazy. You can't get away with this."

Relief hit John, warming and heating his body, easing the suffocating terror that gripped his mind. She was okay. All she had to do was keep on talking.

"Oh, I beg to differ," Spalding words carried through the brick, mortar and drywall to John. "Two guns—

Shit. She was with Spalding. Rage spiked savagely into his fear and propelled him down another hallway. He saw the door at its end. Finally. The garage.

"—a tragedy that the thief got away."

Like hell. Spalding wasn't getting away with anything.

"—I'm actually going to enjoy this—"

"No!" John launched himself at the garage door. He felt his

body hit the barrier, felt the door's brief protest, and then heard the groan of metal, the shriek of cracking wood.

The door crashed open. John burst into the garage. He stumbled over the body on the ground. Pulling back in shock, John stared down at Katherine's father flat on his stomach and with a pool of blood by his head. Dead. After hearing Alex on the other end of the cell at Sharon's office, he'd known about the man's involvement, but he hadn't expected this.

Jerking his gaze away from the lifeless body, John spotted Spalding standing by the hood of a car and Katherine fleeing in the opposite direction. More importantly, John saw the gun aimed at Katherine's back.

"Spalding! You pull that trigger—I'll kill you!"

Spalding turned. For a brief pulse point, their gazes collided across the car. John saw the alarm then the fear flash in his eyes, but that was only a token of what John wanted. He wanted to rip Spalding's face off. He wanted Spalding to experience the same terror and horror of John's co-workers and the kids at the shelter. Spalding not only shattered Katherine's innocence but murdered so many others. All for—

Nothing.

He didn't give Spalding a chance to react. He leaped over the hood of the car and tackled him. Cloth tore. A whoosh of breath. A cry of pain. Chips of drywall flew into the air as they hit the wall. They landed with John on top. Scrambling up, John wedged a knee into the back of Spalding, who lay limply beneath him with an arm twisted at an odd angle. He pressed his hands around the base of the other man's neck.

Spalding had been about to kill her. His Katherine. The woman he adored, the only person who'd always believed in him. One moment later, and John might not have been able to save her. His hands tightened around the collar of Spalding's jacket.

John wanted to kill him. Easy enough. One twist of the neck. No one would ask questions. After all, the assailant had a gun. Simple self-defense.

~~*~~

"Don't!"

Katherine stood with a hip and a hand against the side of the car. She wouldn't let John ruin his future. Not after all he'd been through.

"Please, John. You'll live to regret it." She lifted a trembling hand. "Come here. I need you. I need to hold you—know you're real and not going away."

After a long, torturous moment, John looked up and seemed to hesitate. Then he slowly rose and stepped away from her uncle. Katherine sagged against the car. For a wild moment, she'd thought John might actually kill him, and she thanked God he hadn't. Not because her uncle didn't deserve it. No, she was thankful because she knew how much it would hurt John. Being responsible for someone's death—no matter how fitting— would have eaten at his soul. She didn't want that for John. He was far too special, and not because she loved him, but because he was what he was. Strong, solid, steadfast, filled with principles and strong convictions. A good man.

Voices carried from inside the house, and a security guard stepped from the mutilated doorway and into the garage. She caught the man's stunned expressed before John strode over and caught her up against his chest.

"I'm here, Katherine. Right here. I'm not going anywhere." John clutched her tighter as the sound of a siren in the distance steadily increased in volume. "Everything's going to be okay. We'll let the police take care of him and his bony little henchman. But they're probably going to have to get your uncle to a hospital. I think I broke his arm," he whispered the last against her temple.

Half-laughing, half-crying, Katherine wrapped her arms around John's middle, feeling the heat of his body beneath her hands, the whisper of his breath across her brow. She loved the clean, woodsy, thoroughly male scent of him. She loved every-thing about him.

Over John's shoulder, she saw her mother stumble into the garage with several other people. The unguarded look of horror, fear and shock that flashed across Sharon's features confirmed that her mother hadn't known about her husband, Mitlronics, or the shelter. She met her mother's gaze across the distance and felt a deep, aching sadness for a lost relationship and a childhood she'd never had. She didn't know if this tragedy would bring them together, or forever tear them apart.

But either way, she'd be fine. Because there was John. There would always be John.

EPILOGUE

STANDING ON THE balcony, Katherine looked over the shore from their villa in Cabo San Lucas. The sun had dipped into the ocean, staining the water with fingers of orange and gold. She wrapped both hands around the baluster and leaned forward as a cool breeze, scented of sea and sand, stroked her skin and ruffled the silk hem of her skirt.

She smiled. Life was a beautiful. This day, this moment would become a memory of pleasure and wonder, while the future, well, the future held so much more promise.

Two strong arms wrapped around her waist and pulled her up against a hard chest. John. Sighing with happiness, she clasped his arms and sank deeper in the circle of his embrace.

"Any regrets?" he murmured, resting his chin on the crown of her head.

"Never."

"Even with the risk of bodily injury from a guy who has this terrible habit of breaking things?" His breath whispered against her hair. "It doesn't look like I'm going to lose these powers any time soon."

"Then I guess I'll just have to carry around some super glue for my super man," she teased, glancing down at her left hand and the large diamond ring and matching band.

John had insisted they wait several months to get married

until Katherine's pain had eased from the trauma of her father's death and her family's betrayal. With John's full cooperation, the police compiled enough evidence to keep her uncle, Jason and several others behind bars for life. Even with John cleared of all wrongdoing, Katherine still knew guilt plagued his thoughts from so many needless deaths. They did make a small atonement by ensuring Luke, the boy who died in the car accident in Arizona, receive a proper burial. The small ceremony consisted of just the two of them and the kids from the Morning Dove.

The public outrage over Miltronic's experiments and her father—she still had a hard time thinking of him differently—and uncle's involvement eventually died down and was replaced with another more tantalizing scandal, and life went on. John's physical abilities hadn't diminished in time, and they stayed a secret, one which they intended to keep.

Sadly, her relationship with her mother, already filled with too many years of neglect and secrets, continued its downward spiral. It hadn't helped when Sharon sabotaged the shelter with the misguided belief that once the Morning Dove closed her daughter would pursue a career more appropriate to her education and social status. And her mother's continued refusal to talk about Katherine's natural father further disintegrated what little bond remained between them. Katherine only managed to get her father's name and find out that he died years ago.

There'd been talk of impeachment for her mother, but it had died down, and she would complete her term in office. But it was a good guess her career as a Senator or, for that matter, a position in any political office was dead.

The Morning Dove hadn't changed. Katherine would never give up on the lost, battered and troubled teenagers who sought a haven within the shelter's walls. The case of Tracy's situation was encouragement enough that she was doing the right thing. She'd managed to get Tracy's sister out from under their father and into a foster home after charges of abuse were filed.

"I have something for you."

Smiling, she squeezed his arms tighter around her middle and snuggled her bottom against his hips. "I thought you already give me that "something" numerous times over the last twenty-four hours."

"You wicked, wicked woman. I'm talking about your wedding gift."

Turning, she looked up into his eyes and her chest expanded at the love that glittered in his slate eyes.

"It's on the bed." He tugged her away from the balcony.

"Oh...really. On the bed, did you say?"

John laughed, a deep throaty chuckle that Katherine absolutely adored.

"There you go again—getting those naughty thoughts." He nudged her into the bedroom. "I promise a little later I'll get very wicked. So wicked, that I'll curl those delectable toes of yours."

That "something" turned out to be a large box wrapped in silver and white. A huge jaunty bow sat on top of it. Sinking down on the edge of the bed, Katherine took the package and looked up at John. She hadn't a clue what it was.

"Go on," he urged, looking eager yet nervous.

Carefully, she peeled off the wrapping to find a plain brown box. She pulled the lid off and found a framed photo of a man. Her heart skipped a beat, and the box trembled from hands that couldn't stop shaking. She was afraid to ask.

"Your father," John whispered. "Inside are also several news clippings from his hometown. I even uncovered a yearbook from his high school. He was on the basketball team."

Katherine brushed a tear on her cheek with the back of her hand. "I don't know what to say."

She eased the picture from the box and looked at the photo of a man who looked to be in his mid-twenties. Under the shade of a big, oak tree, her father grinned back at the camera. Her gaze slowly ran over the blond hair cropped close to his head, the strong jaw and brow, the confident stance. He had an open, honest looking face.

"Terry Burke," Katherine murmured, running a reverent finger along the silver frame.

"I think you'll get some idea of what type of man he was.

After his stint in the Army in the Middle East, he'd planned on going back to school for a degree in psychology, but he never made it back. When I was compiling his background, I realized the similarities. You're very much your father's daughter. He really cared for and about people."

Easing down on the bed beside her, John slid a gentle hand down the length of her back. "Are you upset with me? I'd thought you'd want to know something about your father."

With trembling hands, she placed the box and frame on the other side of her, turned to John and pressed a palm against his cheek. Tears flowed unheeded down her face. She blinked until his beloved face reappeared.

"Now I know why I fell in love with you," Katherine said, her voice husky with wonder, love and humility. "No one's ever given me something so beautiful. I—" She cleared her throat. "I couldn't have asked for a better wedding present. I'll cherish it. Always."

"As I'll cherish you. Always."

Katherine looked into John's intense, gray eyes and knew it to be the truth.

THANK YOU!

THANK YOU FOR reading all six episodes of Duplicity. I hope you enjoyed it, and if you did, don't forget to leave a review.

For news on latest releases, contests and other news, you can signup for my newsletter (http://www.hdthomson.com). Also, if you feel like contacting me, you can always catch me on Facebook (https://www.facebook.com/authorhdthomson).

COMPLETE LIST OF TITLES

ROMANTIC SUSPENSE

SMOKE & MIRRORS SERIES

ANXIETY #1
DUPLICITY #2
IDENTITY #3

PARANORMAL ROMANCE

ONYX & MERCURY SERIES

A KISS BEFORE DYING

SHADES SERIES

DEADLY SHADES #1
SHADES OF HOLLY #2
KILLER SHADES #3
KILLER SHADES BOX SET - BOOKS 1 THROUGH 3

CONTEMPORARY ROMANCE

THE LONG ROAD HOME
PROTECTING KATIE

ABOUT THE AUTHOR

H. D. Thomson moved from Ontario, Canada as a teenager to the heat of Arizona where she graduated from the University of Arizona with a B.S. in Business Administration with a major in accounting. After working in the corporate world as an accountant, H. D. changed her focus to one of her passions–books. She owned and operated an online bookstore for several years and then started the company, Bella Media Management. The company specializes in web sites, video trailers, ebook conversion and promotional resources for authors and small businesses. When she is not heading her company, she is following her first love–writing. You can read more about her and her books at HDThomson.com.

What they're saying about H. D. Thomson's books:

"My applause to the author on an entertaining read." – *Romance Novel Junkies*

"Author H.D. Thomson does a great job of keeping the reader guessing." – *Paranormal Romance Party*

"Bravo H. D. Thomson!" – *Writer's and Reader's of Distinct Fiction's Top Read.*

"Thomson's writing is spot on…" – *Confessions of a Bibliophile.*

www.ingramcontent.com/pod-product-compliance
Lightning Source LLC
Chambersburg PA
CBHW021110110726
47900CB00007B/2120